Hi Sa

SMOKE & MIRRORS

FORGED IN FIRE

SKYE JORDAN

Enjoy!
XO Skye Jordan

1

Isabel

It's almost midnight when I pull into the Cockloft's parking lot.

I stare, blurry eyed, at the red neon sign. "Only a man would name a bar the Cockloft."

The term evidently relates to fire in some way. Tucker tried to explain the significance of it, but he may as well have been speaking pig Latin.

I leave the engine on to keep the heater going as flurries of snowflakes melt on my windshield. When I left New York, it was a balmy and beautiful sixty-five degrees. Three days later, I'm now in Oregon, and it's—I glance at the temperature reader on my dash—twenty-seven degrees.

I wasn't expecting snow in Oregon in October, but then I haven't been back to this state in a decade. And I've never been to Hood River, a little town an hour or so from Portland.

My fuzzy mind pulls up the memory of Portland from my childhood, and the dusting and slush that disappointed me every season. But that's certainly not the case here tonight. The snow grows heavier, falling from the dark night like confetti.

As a combo bar and grill, the Cockloft closes around 10:00 p.m., but there are four trucks in the parking lot, not including my brother's, and all of them have firefighter decals on their back windows. I search my mind for the day of the week and realize I've shown up on poker night.

I drop my head back against the seat and close my eyes. "Dammit."

I'm not prepared to see anyone but Tucker. I would pay dearly for Tucker to be the only one here—I mean, if I had any money left. Currently, I'm down to forty-eight cents. Forty-eight cents to my name. One quarter, two dimes, and three pennies.

"How in the hell is this my life?"

After driving three thousand miles in three days, stopping only to load up on cheap snacks and nap in the Jeep, my butt is numb and every other part of my body aches—back, arms, hips, legs. My neck is as tight as a steel rod, creating a killer headache. I can't take one more minute in this driver's seat.

I shut down the engine, grab my jacket from the passenger's seat, and step out into the night. Silence crowds me. Deep, moving silence. The kind you can't find anywhere in New York city, or Portland, for that matter. The kind I've never experienced before. The kind I didn't realize I needed until right this minute.

I slide into my parka as the darkness wraps around me, and the snow tickles my face like angel wings. I take a deep breath, and the scent of clean, cold, fresh, pine-filled air fills my nose, my lungs, my head. It's so intense and stunning, it overwhelms me for a moment. I float for several long seconds in this new place, my new reality, caught between excitement and fear, unsure if I'm on the verge of a mental break*down* or a mental break*through*.

"Holy shit," I say on a deep exhale. "I wasn't as ready for this as I thought." I look around at the unfamiliar surroundings, and tears burn my eyes. "What in the fuck am I *doing*? Who in the fuck *am* I?"

I feel like Alice in Wonderland, and I've just dropped through the rabbit hole. But somehow, I don't see a noble destiny ahead. Unlike Alice and her quest to end the Red Queen's reign, I'm just trying to get back on my feet.

I have to pull myself together to face men other than Tucker. I drag the band out of my hair, and the bird's nest goes everywhere. With the help of melting snow, I work the insanity into loose waves, then use the side mirror to touch up my lip gloss and add concealer to the bags under my eyes.

I straighten and look down at my clothes. The torn jeans work, but I get back into the car to switch out my grubby sweatshirt for a black off-the-shoulder Tom Ford cashmere. I always get a rush of pride when I wear this treasure. It retails for over fourteen hundred dollars, but I grabbed it at an industry sale for seventy-five bucks—obviously mispriced by an intern. Still, I ate rice and beans for the following two weeks to keep the apartment's lights on.

When I look about as good as it's going to get, I take a deep breath and enter the bar. It's bigger than it looks from the outside. And way nicer inside than portrayed in the pictures Tucker sent me when it was newly renovated. Another rush of emotion fills my chest. Tucker deserves good in his life.

A round of hearty laughter pulls my gaze toward the back of the empty dining room, where five guys sit around a table littered with half-empty beer glasses, cards, and poker chips. A table nearby holds ravaged snack containers and empty pizza boxes.

I recognize Tucker immediately, and my heart squeezes. He's facing away from me, and I take the second I need to push the emotions into the background. I haven't seen him in way too long. And I see Cole sitting to Tucker's right. Two others at the table are young, guys I don't know, but I'll bet my next influx of cash—which I foresee coming in the next hour—that the man sitting on Tucker's left, the one with a head of jet-black hair, is Logan Roberts.

Right on cue, my stomach lifts, then coils. I know I'm together enough to fool Tucker, probably Cole too, but Logan... He's always been more astute than most.

I slide out of my jacket and start toward the table. One of the guys I don't know sees me and smiles. "Hey, there, ma'am. I'm sorry, but we're closed."

"Buchanan," Tucker says, "did you forget to turn off the sign again?"

"Oh. My. God." Cole puts down his cards. "No fucking way." He pushes his chair back and stands, arms open to me. "Damn, girl. Look at you. All grown up and gorgeous."

I feel all eyes are on me as I walk straight into Cole's embrace. "And you're all grown up and buff as hell."

By the time Cole releases me, Tucker and Logan are standing. I mean to look at my brother, but all I need is a glimpse of Logan to be completely distracted. I categorize him in three seconds—built, hot, and still broody as hell. Those New York models pale in comparison to this guy.

Tucker hugs me hard and quick, then pushes me back by the arms and frowns at me. "You're too thin. What's wrong? Why didn't you tell me you were coming? How did you get here?"

"A girl can *never* be too thin. Everything is fine." I toss my jacket over a chair nearby and tousle his hair. "You need a haircut. Let me say hi to Logan."

I sidestep Tucker and face Logan. His smile is...I can't quite figure it out. Sort of sweet, sort of amused, sort of...wary? Or maybe concerned?

"Don't look at me like that," I tell him as I walk into his arms for a hug. Christ, he smells orgasmic, like fir needles, cedarwood, bergamot, and leather.

"Everything is fine." I pull back, light-headed from his scent, and look him up and down. "Including you. You're lookin' good, Roberts."

That warms up his smile and quiets some of the suspicion in his eyes. Eyes that are even more striking than I remember. Bright jade green, rimmed in thick spiky black lashes. Eyes a woman could melt into.

"You too," he says. Always a man of few words.

I turn toward the other men at the table. "Hi, I'm Isabel, Tucker's little sister."

"Carter." One of the guys lifts his hand. He's dark skinned, dark eyed, and handsome.

The other guy waves from the other side of the table. He's an all-American sweetheart. "Royal."

The only thing missing from this setting is Evan. The fourth of Tucker's band of brothers growing up. He died in a fire almost three years ago now, and his absence here hurts.

"Where have you been hiding her?" Carter asks Tucker.

"New York," I answer for him. "What have you all got goin' here?"

"Just poker night," Tucker says. "We were playing our last hand anyway."

"Don't leave on account of me." I pull a chair from another table and slide it in between Tucker and Cole. "I'd play a few hands with you, but I've used up all my cash getting here."

"You really want to play?" Tucker asks. "You just showed up out of nowhere. Do you need to talk?"

"Nothing we can't talk about over a game." I shrug. "You taught me in high school, didn't you? I should be able to figure it out."

"Spot her, Medina," Carter says. "You've got all our money."

I see a familiar glint in Carter's eyes—a shark spotting a

minnow. As for Tucker having everyone's money, it looks to me like Carter's got a pretty big pile for himself.

"Yeah, Tucker," I say, bumping his shoulder with mine, "spot me."

Tucker passes the cards to Logan. "You can deal." Then he turns his gaze on me. "Is everything okay?"

"Of course. I just miss you, and the spring-summer fashion season is closing out. Great time for a break. And since I've never been here, I decided a visit was long overdue."

"Why didn't you tell me you were coming?" Tucker asks.

Logan tosses cards to everyone, and I feel the weight of his stare, but I stay focused on the table or Tucker.

"I couldn't surprise you that way, could I?" I pick up one of Tucker's poker chips. "What are these worth?"

He gives me the monetary denomination of each chip and slides a pile worth fifty bucks toward me.

"Thanks. I'll pull cash from my bank tomorrow. Too bad there's no system to bet off an ATM card." I look up. "There isn't, is there?"

The guys give me a you-silly-girl chuckle.

When I reach for my cards, I purposely knock the chips over. Once I see I've got a hand full of absolutely nothing, I set my cards down faceup on the table to straighten the chips.

Tucker's grinning. "You're supposed to keep these hidden."

"Oh, right."

He tosses my cards back to Logan, who deals me a new hand, and I end up with a much better spread.

Everyone takes stock of their cards. Tucker glances at his before putting them down and focusing on me. "Did you fly in today? Rent a car at the airport? I wish you'd told me. I would have picked you up."

"Aw, that's sweet." When it's my turn to add chips, I stare at the pile, then glance around the table. "What am I supposed to do now?"

Carter gives me a quick lesson, and I toss in a few chips to the pile.

"Man, it's good to see you." Tucker's smiling at me, and the cold night melts away.

I love this guy so much. No one could have asked for a better brother. Though, he sure could have gotten a better sister. I've failed miserably in that arena. Among so many others.

I squeeze his shoulder. "It's good to see you too. Sorry it's been so long."

"How long are you staying?" he asks.

"Maybe a couple of weeks."

"Maybe?" Tucker says. "That's..."

"Vague," Cole offers.

"Cryptic," Carter says.

"Mysterious," Royal adds.

"Cryptic is the same thing as mysterious, dope," Carter teases.

"Okay, then..." He's thinking hard, and his lack of verbal sparring with these men tells me he's probably even younger than he looks. And he looks twelve. "Indefinite."

The guys laugh and rib him over the lame description.

The last time I saw Tucker, he'd flown to New York for Christmas about four years ago. I borrowed a high-priced Manhattan apartment from an investment banker who frequented my blackjack table at the New York Poker Club— just one of the many moonlighting gigs that kept me in a shitty walk-up in the Bronx while I waited to break into the upper echelon of the fashion world. The guy used the stunning apartment as a hookup pad and really didn't want that information shared. Especially not with his wife. So, he eagerly granted me the use of the apartment for the week Tucker visited.

I never did break into the fashion industry, but I felt like Cinderella that week, showing Tucker all the amazing parts of

New York as if I really belonged there. We wandered through the Upper East Side shopping district, ate in Soho, scouted the amazing East Village neighborhood. We also did the touristy things like the Statue of Liberty and Rockefeller Center to see the iconic Christmas tree.

One of the very best weeks of my life, for sure. I'm struck by how pathetic that is—the best week of my life was a visit from my brother where I lied through my teeth and pretended to be something I'm not. Nor would ever be, as it turned out.

I lose the first three hands while I try to catch up with Cole, but end up fielding all kinds of questions from Carter and Royal about New York and the fashion industry.

I'm having a hard time addressing the questions without lying, something that has always come so easily to me. Only now, sitting beside my amazing brother and his amazing friends who are literal heroes every day of their lives, do I find the lies drying up. Somehow, it feels deeply wrong to lie to such real, selfless men. And I'm so over trying to be someone I'm just not.

Now, Tucker breaks into the questions to ask one of his own. "What's going on?"

"If you must know," I say with extra melodramatic flair, "my company merged with another, and the job they offered me in the switch wasn't one I wanted. So I'm in between gigs at the moment."

The *whole* truth is my company did merge with another—a year ago. And they *did* offer me another position that I wasn't interested in—but I took it anyway because the fashion industry in New York isn't just cutthroat, it's decapitating. And I *am* also between gigs at the moment. No one needs to know that none of those facts relate to the other or that it doesn't explain why I'm here.

"Is that good or bad?" Tucker asks.

"I was ready to make a change." A change from the fashion

rat race where I was pigeonholed into assistants' positions and odd jobs that barely paid minimum wage. Assistant merchandiser, assistant stylist, assistant editor, assistant inventory manager. And finally, the one assistant position that really was a step up in the industry—assistant designer. The one I quit all my other odd jobs for. The one I lost after just a couple of months.

It really was the death knell for me in New York. The fact that it happened within weeks of my five-year self-imposed deadline for making it in this industry just made the decision to leave a little easier.

When I find Tucker giving me a skeptical look, I say, "*It's good*. And don't worry, I've been getting offers from a bunch of other places. I'll have an incredible new job in a week, which is why I want to spend this time with you. New jobs are always demanding. Have to prove yourself, you know?"

"Oh, how well I know," Royal mutters, making the guys laugh.

"So, catch me up on things here." I start with Cole and learn he's with Natalie, a woman who was married to Evan. I imagine Cole took a beating for claiming another firefighter's wife even if she was a widow. Cole and Evan were best friends growing up. That couldn't have been easy on either Cole or Natalie. I admire the dedication required to overcome that kind of judgment.

I make sure I win only one out of the next four hands while I get to know Royal and Carter. The two men have been with the team roughly the same amount of time, and there can't be more than one official probie, so while Carter was teased early on about his probie status, he came to the station older than Royal and with more experience, which nailed Royal with the official title. A title he'll keep until the next new hire.

I glance at Logan, who hasn't said a word, but he's soaked in everything that's been said. "I see you're still the strong, silent type."

I get a smile, but there's a lot going on behind those eyes. I can't help but remember the look in his eyes the last time I saw him, shirtless, jeans riding low, hips deep between my thighs, hands in my hair, so much raw desire and affection in his expression as he gave me an unforgettable and amazing first time. It's been fodder for fantasies ever since I learned most men's A game is Logan's Z game.

But that was a lifetime ago. Before I got a heavy dose of idiocy and desperation. Before I betrayed my best friend— Logan's sister—and left town without saying goodbye to anyone.

To be fair, it's not like I broke Logan's heart. We weren't dating at the time, not even into each other. We were always just friends. And, as friends, we made a pact that if we were both still virgins by the time we turned eighteen, we'd be each other's firsts.

Something shifted between us that night. Something unexpected and terrifying—at least for me, and romantic feelings weren't part of the deal. My mom's relationships cured me of ever wanting one for myself, and Logan's parents sure hadn't imprinted anything good on his heart.

I learned young that love isn't forever. Nor is it good or sweet, like in the movies. And that men you thought you could trust can turn on you and act like someone you've never seen before.

I suddenly need a break from this. From the questions and the curiosity and the man with the thick black hair and bright green eyes, who's even better looking now. His jaw has squared up, his features sharpened, those naturally straight white teeth still gleam. He's almost too pretty to look at. But it was the least the Lord could do after giving him such hideous parents.

He's checking me out in a way that makes it seem like he

can see through my farce, which is ridiculous given how different we are now. But I'm starting to wonder if I've changed all that much from the selfish, desperate girl who left here.

As if to prove it, the forty-eight cents in my jeans' pocket takes on weight, reminding me that I'm in a similarly desperate situation as I was ten years ago. So I fall back on old skills and make quick work out of getting the guys to toss money into the pot before I demolish them with a royal flush. A girl's got to take care of herself.

"How exciting. I never win." That much is true. You can't win if you don't play, and I don't play. I just deal. Or I used to.

I reach for my winnings, and the sleeves of my sweater slide up my arms. It takes me a second to realize my bruises have slipped into view, and I hurriedly pull in the cash and tug the sleeves back to my wrists. My heart is skipping over that slip, but I've learned how to hold myself together through almost anything.

Breathing deep to settle my nerves, I separate fifty dollars' worth of chips and slide them toward Tucker's dwindling pile, leaving me close to two hundred bucks.

Maybe I ought to just accept fate and embrace my future as a hustler.

"Thanks for spotting me, Tuck," I say. "If someone could cash me out, that would be great. I'm going to see if the kitchen here is as amazing as the rest of this place."

I wander through the restaurant, admiring the clean masculine lines of the architecture, the heavy furniture, the high ceilings, above which is the loft where Tucker's living.

I hear one of the guys say, "I think we've just been hustled," and I'm grinning as I push into the kitchen.

Of course, the kitchen *is* just as nice as the rest of the place. Stainless steel countertops, a huge center island, Wolf ranges, equipment neatly lined up or tucked away, shelves of pantry goods. I turn to face the massive industrial refrigerator, and my stomach growls. I'm going on eight hours without anything to eat. Forty-eight cents wouldn't even get me a decent candy bar.

My cell buzzes in my back pocket with an incoming call. I already know who it is. No one else would be trying to contact me. I pull it from my pocket and send the call to voicemail without looking at the screen. A flurry of texts come in, but I ignore those too.

I have more pressing matters, specifically an angry stomach. I leave my cell on the counter and pull open one massive refrigerator door. I'm greeted with shelf after lighted shelf of meats and cheeses and fruit and—

I gasp and reach for a pie with a clear plastic cover. There are a few slices missing. It's chocolate on the bottom and whipped cream on the top, and I'm drooling by the time I find a fork.

I return to the fridge, holding the door open with my shoulder to remind me I have to put it back. Then I load up the fork and open wide to get all the luscious goodness into my mouth at once. It's sweet and light and chocolatey with a graham cracker crust that melts in my mouth.

I've died and gone to heaven.

2

Logan

I fold early in the next hand so I can stare at the kitchen door and try to puzzle out what just happened.

"Don't you think that's strange?" I say to Tucker. "Her showing up out of nowhere?"

"She's a creative genius. There's no telling what she'll do. Plus, she works her ass off. She deserves a break."

I might believe that if it weren't for those bruises on her forearms, the shadows under her eyes, the way her fingernails are bitten to the quick, the polish chipped off. And, yeah, Tucker nailed her weight—she's too thin.

But my biggest concern revolves around not only the bruises, but the way she tried to hide them.

Old images from my past rise from the shadows. My mind superimposes Isabel's image over my mother's, and the mere idea that someone put their hands on Isabel in a hurtful way makes me want to put my fist through a wall.

"She dating anyone?" I ask, trying to keep my protective temper on simmer.

"I don't know," Tucker says without looking up from his cards. "No one serious. She hasn't wanted me to meet anyone."

Tucker is a good guy. He really is. He tries to act aloof and untouchable, but I know he loves fiercely—his friends, his firefighter brothers, Isabel. But he's also a little on the dense side, as shown in the careless way he tosses aside the major warning sign of Isabel showing up from across the country, unannounced.

"You can be intimidating," Carter tells Tucker.

"Pffft, me?"

"Yeah," Royal says, "all six foot four, two hundred pounds of you."

"Exactly," Carter says. "I wouldn't want to be the guy who gets on your bad side."

"Same, man," Royal says. "Same."

"Don't be pussies," Tucker says. "I wouldn't hurt a fly."

His gaze lifts from the cards and meets mine. Maybe he's not as dense as he pretends, because I know our thoughts have drifted to the same place—Portland, eleven years ago, and the way Tucker beat one of his mother's boyfriends to a literal pulp for coming on to Isabel when she was just seventeen. Their mother called the cops and had Tucker arrested, forcing Isabel to go public with the awful experience of attempted sexual assault to get the cops to drop the charges.

Tucker hands me the cards. "Deal."

I pass the cards to Carter. "I'm out this hand. I'm going to see how she's doing."

How she's *really* doing.

When I reach the kitchen door, I hear her moan. The sound that sparks an old memory and shoots tingles straight up my spine.

I push through the door and find her behind the open fridge door. "What did you find in there?"

She startles and gasps.

I lean my butt against the counter and cross my arms as she turns with a forkful and a mouthful of pie, a little cream left on the edge of her upper lip.

The idea of licking that away is way out of bounds. Right?

"Came in here to check up on me?" she asks with a sassy smile.

"I had a feeling you'd scope out my pie. You always loved chocolate."

Her eyes go wide, darting between the pie and me. "Oh, shit. This is yours?" She moves to the counter, sets down the pie, and tries to re-cover it, but the plastic keeps popping off. "I'm sorry. I just figured it was restaurant food."

I put my hand over hers, and she freezes. The flash of something just this side of fear darts through her eyes, then it's gone, making me believe I imagined it. "It's fine. You can have all you want."

"You sure?"

I nod. "I can get more from Natalie anytime."

She relaxes. "I'm going to have to make friends with Natalie."

I forget that Isabel doesn't know Nat. She couldn't get time off work to come for Evan and Natalie's wedding. Then two years later, Evan was gone. She missed his funeral too, but I don't blame her. It was a drawn-out torture fest with all the fallen firefighter bells, whistles, and bagpipes.

"That's easy to do," I tell her. "Nat's amazing."

She nods and slows her pie demolition. "Must have been... awkward for her and Cole, Evan being his best friend and a firefighter and all."

"They've had a rocky road, but it all turned out okay. They both say it was worth the struggle."

"That's nice to hear. Cole's such a great guy." She stares at the pie as if it has magical qualities. "This is incredible. Dangerous, actually. Maybe I shouldn't befriend Natalie."

I move back to the counter and watch her hunger fade when she's got the pie whittled down to a small wedge. She sighs, sets it down, and replaces the cover.

When she's within reach, I lift my hand to wipe the whipped cream off her lip. She flinches, startling me.

I freeze, my hand a couple of inches from her mouth, with a chasm of molten lava swamping my chest. A fiery anger that's caused me to act rashly in the past. One I've learned to control. Or I thought I had.

"Sorry," she says, going for upbeat self-deprecation but not quite getting there. "You surprised me."

I let my hand continue on its path and barely graze her lip, wiping the whipped cream away with my knuckle.

She smirks. "I was saving that for later."

That makes me laugh, despite the river of anger running deep in my veins, and I lick the cream off my knuckle.

She puts the empty fork back in her mouth upside down, sucking off whatever's left. Her smile is embarrassed, but sweet. "I'll, um, just put it back. Left a few bites for you."

She's got the pie in one hand, trying to juggle things around in the fridge to find a place for the pie. "What the heck? How is there not room for this when I just took it out?"

"Probably because it was shoved in there to begin with." I push away from the counter to open the door wider. "Let me help."

"I got it." Her cell rings.

"Want to get that?"

"No. Probably just job offers. I'll call them back at a decent hour. Fashion. I swear, the industry never sleeps."

The phone goes silent, then immediately rings again while Isabel is still moving food around.

"Someone certainly wants to talk to you." I glance at the phone on the counter and catch the display, which reads Cocksucker, just as she swivels and grabs the phone, pocketing it without looking at who called.

"If Cocksucker is calling to offer you a job," I say, "we need to have a serious heart-to-heart."

She laughs. "His full name is Motherfucking Cocksucking Loser, but it was too long to fit on the screen."

I break out laughing. She laughs too, and we find equilibrium again with her leaning against the fridge and me against the counter, smiling at each other.

"He sounds like a gem," I say.

She shakes her head and closes her eyes for a split second. "I absolutely *do not* know how to pick them."

After she grew up with a mother who had a revolving door of men, I imagine Isabel doesn't have much of a positive role model in that department.

The one-shouldered black sweater she's wearing is making me a little crazy. It shows a healthy amount of smooth skin while also hugging all her curves. I love my chocolate silk pie, but I'd give it up for an eternity just for a few minutes with my hands on that body of hers.

Her jeans hang low and mold to legs longer than I remember. Rips in the fabric show the same smooth skin on her thighs. Her hair is still a rich dark chocolate, her eyes just as dark, just as mysterious as they'd been as a teenager. Even if we didn't already know Tucker and Isabel had different fathers, it's obvious by their coloring—Tucker a blue-eyed sandy blond and Isabel an olive-skinned, dark-eyed beauty.

The longer I look, the more I like, from the multiple piercings in her left ear to the hint of a tattoo peeking out from the edge of the sweater. On the one hand, ink on that perfect skin seems unthinkable. On the other, it's sexy as hell.

"You look great." In fact, she's mouthwatering. All grown up, confident, independent, sassy. She's got a sophistication to her that's hard to describe. An elegance. Yet I still catch glimpses of that dreamy, emotional, scrappy seventeen-year-old.

"You too," she says. "How have you been?"

I shrug. "Life's good. Can't complain."

She smiles like she's thinking something funny to herself. Those dark eyes spark with humor, and a dimple pokes into her left cheek. The sight softens my bones, and I brace my hands on the counter behind me.

"Tell me about life in New York. You know, the story you didn't tell everyone else." I pause before adding, "You used to be able to tell me anything."

The micro changes in her expression are fascinating: the quiver of a smile, the shift of her eyes, the softening of her shoulders. It's like watching her walls come down, one by one.

And not until just now do I realize I've always been into her. Even when I didn't think I was. Even when I told myself the sex was nothing but friends taking the next step toward adulthood together. Even when I swore her vanishing without telling me her plans or where she was going or why she ran didn't damage me on a fundamental level.

"I've been gone ten years," she says. "That's a lot of telling."

"Eleven," I say. "You've been gone eleven years."

"Right. Eleven." Her gaze falls away. "I'm not prepared to talk about this with you tonight, I mean about how long I've been gone, how I left, the decisions I made."

She blows out a long breath and shifts on her feet. Then her gaze returns to mine with the first show of honesty bright in her eyes. "But I did plan on addressing it while I was here. I don't expect either of us to just pretend it didn't happen. I guess it's one of the reasons I took this time to come. To, I don't know, set things right with the people I care about. Or at least make the effort."

"That's good to hear. But for the record, as far as you leaving all those years ago, I know you did what you had to do to take care of yourself. You were right to do it. I wouldn't have wanted it any other way."

She studies me through her lashes, looking so much younger and more unsure of herself than the woman on display in the dining room. It's heartening to see she'll still let her guard down with me. "You mean that?"

"Hell yes." I cross my arms and shrug one shoulder. "Do I wish I could have helped you? Sure. Do I wish you'd told me? Yeah. But after I grew up a little, I realized it wasn't about me. It was about you, and you did the best thing you could for yourself."

"Wow," she says softly. "That's not the reaction I was expecting."

"Maybe you've been hanging out with too many mother-fucking cocksucking losers."

She laughs, and the sound turns back time. "Or maybe I've just forgotten what a great friend you were."

And suddenly, we're in a moment. Soft silence circles us, one that feels like it's steeped in possibility. But I have to remind myself who she is. She might be gorgeous, fun, sweet, and strong, she might seem a lot like what I've been looking for in a woman, but she's also temporary. She's going to walk away the way she did over a decade ago. At least this time, I'll see it coming.

"Two weeks, huh?" I ask.

She shrugs. "Give or take."

That should keep me in check.

Conversation picks up in the dining room, then Tucker pushes into the kitchen, smiling.

"Why do you look guilty?" Isabel asks him, crossing her arms.

"Damn, she sure can read you," I agree.

"Uh, so, where are you staying?" Tucker asks Isabel.

"You sonofabitch," she says without any heat. "You're hooking up with someone."

Tucker winces. "You didn't exactly give me advanced notice, and she did come from out of town, and the loft is really just a loft, if you know what I mean, and..." He laughs, but lowers his voice. "I've been after her for months."

Isabel shakes her head. "You asshole. Fine. I wasn't exactly looking forward to sleeping on your couch anyway. Is there a cheap hotel somewhere close?"

Tucker looks at me, expectant.

"That's cold, dude," I tell him. "You've been merciless about how shitty it is, but because you can't control your fucking teenage hormones, the place is suddenly worthy of family? Isabel's right. You're an asshole."

"You can both hate me, but can we make a decision, please?"

"Honestly," Isabel says, "I'm exhausted. It doesn't matter if it's a roach motel. I'm just going to fall face-first into the pillow and pass out." She pulls her keys from her pocket. "Where is it?"

I give Tucker the I'll-kill-you-later look, then glance at Isabel. "I bought a place recently. It's a motel. Kind of. Sort of. Not really."

"You bought *a motel*?" she says with the same are-you-for-real look everyone gives me when they hear.

"It's old and run-down and I can't rent it out because it needs a lot of work—"

"Whoa," Isabel says, putting her hand out like she's slowing me down. "Wait. You're a full-time firefighter, you own and run part of this bar, and you bought a motel that needs work? Have you always been an overachiever?"

"If I was an overachiever, I'd have the place fixed up. It's currently a dump, if I'm being honest, but I've got the main apartment in good shape. You can stay there."

She gives me a dubious look. "You said it wasn't nice enough to rent out."

"The individual rooms aren't, but the apartment's decent."

She puts out her hands palms up as if to say *explain*.

"It's my place," I tell her. "But I'll stay in one of the rooms. Unlike your brother, I prioritize family over hooking up."

"Only because you shut down all your options after—"

I smack him in the chest before he belts out Emily's name. "Shut the fuck up. You're already on my shit list."

"Mine too," Isabel says, lifting her chin at Tucker. "Get out before I beat you with the gigantor turkey leg in the fridge."

Tucker backs out of the room trying to look contrite when the guy doesn't even understand the concept. I'm left with a rush of embarrassment over exposing Isabel to one of my colossal misjudgments—the motel.

"I love that guy," I say, staring at the door, "but sometimes..."

"He's an asshole," we say at the same time.

"Don't worry," she says. "I'll get him back."

"Can I watch?"

"Only if you help."

I grin and put out my hand. "Deal."

She slaps my hand playfully. "But you and I have to get something straight right now. I'm not taking your apartment. If the rooms are good enough for you to stay in, then they're good enough for me to stay in."

"I—"

"No arguments, or I'll cozy up on one of the booths out there. Please don't make me do that."

All my air leaks from my lungs. "Let's table this until you see the place. You'll change your mind."

3

Isabel

I 'm damn glad I'm following Logan because the road is steep, heavily wooded, and the night is pitch-dark, barely a sliver of moon and not one streetlight.

I'm feeling not just good about being here, I'm a little giddy. It was even better to see Tucker than I expected, and Logan and Cole made me feel like I was coming home, not to a place I've never been after years of losing touch.

And, sure, I'm still ogling Logan 2.0, hot, chill, guarded. Far more mysterious than the kid I knew. I wasn't into him as a kid. He was just another boy. Which made him part of a gender I learned early to distrust and dislike. And he never treated me any differently than he did our friends. I was pretty much just one of the gang. He had a few girlfriends through high school, but nothing significant. The whole virginity pact was just a safe place for us to explore. But he'd always been a good guy. A bit on the broody, dark side, but a stand-up, protective, solid friend.

His blinker clicks on. My mind is drawn back to the

surroundings, and I have a what-in-the-hell moment. Did he seriously buy a shack on the side of a mountain? All I can see outside my headlights are black pines against an indigo sky.

Then he turns into a cracked asphalt parking lot, and the beams of his headlights sweep over a building, followed by mine.

The sight hits me like a brick. My mouth drops open, and I let the Jeep drift to a stop beside his truck. Logan shuts down his engine and gets out, but my headlights are still blazing, lighting up a squat, L-shaped...dump. I can't lie. It's dirty and dingy, siding peeling, a few broken windows boarded up with scrap wood. It looks completely abandoned.

I don't even notice Logan come up to my window, and when he knocks, I jump.

"Settle down," he says through the window. "You were warned." He twists and points behind him, where a light burns over a door. "That's the apartment. Come in and see it before you go scouting all around town at this hour only to end up back here or sleeping in your car and turning into a human ice cube."

I turn off the Jeep and get out. "I'm not going somewhere else. I'm just...um..." I search for a descriptive word that won't hurt the fragile male ego. "It's...very...Bates Motel Chic."

The dark smirk on his face mixes with the reality of the situation and my exhausted state, and I start laughing. I try to stop. Several times. But it's like all my pent-up emotions are bubbling out of me in the form of laughter. I have to bend at the waist to hold my belly against the burn, grab the side mirror of my Jeep to stay upright. I grow dizzy because I'm laughing so hard, I can't breathe.

I have no idea how long it takes me to get my shit together, but Logan is just standing there, hands in the pockets of his hoodie, with that damn, dry smirk, heavy-lidded gaze with a yeah-whatever expression, and snowflakes collecting on his lashes and melting on his face.

"You've seen it, right? Bates Motel?"

"Can't say I've had the pleasure. Can't say I'd like to."

"Okay, honestly, the laughing isn't just about this place. Really. I mean, it started out that way, but my exhaustion kicked in, and I'm really punchy." I sniffle, wipe my eyes, and take a deep breath. "Don't take it personally."

"I'm used to it. I've been getting nonstop shade from the guys since I bought it."

"How long?"

"A few months. Let's talk inside."

By the time I follow him into a small office, then through a short hallway to an apartment, all my exhaustion floods back. While I'm physically wiped out, my brain is spinning like a top —from all the stress over the past month, from all the change.

The hallway opens up to a surprisingly nice apartment. Recessed lights brighten the space, a clean, masculine, open living area in grays and whites, brushed chrome and glass. Large sliding glass doors lead out to a patio or deck of some kind, beyond which I can only see darkness. The kitchen is spotless, the living room neat and simple, with a comfortable-looking, sleek sectional.

"Holy shit, this isn't 'decent.' This is amazing." A flat-screen television covers almost one entire wall. Granted, the space is cozy, and the wall is small, but still. "That's quite a TV. Theater-grade I'm guessing."

"Page 126, section K, part 3 of Guy code," he says. "Have to stay on top of regulation equipment. Can't risk losing my membership."

"Why have they been giving you shit about this place?"

"You haven't seen the rest of it yet."

"Can you show me the rest of this first?"

"Of course."

"Need to hide any forgotten panties? 'Cause I'd rather skip that part of the tour."

"Sheesh." He shakes his head and gestures to two doors in the back corner of the apartment. "I'm not Tucker."

"Good to know," I say as I pass him again. His scent grabs me by the throat, and I stop just a foot away and look up at him. "What in holy hell are you wearing and where can I get a gallon of it?"

He looks confused a second, then breaks into a smile that takes me out at the knees, and I press my hand against the doorframe.

"I'm trying out a new cologne. The guys gave me shit over the last one."

"A: Those guys are idiots. If you want to know how you smell, ask a girl. B: Stay ten paces away from me. You smell completely—"

His brows lift. "Completely...?"

"Never mind. Inappropriate."

"Inappropriate is my middle name," he says. "I smell completely...?"

"Fuckable, if you must know." He's making me light-headed and stupid. "Fuckable, edible, devourable." I press my hand to his chest—shocked by the solid wall of muscle beneath his long-sleeved Henley—and push him back a couple of steps. "Just stay out of reach, will you?"

I pass through the doorway on the right and search for a light switch on the wall. Logan slides in behind me, reaches over my shoulder, and flips the switch.

"Too close?" His husky murmur brushes my ear.

"Asshole," I tease, elbowing him in the ribs.

He's chuckling as I take in the bedroom. It's very much like the living area, but roomier, with the same clean-lined furniture, king bed, side chair with an ottoman, and a side table holding a stack of books.

"I didn't have time to change the sheets." He's got his shoulder against the doorjamb. "No doubt they smell like me."

"If I was on the fence, that would have sealed a big fat no way. But since I was never on the fence to begin with, show me to the musty, dust-inhabited rooms, please."

He chuckles, the sound deep, his smile hot, amusement dancing in his eyes. How could a man I haven't seen in a decade captivate me after only an hour? Especially while I'm *totally* anti-men?

"I kinda like the idea of you in my sheets, unable to sleep," he says, voice a sexy, deep purr.

I smirk as if that idea doesn't make me wet. "Yeah, you do. Keep dreaming."

He steps out of the doorway, turns toward the office, and grabs a ring of keys from a hook on the wall on his way outside.

I follow, arms crossed tight across my middle against the chill. The snow has grown heavier, and I'm glad I was able to keep my four-wheel-drive Jeep. Honestly, I was sure I'd break down on the drive here and was ecstatic that she proved me wrong. I bought it used when I got the assistant designer job—thanks to Aiden. Getting fired was also thanks to Aiden.

Movement in New York, in my opinion, is a bitch. You have to plan for everything from subway maintenance to extreme heat or cold no matter how long the journey. Sometimes I just want the freedom to get in my own damn car and get somewhere, even if that's to the corner five corners away whether it's three degrees outside with a wind chill of negative seven or ninety-five degrees with a humidity of eighty-five percent. Had I known the job would only last as long as I dated Aiden, I would never have bought the car.

Luckily, tonight's poker game gave me one of my overdue payments, staving off repossession a little longer. Plus, they have to find me to take it. I'm hoping I can get ahead of the eight ball before then.

He leads me past several dark rooms with dingy drapes and dirty windows, and my hope sinks with every step. "Trying to get me as far away from you as possible?"

"You're the one who wanted space."

The dark, empty rooms, the dreary condition, and the eerily quiet night are upping this place's creep factor. Or maybe that's just me freaking myself out because of the whole Bates Motel thing.

At a door marked with a 7, which is smack in the middle of the line of rooms, Logan puts a key into the lock. "This is the best room I've got. I started working on it last week."

He pushes the door open and steps aside to allow me in. I move into the doorway, and the scent of freshly cut wood touches my nose. Not what I expected. Again, I search the wall for the light switch, and again, he slides in behind me, his chest brushing my back as he reaches in and turns on the light. I don't bother bitching at him again as that clearly has no effect.

The room is...hard to explain. Construction zone comes to mind. It's really big for a hotel room, double the size of any single room I've ever stayed in. And he's definitely been working on it. One wall has been taken down to the studs, and I can see where old and new merge. Sawhorses are set up in one corner, a circular saw on the concrete subfloor. Drywall is upright and leaning against another wall. The furniture—a bed, a chair, and a dresser—is covered with plastic drop cloths. The bathroom, also oversized, is on the left through an open doorway with no door.

I exhale, long and slow. "Is there heat?"

He steps around me and adjusts a thermostat on the wall. A wall heater I hadn't noticed kicks on.

"Running water?"

He steps into the bathroom and turns on the sink. Water runs, and he nods, as if even he wasn't sure there was running water.

"Okay. I can do this," I tell him. "I really appreciate you letting me stay here. I didn't have the energy to kick Tucker's ass."

He faces me. "Please take the apartment."

"Nope. I'm good."

He shakes his head with an exasperated look. "I don't have the energy to argue with you."

With one swipe, he yanks the plastic off the bed, rolls it up, and puts it beneath a sawhorse. The mattress looks surprisingly new. Most definitely nicer than other mattresses I've slept on over the years. "This isn't as bad as you made it sound."

"I'm replacing the Sheetrock, pulled up the carpet, cleaned it up, but not much else. I—"

"Wasn't expecting guests." I'm looking at the concrete floor, and a grin slides across my face. "There was an episode of Bates where they roll a dead body in the carpet they're getting rid of in the renovation, and a cop comes to the room while they're bent over the body inside the rug. I loved that series. We should stream it while I'm here. I think you'd like it."

"And I think you'd like the apartment."

The heater's taken the chill off the room, but I'm looking at the large plateglass windows with no coverings. I'll have to do something about that, or I'll never get to sleep. But I'll worry about that after he's gone.

"I have everything I need," I say. "I'll pull my suitcase from the Jeep and settle in."

I move past him and out the door. Once I'm out in the cold, snowy air, I breathe deep.

He laughs. "You were holding your breath when you passed me."

"Was not."

He follows me to the Jeep in a lazy stroll. I wait to open the door, which is awkward, because he's watching me wait.

"Go away, Roberts. I can take it from here."

He doesn't respond. He's standing in front of the Jeep, staring through the windshield—the only window that's not tinted. His smile has faded, his brows dip, and, after a second, he steps back and glances at my license plate.

Shit.

His gaze rises to meet mine, puzzlement and concern in his expression. "Isabel—"

"Not tonight, Logan." My shoulders droop. "Please?"

His gaze swings back to my Jeep, packed to the roof, then drops to the New York license plate. He's clearly connected the dots and knows I drove here with all I could fit stuffed into the Jeep.

I can tell by his tense posture and jumping jaw muscle, he doesn't want to let it go, but he finally nods. "Yeah. Okay."

"Thank you."

"Give me your cell number," he says, then enters the numbers into his own phone. "Call if you need anything."

Once he goes inside the apartment, I breathe a little easier. There is so much I can't face right now. And I'm suddenly bone tired. From the past. Over the future. I know the only thing I can do is focus on right now.

I drag in my pillows and a few blankets that I use to cover the two windows. Then a small suitcase with the basics— pajamas, toiletries. The room is warm and quiet, and I'm really looking forward to sleeping in a bed for the first time in days.

The mattress is probably just okay, but right now, my body thinks it's a cloud. Yet when I try to get comfortable in sweats, my hair in a messy bun, my teeth brushed, I can't get my mind to quit spinning. I'm not ready to turn off the lights and find myself missing the rumble of the city.

My gaze slides across the ceiling, which I can see now is a drop ceiling with water-stained square panels, a few askew, exposing the metal framing above. I roll to my side, and my gaze catches on the old heater, chugging out warmth. The paint on the metal unit is thick and flaking.

My mind tries to work its way back to Aiden, New York, all the humiliation I ran from. Then races ahead to what the hell I'm going to do next. I've had a lot of time to think about it on the drive, and out of all the possibilities, San Francisco and Los Angeles are my best bets—that is if I want to continue to beat my head against the fashion industry's bulletproof glass ceiling.

But maybe I could find something in Portland. A buyer for a department store, maybe? I could start as a window display artist and move up through the ranks. Then I realize I'd only be repeating the same mistakes, expecting different results.

I give up on sleep for now. I take clothes out of my suitcase and open a dresser drawer. A squeak coincides with a flurry of movement.

Mice. I recognize the situation immediately. I've lived in enough shit holes to know.

Everything happens at once. One mouse runs, hopping over the back of the drawer, scurrying down the inside of the dresser. I suck in a breath and jump back, hoping it doesn't find the floor and run up my pant leg.

Inside the drawer, there's a nest, much like a bird's, with half a dozen squirming jelly-bean-sized babies. The adult mouse that didn't run stands on its hind legs and gnashes its itty-bitty teeth at me. It's the strangest, eeriest noise I've ever heard. Ten times worse than fingernails on a chalkboard.

I'm guessing it's the father. The male mice are the more aggressive, especially around a nest—the things you learn dealing with exterminators too often.

"Okay, big boy," I say, almost a whisper. "Everything's okay. I don't want to hurt your babies."

He drops back to all fours as if he understands and starts a worried pace along the front edge of the nest.

I slowly climb onto the bed, rest on my knees, and Face-Time Logan.

He answers with a big grin and a teasing "I knew you were going to change your mind."

"Actually, I was just wondering if I get a discount for roommates."

His face falls into confusion. "What? Roommates?"

"Hold on." I flip the camera to face forward and zoom in on the mice family.

"You've got to be fucking kidding me," comes from Logan. "I'll be right there."

"No. Not now." I turn the camera back to face me, and I can't help but laugh. "It's a family, so it's going to take more than a trap or a shoebox to get them out."

"Why aren't you screaming your head off like ninety-nine percent of the female population would?"

"Let's just say this isn't my first rodent rodeo."

"Are we still talking about the mice?"

Laughter bubbles out of me. "While I've got you," I focus the camera on the flaking paint. "Is that lead paint?"

"I don't know. Just don't eat it, and you'll be fine."

"And..." I zoom in on the ceiling tile. "Is that asbestos?"

"I don't know. Just don't—"

"Breathe?" I ask, turning the camera to face myself again. "And I'll be fine?"

Now he's laughing. "Seriously, would you *please* swap rooms with me?"

"Nope. Just wanted to let you know you've got squatters. Sweet dreams."

I disconnect and slowly, slowly, painfully slowly, slide the dresser drawer closed. Then I sigh in relief. I flop back on the bed and close my eyes. It's almost 2:00 a.m., but my mind is still grinding. What am I going to do for money? Where am I going to stay for the next few weeks until I figure out a plan? I expected the loft to have a separate bedroom. I can stay at Tucker's while he's on duty, I guess. At least that's half the battle.

I know from lots of experience that with a mind this busy, I'll never sleep without some sort of intervention. I push into my cross-trainers, throw on my jacket and head to the Jeep. The snow is still coming down, but I don't feel as cold. My body temperature warmed up enough to buffer the subzero chill.

It only takes me a minute to find my sketchbook. It's really a journal and a sketch pad and a to-do list and a planner all in one. It's basically a physical manifestation of my mind dumps. And boy, oh boy, do I have shit to dump tonight.

I straighten from the Jeep and shut the door, only to have my gaze drawn toward the apartment. The lights are still on, the blinds up, and I catch glimpses of Logan moving around in the living area. He suddenly and unexpectedly drags his shirt off over his head and tosses it in the direction of the sofa. I suck air, and my mouth hangs open.

"Jeeeeezus." He doesn't look at all like the kid I knew in school—average height, average weight. Maybe even on the skinny side.

There is nothing skinny or average about Logan the man. His chest, abs, and arms are thickly muscled, and while I can't see detail from this distance, I can sure as hell see enough for my body to shoot off fireworks beneath my skin. He picks up a drink from a side table and points something toward the TV, presumably the remote.

I turn to face away from the apartment, drop my head back, and welcome the snowflakes on my skin. I definitely need to cool down.

My cell vibrates. I look at the display expecting to find Logan's name, but Cocksucker fills the screen. I'm so over all this bullshit.

I tap the green button and answer. "Hello?"

"How long are you going to do this?" Aiden sounds...mildly annoyed. Like I'm still an inconvenience, even though I officially broke up with him over a month ago. But his voice sounds loud in my ear, so I tap the volume button down a couple of times.

"I'm sorry," I say. "I just got a new phone. Who is this?"

"You know it's Aiden. And I know you can't afford a new phone."

"Oh," I say, drawing out the word. "That makes sense now. The caller ID reads cocksucker."

"Not funny."

"Not joking."

"You're such a bitch."

What in the hell did I *ever* see in this guy? "You sure know how to turn a girl's head. I'm talking *The Exorcist*."

"Where the fuck are you?" he yells, and my eardrum rings. "I've called all your friends, been by all your jobs."

"Therein lies the problem. I have no friends and no job, thanks to you."

"Come on. This is stupid. Let's talk about it already."

"Happy to talk as soon as my money is back in the bank."

"I'll put the money back as soon as you return Valerie."

He's a broken record. Right now, I have the leverage, and he'll have to pry it from my cold dead fingers.

"Undamaged," he continues. "Unfired. In her collector's box."

"I see hell freezing over in your future."

"*Get the fuck back here* and bring Valerie with you."

"I always thought she was more of a Sterling or Ivory," I say, reminding him of the finishing touches he loves about the antique rifle. "I got a killer offer on her today, and it will bring us even, so if you don't want her back, just let me know. We'll call it good and go our own ways."

"*Don't you dare fucking sell her.*"

I wince and leave the phone a couple of inches away from my ear to bring this conversation to a close. "Sell her? Hell no. I'm gonna pawn her."

"That's worse."

"I know. Drop me a note when the money has been returned, and I'll let you know if I still have Valerie or not."

He's swearing up a storm when I disconnect. My shoulders rock with a deep breath of relief. Oregon is the perfect place to get a great price on the rifle. Lots of gun owners in the mountains. I really don't want to sell it, but I need the money he siphoned from my account. He also bought that gun with my money. I'll get it back one way or another. His choice.

I'm still intensely annoyed I've lowered myself to this slimy level. It's like one more confirmation that I belong right where I am—a broke failure. But if there's one thing that has stayed constant from the second I left Oregon, it's the knowledge that I can take damn good care of myself. I don't need a man. Hell, I don't even want one.

I turn toward the room and startle at the sight of Logan standing beside my open door, blankets in one hand, a flashlight in the other.

"Oh my God, you scared me. What are you doing?"

"I lose power out here sometimes. Haven't upgraded the service yet." He lifts the items in his hands. "Just in case."

We just stare at each other a moment that feels like it expands and twists.

I cross my arms and feel all my walls go up. "How much did you hear?"

"Given it was about a five-minute call, I'd say all of it."

I close my eyes and pinch the bridge of my nose. "I'm sorry you had to hear that mess."

"I'm sorrier you're in it." His voice softens. "Sounds like you need a friend. Please tell me what's going on."

"It's late, I'm exhausted, and you have to work in the morning. Let's table this discussion for another day."

"You're still as stubborn as you always were." He offers me the blankets and puts the flashlight on top. "Those may or may not smell like me. Sweet dreams."

"Asshole," I say to his back, only to get another sexy chuckle.

4

Logan

The woman on the ground in front of me is far too young to die. In fact, I'm pretty sure she's only a few years older than me.

Jake Bryant, one of our volunteers and an off-duty ER nurse, pumps her chest in a steady rhythm as I set up the defibrillator. The sickening scent of burnt flesh mixes with the smoke coming from the apartment where she lives, and my stomach makes a slow roll toward my throat.

"She really pulled a Pryor this time," Jake says, referencing the alcohol still soaking her T-shirt and the burns on her face, neck, and arms from freebasing crack, the same activity that set the apartment on fire. "At least she was too high to feel much pain."

I've been doing this long enough to know with relative certainty which patients will come back, and which won't. In this case, I also have the woman's history—a crack addict who failed out of recovery several times. Crack is a wicked, wicked drug, and after her years of addiction, I don't see her heart starting again no matter what we do. But despite what I might think, or how many odds are stacked against us, I always, always, *always* go the extra mile with every patient, just in case their spirit is undecided over which world they want to live in.

"Clear," I say for the third time. Jake sits back, and I shoot jolts of electricity through the woman's worn body, but nothing is restarting her heart today.

Jake starts compressions again. "She's not coming back."

"I know." But I stick with protocol and deliver epinephrine, my last-ditch effort to give her a kick start.

Suzy Blunt is a frequent flier. All the paramedics, cops, fire, and emergency room personnel know her. She's a nice lady, but the drugs had a grip on her she couldn't shake. I knew there would come a day when I was called to the house and I wouldn't be able to save her.

Looks like today is that day.

I check my watch. Our most up-to-date field procedures call for twenty minutes of CPR on scene. If the patient's heart restarts during that time, we transport to the hospital. But today, it looks like I'll be calling the coroner.

"We've got about seven more minutes before we tap out," I tell Jake. "Want me to take over?"

"Nah, I've got this."

I look toward the house. The fire is out, and Cole, Tucker, Royal, and a handful of volunteers are mopping up the mess. Neighbors have gathered, and local police are holding a perimeter.

"I'm gonna go help the guys," I tell Jake.

"Yeah."

If it were anyone else, I'd stay and run out the clock, but the truth is that even after I've spent ten years in the field, Jake may be more experienced in emergency medicine than I am.

Royal's at the engine, coiling hose, so I head inside and help haul it down the stairs and out of the apartment. The place is gutted and blackened. The fire started in the living room, burned across the first floor, through the ceiling, up the stairs.

Royal meets me at the front door and takes the hose. I wander through the remnants of the house. Multiple liquor bottles managed to survive the fire, as did some of the drug paraphernalia. I've seen this a lot during my time as a paramedic, but it still strikes me as sad.

I grab an axe and a halligan leaning against the wall and step out of the apartment.

A whimper touches my ear, and my feet stop. The hair on the back of my neck rises.

Tucker exits the front door. "Guess we won't be coming here every other shift anymore."

I follow his line of sight and find Jake covering Suzy with a plastic tarp.

"Was she the only one here?" I ask.

"Yeah, why?"

Another whimper comes from somewhere, but it's so weak, I almost think I'm imagining it.

"Shit." Tucker's eyes go wide, and he spins toward the sound. "Where's that coming from?"

Cole and Royal come into the house talking, and Tucker and I shush them at the same time. Everyone goes quiet.

Cole finally whispers, "What are we—"

Whimper. It's an animal. Probably a dog.

"The kitchen." The apartment is small, and it only takes me three steps to get there. Tucker and Cole follow. Everything is smoky and covered in soot. I start opening cabinets, Tucker checks closets, Cole opens the refrigerator. What addicts and mentally ill people do to people and animals is beyond me. A baby in the fridge is—sadly—no stretch. But it's empty, as are the cabinets and closets.

"Maybe it was just—" I start.

Another whimper makes me swivel toward the trash can.

"Motherfucking sonofabitch." Inside, a small animal lies in the trash, covered in soot and garbage. "What in the fuck was she thinking?"

I start to reach in, and Cole pulls me back by my turnout jacket. "Don't put your hand in there. It could be something feral."

The animal scrambles amid the trash, and the sounds identify it as a dog. I snatch it from the garbage can. He's small, barely double the size of my hand, and weighs maybe a pound or two.

"It's a puppy, for fuck's sake." I brush at the soot on his fur. "People are so goddamned sick."

"She was higher than a kite," Tucker says. "She wasn't thinking about anything but her next hit."

The dog's got the shape of a Lab. He's a mottled mess, but I take his snout in my hand and look at the face. Its eyes are barely open, but they're bright blue. I've never seen a Lab with blue eyes. "I think it's an Australian shepherd."

When I look at the guys, I find them staring at me with here-we-go-again expressions. Cole's got one hand on the countertop, the other at his hip. Tucker's got his arms crossed.

"Oh, come on," I say. "You two are narcissists if you don't care about this pup."

"You already have two house cats," Tucker says.

"And this is the sixth animal you've wanted to make a pet of this year," Cole says.

Tucker lifts his fingers and ticks them off. "Rabbit, guinea pig, turtle, iguana."

The puppy's breathing is raspy, and it closes its eyes and goes still.

Royal comes in. "What's going on?"

"Give me your BA," I tell Royal, using gimme fingers. "Come on."

"What in the hell are you doing?" Tucker wants to know, his voice dripping with *you idiot*.

"Fuck you, Ice Man. You let your sister flail for a place to say so you could get laid and now you're against a defenseless puppy? Just because you have a scarecrow's heart doesn't mean the rest of us do. And last time I looked, Cole's the one with brass on his collar. You want to boss people around, take the fucking test and promote."

"Wasn't it the tin man who wanted a heart?" Royal asks, offering his breathing apparatus.

"The scarecrow wanted a brain," Cole affirms.

I lay the BA over the pup's head, but he's so small, the mask covers half his body too. I take off my helmet and put it on the counter upside down, then drag off the soft fabric of my head and neck cover and bunch it in my helmet. I lay the pup on top and cover him with Royal's BA again.

"Now I've seen everything." Tucker shakes his head. "I need some damned ruby slippers so I can get the hell out of this place."

"Let the door hit you on the way out," I tell him. To the puppy, I say, "Yeah, he's an asshole. You're lucky I'm the one who found you."

"That's a great name," Royal says. "Lucky."

"I think we're going to keep you around, kid," I tell him.

"Last time I looked," Tucker parrots dryly, "Cole's the one with brass on his collar. You want to make decisions, take the fucking test and promote."

"Asshole." I collect the helmet, the BA, and the puppy and shoulder my way past Tucker and Cole on my way out. "Seriously, you should find a Narcissists Anonymous."

Royal's beside me, enthralled with the dog. "Dude, I think that's a Dalmatian."

"How can you tell?"

Outside, I pause, and Royal fluffs the pup's fur, loosening

some of the soot. Sure enough, the fur color is light around at least one very distinct black circle. "They aren't born with spots, so he has to be older than four or six weeks."

"You've got an eye," I tell Royal. "We gotta keep him now."

Outside, we pause to watch the coroner load Suzy into the back of their van.

"Why do you think she put him in the trash?" Royal asks.

"High people do crazy things, including become paranoid and have hallucinations. I can think of half a dozen ways the dog ended up in the trash."

Still, Dalmatians aren't the kind of dog you just pick up from a box in front of Walmart. Was she holding it for someone? Did she steal it hoping to sell it for drug money? If so, why was he in the trash? The can was too tall for the pup to get in there himself.

The crowd milling around the edges of the scene would be the perfect group to ask, but that meant I'd risk having someone claim him. Still, it's the right thing to do.

I approach Dalton Conway, a local cop, who is now dating Emily, my ex, and the reason I put my sex life on hold. Everyone in EMS knows everyone else, regardless of their position. Cops, firefighters, and EMTs cross paths every day. In this case, there are no hard feelings. I was happy to have Emily move on with someone else. It ended the headache she was hell-bent on giving me.

"Hey," Dalton says. "What have you got there?"

"Dog. He was in the trash can."

Dalton shakes his head in disgust. "It alive?"

"Yeah. I know you come out here quite a bit," I say. "Do you know anything about it?"

"No. What the hell would she do with a dog? It would cut into her drug budget."

To the small crowd, I say, "Does anyone know about Suzy getting a dog?"

I get a lot of shaking heads and murmured nos, then a guy from the back says, "I think she was going to give it to her boyfriend for his birthday."

"Puppet?" Dalton asks in disbelief. Puppet is a low-life local drug dealer—the worst person on the planet to care for anyone or anything other than himself. "Are you serious?"

The guy shrugs. "I'm just telling you what she told me."

"Why a Dalmatian?" I ask.

"She said he had one as a kid."

Dalton looks at me. "Take it if you want it. Or drop it at a shelter. Anywhere is better than here."

"I'll hold on to him. If someone comes forward, let me know."

"Sure thing."

"Dude," Tucker says to Cole at the truck, where he's putting away the fire hose with volunteers. "Nip this in the bud. You know how much trouble puppies are."

Cole's gaze swings toward me. He was promoted to captain not that long ago, and I know he constantly finds himself between me and Tucker, his two best friends.

"I'll take care of him," I say. "I promise."

Tucker laughs. "You still sound five years old. 'Can I keep this racoon, this bird, this snake, this dragonfly, this ladybug, this salamander?' You're going to be an animal hoarder when you're an old man."

"The racoon was the best," Cole says. "Remember how he'd get loose and dump over all the garbage cans in the neighborhood, and Logan had to go around and pick them all up again?"

"Bandit," Tucker says, grinning. "Such an original name."

"What will you do when someone wants it back?" Cole asks, turning the conversation back to the puppy.

"I'll cross that bridge if it appears." I step close and show Cole the fur Royal roughed up. "Look, it's a Dalmatian."

Cole sighs. "I don't care whether or not you keep the dog, but you're going to have to get it past Sorenson."

Tucker snorts a laugh and shakes his head. "You're such an enabler. Always have been. And Sorenson will never go for it." Then to Logan, "If you really want it, keep it as your own."

"I can't take care of a dog on my own, not with our schedule."

The broody sky opens up, dumping rain.

"Let's get something to eat before we're called—" Tucker starts.

"Rescue one," the dispatcher's voice comes over the radio. "Shortness of breath reported at 622 Waldorf Street."

I offer my helmet to Royal. "Keep Tucker from getting his hands on the dog."

"Will do." Royal scoops the pup from my helmet and climbs in the engine. I head to the rescue, and we all start toward Waldorf Street.

5

Logan

I t's 7:00 p.m. when engine one pulls into the driveway of the firehouse, me right behind them in the rescue.

This has been a nonstop day, call after call after call. Normally, I love these days. Time flies and we're having fun. There's always a lot of energy in the house on days like this. Only today, I'm stressing over leaving the puppy alone.

I've barely had enough time to check his water and clean up his poop before we're out on another call, though I did get in a shower earlier and took him in with me, soot flowing down the drain, mostly from the pup. And Royal had been right, the dog turned out to be a beautiful and devilishly cute Dalmatian, covered in black spots of all sizes, his eyes an even brighter blue than I thought.

The scent of cooking food and spices hits my nose, and my whole body tenses up. We haven't eaten since breakfast, but I'm going to have to deal with the puppy before I can sit down to eat. Natalie, Cole's fiancée, knows we've been out all day, so she came to cook for us, which we all deeply appreciate. It would have been torture to wait for delivery, and no one's in shape to cook.

I shed my gear and file into the house with the others, pausing at the open door to the half bathroom on the bottom floor, where I've been keeping the puppy. But he's not in the room and the floor is clean.

For a second, I think someone claimed him and he's gone. I can't lie, my heart drops to my stomach. Then I hear yips coming from the kitchen, and relief flows through me.

"Roberts," one of the guys calls down the hall. "Your kid wants to see you."

I move into the house and find Natalie in the kitchen, which is open to the rest of the living area. This station is relatively new, and it's pretty posh, with a big U-shaped kitchen and quartz counters. Actually, everything in this kitchen is big—the stove, ovens, fridge.

Natalie has blocked off the kitchen so the puppy can't get out, and he's pacing the row of boxes and buckets, yipping. As soon as he sees me, his whole body wags on overdrive, he pops his paws on the barriers, and yips at me while trying to reach me.

Only he tips one of the buckets over just enough to swallow him up, and he drops to the bottom of the bucket with a thump.

The guys bust up laughing. I don't blame them, it's funny, and the pup is okay, just scrambling to get out of the bucket.

"Hey, buddy," I say, laughing as I lean in and pick him up. Oblivious to his misstep, he wiggles and licks my face.

Yeah, Jesus, I'm going to be so damned disappointed if I lose him.

Natalie's mom, Betsy, is sitting on the other side of the kitchen counter. "He's adorable, but he's pretty energetic. You'll have your hands full with him. He's smart and fast and feisty."

"Aw," Natalie says. "He sure loves you."

"Dogs can smell stupid a mile away." Tucker's comment makes the others laugh.

"Then I'm sure he'll warm right up to you," I tell him, which gets an even bigger response.

"Your headache," Tucker says, shaking his head. "But Sorenson will never let you keep him."

That reminds me this pup is going to be a hard sell. With him secured close to my body, I jog up the stairs and grab the form I created earlier in the day from the printer, then return to the family room. Unless I get the other firefighters on board to keep him, I'll have to give him up. With my work here and the bar, I'd have to crate him a lot of the time, and that's no life for a dog.

I stop in the kitchen. "That smells amazing. "What are you making, Nat?"

"One of your favorites, spaghetti and meatballs."

The guys cheer from the rec room.

Natalie has a way with food. Her sauce tastes like it comes fresh from the garden, her meatballs spiced to perfection. She adds cheese to her garlic bread and makes a feta and walnut salad that changed my mind about the worthlessness of lettuce, but is still mostly a vehicle to get her champagne vinaigrette into my mouth.

"God, I can't wait." I groan the words. "Thanks for coming. We'd all be scrounging in the fridge without you."

"I love cooking for you guys. And that puppy is heart-stoppingly adorable."

Mention of the puppy makes me realize he's quiet, and I look down to see he's fallen asleep. "Thanks for watching him."

"Not a problem. He's a good pup."

I was going to grab another shower, but with the dog asleep, I join the guys in the rec room instead. "Okay, guys," I say to the room at large, "this is the puppy petition. Everyone who wants to keep the pup needs to sign it."

"You think signatures are going to sway Sorenson?" Tucker asks.

"It can't hurt."

Royal speaks up first. "I'll sign it if we can name him Lucky."

"Lucky it is." I hand him the paper, and Royal signs even though I'm not ready to name the dog. That feels too permanent for something I don't know if I'll be able to keep.

I turn to Carter. He looks at the paper, then the pup, then me. "I've got tickets to Santana next month. Take my shift so I can go, and I'll sign."

I don't have anything coming up, so I agree and get my second signature.

Cole is next. "Natalie and I want to go to Hawaii on our honeymoon."

"You haven't even set a wedding date."

He shrugs. "Cover me for the trip. We can work out the dates later."

"Fine." I hand him the sheet.

"Dinner's ready," Nat calls from the kitchen.

We sit at the table, and the movement wakes the pup. He scrambles out of my lap and wanders around under the table while I negotiate for signatures over dinner.

Smitty wants Christmas off.

I look at Tucker. "What do you want?"

"New Year's," he says as if that's a given. "And the phone number for that insanely hot chick we picked up at the gorge last month. The blonde. If you're not going to use her number, I will."

I think back and remember her as a rough-around-the-edges beauty who wore her sexuality on her sleeve. She'd been jumping from the cliffs into the water and slipped, scratched up her arm pretty good, but she refused a trip to the hospital. After I bandaged some superficial cuts, she gave me her phone number. Even as I was saying I can't date patients, she stuffed it into the breast pocket of my uniform.

"That flight attendant must have really stolen your heart. You waited a whole"—I glance at my watch—"twelve hours before chasing another chick."

"She'll be coming back through in a couple of weeks," he says, "but in the meantime, I'll touch base with the gorge chick. Always gotta keep your iron in the fire. Besides, you're the one wasting the opportunity. You've got to get over Emily's bullshit and get back on the horse, dude. You're headed into pathetic territory."

"Says the guy who's never been scared out of his skin by those two fatal words—'I'm pregnant.'"

"That's because I'm not stupid enough to trust anything a woman tells me."

"Fine. I'll look for her number." I give up. Tucker's got a comeback for everything. "Have I told you what a prick you are lately?"

"Now, boys, stop ruffling each other's feathers." Betsy stands and hands me a piece of paper. "There you are, honey. All the promises you made so you can keep track."

Fucking perfect. "Thanks."

I'm annoyed with the guys—until Nat puts food in front of me. Before I can shovel in my first bite, Jake pushes his chair back from the table, laughing. "Dude, your dog untied my shoelaces."

I put down my fork, move around the table to take the dog from Jake, and return to my seat. But now, with the pup in my lap, the table is in his direct line of sight, and he's eyeballing my plate.

"Shit, I didn't get dog food."

"I gave him a can of tuna," Nat says. "He should be fine."

"Okay," I tell the pup, "you've eaten. This is mine."

Eventually, the dog yawns and curls into a comma on my

lap, little head on little paws. Animals are so trusting. Maybe that's why I'm so drawn to them—no lies, no bullshit, no betrayal.

Isabel crosses my mind. She's got that trio against her for sure. She's lying about what happened with her ex, whipping up all kinds of bullshit to cover why she's here, and while she hasn't betrayed anyone—that I know of yet—she did a damn fine job of it when she left town all those years ago.

"Cole said Isabel is in town." Natalie sets a plate in front of her mom at the counter, along with a glass of wine, and takes a stool beside her. "Is she staying with you, Tucker?"

Tucker's gaze meets mine across the table.

"No," I say for him. "Tucker prioritized sex over family. She's staying with me, in one of the motel's rooms."

"Tucker," Natalie chastises. "She's family."

"If she'd told me she was coming I could have rescheduled," Tucker says.

"I put her in seven," I say. "She didn't seem to mind. It's the best room I've got."

"It's also the only room with running water," Carter says.

"Last I heard," Tucker adds, "it wasn't hot water."

I didn't remember that until this morning on my way to work. "I offered her the apartment—twice—but she wouldn't take it."

"Honey," Betsy says. "Did you offer her the apartment with you in it or out of it?"

"Out of it, of course."

Betsy grins. "There's your problem."

Everyone breaks into laughter. Betsy's become a den mother of sorts, and she's fun to have around. "Ha, good one."

While the others are laughing, I'm eating. One touch of Natalie's magic sauce on my tongue and I can't get the food in fast enough. "Oh my God, Nat, this is amazing."

The others agree, and the room goes quiet. Someone walks

in through the door between the garage bay and the house, but we all ignore whoever it is, focused on the food.

When the person stops in the doorway, I glance up, expecting to see a volunteer, but it's Isabel, and she looks like she just rolled out of bed. She's wearing the same clothes as yesterday, and a ball cap with her hair pulled through the back in a ponytail.

"Is that my baseball hat?" I ask.

"Good morning, afternoon, evening—whatever—to you too," she says. "It was in the room, which is as good as the lost and found."

"Well, look what the cat dragged in," Tucker says.

"There's a cat?" She's got a deadpan expression and she looks tired, like she barely slept. "Send it to room seven. My roommates partied all night long. It's time for an eviction."

"Roommates?" Royal says.

"Don't ask," I tell him, and since Tucker's being rude, I use my fork to point to each guy and introduce them to Isabel. There are way too many names to remember. I can't even keep track of half the volunteers myself. "This is Isabel, Tucker's sister."

Isabel gives the table a wave. "Hey, guys. Why aren't there any girl firefighters?"

Carter's face breaks into a big grin. "Because we're lucky?"

More laughter fills the space, but now I'm hyperaware of Isabel. She seems to take up every brain cell.

"And what happened to all of you?" she asks. "You're a mess."

I imagine seeing us all through Isabel's eyes. We're dirty, sweaty, smoky, and a few of us are cut up, including me.

"It's been a rough day," I tell her.

Lucky lifts his head, wags his tail, and whines while looking at Isabel.

"Are you picking up strays again?" she asks.

"He picked you up, didn't he?" Tucker asks.

"You're an ass," she tells him. "Can I use the shower here?"

"You just called me an ass."

Her gaze turns to Cole. "Can I?"

"You could have used the shower in my apartment," I say before Cole answers. "If you'd called, I would have told you where the hide-a-key is."

She just shrugs and addresses the table. "Everyone in favor of letting me shower here, raise your hand."

My arm wants to shoot skyward, but I don't want anyone to get the wrong idea, because I'm totally not into her. The others don't have any such limitation, and every hand shoots straight up, Carter's and Royal's first, like they were already thinking about her upstairs in the shower.

"Majority rules," Isabel says. "Thank you. I will reward everyone who voted for me—which specifically excludes Tucker and Logan—with pizza one night very soon."

All the guys cheer and high-five each other.

"Point me in the right direction." Isabel barely gets the words out before Carter and Royal shoot to their feet with "I'll show you" in stereo.

"I said it first," Royal says.

"But I've got seniority," Carter says.

Isabel laughs. "Aren't they adorable?"

"Heel, boys," Tucker says, then tells Isabel, "Up the stairs, first door on the right."

She turns for the stairs, and everyone's gaze follows her until she's gone.

"Where you been hiding her?" Jake wants to know, clear interest in his voice.

"New York," Tucker says. "Don't even think about it. She'll be gone soon anyway."

"Oh, heck." Smitty puts down his fork. "The towels are in the drier."

Tucker leans back toward the staircase and yells, "Isabel, the towels are—" The door shuts, and the remainder of his words escape on an exhale. "In the drier."

All eyes turn to Natalie, a silent suggestion she bring the towels upstairs. But the oven timer dings, and she slides off the stool with "You want me to finish your dessert or pass out towels? 'Cause I can't do both."

"Dessert" is everyone's answer.

"You should bring her the towels," Natalie tells me on her way to the oven. "You did make her sleep in a third-world motel last night."

"Didn't you notice the puppy on my lap?" The thought of standing on the other side of a door from a naked Isabel shoots a zing of panic up my spine. "And why is Tucker's disrespect my problem?"

"He's right, Tucker," Betsy says. "You should know hookups always come second to family."

I snort a laugh.

"We all know you're a better guy than Tucker," Natalie tells me. "Do the right thing, Logan."

Tucker sits back, palms up. "Why the hate?"

Carter and Royal look at each other, and I see the competition streak through their eyes. They both stand at the same time and say, "I'll get them for her."

"Once again," Royal says, "I said it first."

"And once again," Carter says, "I have seniority. Besides, you owe me for spotting you in the workout yesterday."

"Oh, good God," I mutter, collecting the sleeping bundle of puppy and pushing to my feet. "Both of you sit the hell down. I'll do it. But if anyone—and I mean anyone, including you beauties"—I aim my fork at Natalie and Betsy, making them both laugh—"touch my food, it will be a declaration of war."

Once the guys sit down, I put the dog in Royal's lap. He sits back. "Dude, I'm eating."

"Two seconds ago, you were willing to bring towels upstairs."

He accepts the pup and shuts his mouth, just like he should.

In the laundry room, I messily fold the towels, still warm from the drier, and head up the stairs. Everyone is back to talking and laughing around the table, and I'll bet that my food won't be there when I get back. It's a given. I should have let Carter or Royal take them.

The water is running, and I pause in front of the door. God, I wish my mind would stop picturing her naked. I raise my hand and knock. "Isabel, I have towels for you."

From experience, I know she won't be able to hear anything in the shower. I knock again. Still get no answer. "Jesus."

I finally try the door, find it unlocked, and roll my eyes. I open it just enough to reach in and put the towels on the sink while lifting my voice to say, "Isabel, it's Logan. I'm leaving towels—"

Movement pulls my gaze toward the shower, to Isabel standing naked, her back toward me, her hand testing the water temperature. In split-second snapshots, I take in all the smooth skin, all the sexy curves, and yeah, I get a really good look at her gorgeous ass, before my attention is drawn to the bruises on her arms and fury spikes.

They no longer look like mottled yellow and purple areas. They've faded to a brownish yellow and are in a distinct finger pattern. There's also a healthy bruise on her hip and one on her calf.

Isabel's gasp pulls me back, but not in time to see her full-frontal nudity before she's standing right in front of me, the stack of towels covering a good chunk of her luscious body.

"Isabel." I hope my voice is less punishing than it sounds to me. "You didn't get those bruises carting luggage."

"You don't know that. Have you ever driven across the

country having to handle all your own luggage?" Then she adds, "As a girl, I mean?"

My sense of humor has evaporated. The sight of those bruises cuts me deep and draws all my protectiveness to the surface. "If anyone knows what abuse looks like, it's me. I'm not going to just pretend yours doesn't exist. You can tell Tucker and let him handle it, or I'll handle it, or you and I can handle it together. Those are your choices."

Her brow is pulled into an angry scowl. "Since when are you my keeper?"

"Since you're staying in my place and since I saw those bruises. I'm not trying to come down on you, but I can't just pretend I didn't see them."

She takes the towels, closes her eyes, and sighs. "Can we talk about this when I'm not naked?"

Oh, shit. "Of course, I forgot, sorry."

I back out of the room, but catch a split-second side view of her in the mirror. Her arms and the towels cover her breasts, but I definitely got a glimpse of her flat belly before I close the door again. I turn and rest my back against the wall, eyes closed, and every little visual detail rushes back at me.

It's not like I never see naked women. Sure, I haven't dated since I got rid of Emily months ago, but I'm regularly exposed to nakedness of all kinds in my job. This, however, isn't the same. Not even close, and my body agrees.

I shake out my hands, run them through my hair, and do what I can to cool my body before heading back to the peanut gallery. Even before I sit at the table again, I can see two of my meatballs are gone, but I don't have the energy to play this game.

I cut the one I have left with the side of my fork and glance at Natalie. "Any more meatballs?"

"You know I cook for fifty," she says on her way to the stove. "Figure that will keep you all in dinner for two nights, tops."

She brings a plate with two meatballs.

"Thank you," I tell her. "Just make sure whoever took mine doesn't get dessert."

"You were up there awhile," Jake says. "What'd you two talk about?"

"She wanted me to get in with her, and I had to explain all about the no-sex-at-the-firehouse rule, one her brother has conveniently forgotten a number of times," I say with a heavy dose of dumb shit. "What do you *think* we talked about?"

The guys laugh, then pick up conversations that don't involve me, which is good because I can't think of anything but those fucking bruises on Isabel's skin. Or how she might have gotten them. I watched my mom get beaten often enough to know what attacks result in what injuries, and in my head, Cocksucker grabbed her arms in anger and held tight while she tried to get away. Then he shoved her into something, furniture probably, resulting in the other bruises.

Then the conversation I overheard slides in to provide another layer of context.

My appetite is suddenly gone. I don't have the right to mess with her business. I know that. But I also can't just stand by and let it continue happening. I may not have talked to her in ten years, but we grew up together, were great friends before the bottom fell out and she disappeared. Besides, she's Tucker's sister. We'll always be family.

I heard about eighty percent of her conversation with Cocksucker and I know there is a dispute over money, and possibly someone named Valerie. What I could also hear was the condescending arrogance in his tone and the sense of ownership in his demands.

I push spaghetti around on my plate, pissed I have no real right to butt in.

"That smells amazing." Isabel's voice brings my head up.

She's wearing fresh jeans and a dark green sweater that

hugs her body. Her hair is still wet, loose, and falling in soft waves. She still looks even more beautiful without makeup. And fresh out of the shower, she's sexy AF.

"Sit," Natalie says. "I'll fix you a plate."

"Bless you."

6

Isabel

"He *forgot* I was naked," I tell my reflection, turning to get a better look at the bruise on the back side of my hip. "*For-got.*"

That's all kinds of painful for my tattered ego. "What man forgets a woman is naked?"

My reflection doesn't have any decent answer.

I dress in my last set of clean clothes, finger comb my hair, and head downstairs. I left all my toiletries at the motel because I was half-asleep and disoriented.

In all the years Tucker, Cole, and Logan have been firefighters, I've never been in a firehouse. I left town before they joined the fire service. At seventeen, I grabbed a scholarship that wasn't truly mine and ran to New York, a fashion designer wannabe. I liken it to women who come from the Midwest for a shot at Hollywood. And just like ninety-nine point nine percent of those women, I washed out.

When I walk into the dining room, all eyes turn to me.

There are eighteen people here, not counting me. Sixteen guys plus Natalie and Betsy.

"That smells amazing," I tell Natalie.

"Sit," Natalie says. "I'll fix you a plate."

"Bless you."

I go for an icebreaker. "Okay, let's see if I can get all your names."

"Twenty bucks she gets them all." Tucker pulls out a twenty and slaps it on the table.

"No way," Carter says, tossing out another twenty. "Ten out of eighteen."

Betting is clearly a thing with these guys. They toss bets at Tucker, and he jots them down on a napkin. Wallets come out of back pockets and money appears on the table. With most of the guys tossing in twenty bucks—everyone except Logan and Cole—there is quickly nearly three hundred bucks on the table, which looks very appealing to someone who hasn't seen that much cash since Cocksucker drained her bank account.

"What do I get out of this?" I ask.

"If I win," Tucker says, "I'll split it with you."

"But I'm doing all the work. Eighty"—I point to myself, then to Tucker—"twenty."

"Sixty"—he points to himself, then to me—"forty."

"Seventy, thirty," I say. "Final offer. You're treating me like a circus act. I should be compensated."

"She's a shark," Royal murmurs.

"She's Tucker's sister," Cole says. "What did you expect?"

"Fine," Tucker says. "Go."

I look around the table and let the silence linger. I swear all the guys are leaning in, on the edge of their seats, waiting. Tucker is kicked back, arms crossed, smiling like a cocky playboy. If I didn't need the money, I'd lose on purpose, just to mess with him.

I take a breath and point at each guy as I rattle off all their names in thirty seconds, finishing with "Natalie and Betsy."

When I'm done, all jaws hang open except for Tucker's, Logan's, and Cole's. I've always had a strong memory. Tucker's grinning and reaching for the money. I want to grab my portion and pocket it like a greedy squirrel facing winter, but I'm too aware of the conversation Logan overheard last night. Too mindful of his eyes scanning my face, searching for the answers to his questions, validation for his concerns. Despite my dire circumstances, I still have some pride. Probably too much, or I would have asked for help sooner.

The losers deflate. Everyone moans and mutter things like "That's impossible" and "How'd she do that?" Some lean back, hands clasped on their heads. Others drop their foreheads to the table on a groan. And some try to bargain their way out of losing by claiming I mixed first names and last names.

"She gave the names as Logan introduced them," Tucker says. "Can't argue with that."

A couple of the volunteers say their goodbyes, and Natalie and Betsy fill those seats at the table. While I devour Natalie's amazing cooking, others wolf down dessert, a berry streusel à la mode.

If it weren't for Betsy—who's showing a keen interest in my life in New York—I could have eaten, grabbed the money, returned to the motel, and called the night a success. But she's asking me all the questions most people outside New York and the fashion industry want to know. And as soon as the word "fashion" popped up, all the guys' eyes glazed over. Except Logan's.

He's always been a sleeper, hanging in the background, unassuming, quiet. But I know there's a lot more to him—intuition, street smarts, intelligence, and the most compassionate, protective soul I've ever met.

"Do you love New York?" Betsy asks.

I smile. "There's a lot to love."

"Where do you live?"

Fuck. Where *do* I live?

"Manhattan," Tucker says for me. "Are you still in that killer apartment?"

I just smile.

"What do you do there?" Betsy asks.

"Tucker told us she's in fashion, Mom," Natalie reminds Betsy. I understand there's some concern over a mental decline, but she seems awfully sharp to me.

"What's that like?" Betsy asks. "Is it as glamorous as it looks?"

"Oh, there's a whole different side of the industry that you only see when you work in it."

"Have you done runway shows?"

"I have." Because acting as a changing room assistant to the models counts, right?

"Do you watch *Runway Wars*? Is it that competitive?"

I've never had time to watch much television. I don't even own one. "Oh, it's competitive all right."

Trying to field Betsy's questions without lying is awkward, and I'm exhausted from trying to pretend I have a life I don't. From battling an ex who's been trying to control me for months. From driving across the country, worrying about every penny I spend, and stress over what I'll do next.

I want a fresh start, something I didn't fully realize until right now. I want out of these lies, out of my dead-end jobs, out of my false personas.

Which would mean I'm a big, fat, epic failure. Not only didn't I make it in the fashion industry like I'd planned and told everyone I would, I've passed my five-year mark, the amount of time I gave myself to make it in New York before I gave up, without any notable accomplishments to my name.

I never imagined being in such a complicated mess when

those five years were up. The spider's web I've been caught in has wrapped and wrapped and wrapped around me like an unbreakable cocoon, and the wolf spider living there just spotted me. *Lunch.*

"Check out her Instagram," Tucker suggests to Betsy. "It's amazing."

My stomach falls, and my food sticks in my throat. I force myself to swallow. "You follow my Instagram?"

"Of course. You're all I got, girl, that gives me bragging rights."

I've just stepped into quicksand, and I'm sinking. Fast.

My Instagram has been geared toward showing potential employers what I can do in hopes of getting work. And, yeah, it gives the impression I am what I'm not. My posts don't specify that I created only the *window displays* and not the designs showcased in those displays. Or that I took that low-level position in hopes of climbing through the ranks to become a buyer until something higher in the industry opened up for me.

Then along came Aiden, a manager in the company with enough clout to get me promoted to assistant buyer. I wasn't thinking about that when I agreed to date him. We had a lot in common, a lot to talk about. He's good-looking, successful, and made me feel like somebody. The job turned out to be nothing but glorified admin, but it had potential. The longer we dated, the more controlling and manipulative he became, and when I broke things off, he summarily got me fired. The only thing that keeps me from completely hating myself over that prick is that I didn't sleep with him.

My lies didn't just follow me here, they arrived even before I did. And there are so many, I'm bound to get them mixed up, which is when Logan will pounce. Not in a bad way. I know he cares. But in a way that will rip away the veil I've lived behind for so long. A veil I don't know how to live without.

After only a day here, I can clearly see that ending the lies without giving up any of my secrets or contradicting one of my earlier lies is going to be a tightrope walk—over a lagoon of hungry alligators.

I've got to escape so I can think. "I'm pretty tired from the last few crazy weeks. There's always a lot of cleanup when a season ends. Thank you so much for dinner. I'm going to head out."

"Grab your things and head over to the loft," Tucker says. "You can take the bed. When I come home, I'll take the couch."

"Oh, hell no." I huff a laugh. "I know you. If you washed the sheets after she left, I'll give you all the cash I just won. If you didn't, you give me all your cash."

"Don't be like that. How hard is it to throw sheets into the washer?"

"Beats mice," one of the volunteers says.

"And cold water," another says.

Tucker laughs and tells Logan, "That place is such a dump, dude."

Logan doesn't take the bait, but I can tell from his expression, he's irritated, and as it turns out, he's not the only one with protective instincts.

"Have you guys seen his apartment?" I ask.

"When he bought it a few months ago," Tucker says. "Can't be that much different."

"It must be, because if you saw the apartment I saw, you wouldn't be giving him shit. His renovation is top-shelf stuff."

Cole looks at Logan. "Why didn't you tell us it was finished?"

"It's no big deal."

"You sank big money into that place," I tell him. "Don't minimize its value to you just because these guys have no vision." To the others, I say, "Logan's going to be laughing all the way to the bank while you guys are trying to survive on a civil servant's salary."

"What do you mean?" Tucker asks.

"I walked around the property, looked at the other rooms, did a few quick calculations based on other rentals in the area. Even at only thirty percent capacity, which is extremely conservative, Logan's going to be pulling in at least twice his firefighter's salary every year, just from the motel. I don't see anyone else around here with the self-confidence and initiative it takes to nail down a project like that."

The room goes silent, like all their brains are working overtime. I glance at Logan, and his mouth tips in a barely there smile. A silent thank-you.

"Anyway," I say to Tucker, veering back to the previous topic. "I'd rather live with rodents than clean up after you. I'm fine right where I am." I look at Logan. "If it's okay with you."

"Come on," Tucker says. "Don't make this a big deal."

"Natalie," I say. "Am I making this a big deal?"

"I'd say not. I'd have cut off his cheesecake by now."

I laugh. "An interesting euphemism." I turn my gaze on Betsy, who's watching all this with amusement. "What do you think about all this, Betsy?"

"If he was my boy, his rear end would be tarred and feathered."

Tucker sits back and lifts his hands. "When did everyone get so sensitive?"

"A better question would be, when did you become a jackass?" I look at Logan. "Has he always been this big an ass, or has it gotten worse over the years?"

"Both," Logan says. "And you're welcome to stay as long as you like. I'm working a double, but when I get off, I'll get the hot water working and put in a few mousetraps. Since I'm not using the apartment, you really should stay there. And like I told you," he says with a look at Tucker, "I haven't been hooking up in the sheets."

But they'd still smell like him. I'd never get any sleep.

"Thanks, but I'm okay where I am. While I was trying to unwind last night, I made some sketches of room layout designs and some landscaping ideas to maximize the view. I'll show them to you when you get back."

"View?" Carter asks.

"Yeah. All he has to do is take down a dozen trees or so and the property will have an amazing view of the river. The property value will go through the roof."

When the quiet, dumbstruck sensation fills the room again, I roll my eyes. "You're all such...*men*."

"We're just razzing him," Tucker says. "It's all in good fun."

I look at Logan. He's biting the inside of his lip and his jaw is jumping. He could be pissed at me for bringing all this up, or he could be pissed that no one has been supporting him in this endeavor.

"Is that the expression of someone who's having fun?"

"Ooo," Betsy says with glee in her voice. "I like this girl."

That makes a few people laugh.

I push to my feet and face Logan. "Looks like I'm not the only one who has a hard time asking for or accepting help. Which reminds me, if you give me some cash, I could start working on the place while you're on duty."

"You don't have to—"

"*Stop. It.* It will keep me busy and out of everyone's business."

"Give her the money," Tucker says.

Logan pulls out his wallet and asks me, "How much?"

"Five hundred would give me a good start."

Logan chokes. "What the hell are you going to do with five hundred bucks?"

"It will cost three hundred just to buy the cleaning supplies I'll need." Yeah, I know the figure off the top of my head from cleaning houses while struggling to land a job in fashion.

"It's a good deal, Logan," Natalie says.

"Good deal?" Betsy says. "It's a steal. Give the girl some cash."

"I don't have it on me."

"I've got forty," Jake says, standing and tossing two twenties on the table in front of Logan, then slaps his back. "I want to see this renovation."

"Thanks," Logan says. "I'll get it back to you."

"I'm not worried." To me, he says, "We could use a fighter like you in our ER."

Carter offers a twenty. "Sorry we've been ragging on you, bro. Sounds like we need fresh material."

I grab a pen and napkin from the center of the table and jot down names and amounts. It doesn't take any time at all to rack up four hundred bucks.

When the volunteers are gone and Carter and Royal move into the rec room. I'm left sitting at the table with Tucker, Cole, Logan, Natalie, Betsy, and the puppy. A well-behaved puppy, but one far too interested in me for whatever odd reason.

I ignore the dog whining at me with a tail wag and stack up the bills, straighten them out, fold the wad in half, and stuff it into my back pocket. "That might make a dent." To Tucker, I say, "If you don't step up and treat your friends right, you're gonna lose them. I should know. Learn from my mistakes, Tuck."

"Hey," Tucker says to Logan. "You know we're only giving you a hard time."

"I know."

My phone starts buzzing. It's late on the East Coast. Aiden's been to a couple of bars by now and is drunk texting me.

"You gonna get that?" Tucker asks.

"I'll catch the messages later. Hey, can I pick up work at the bar? You know, to stay busy and get to know people here?"

Tucker's still looking at me sideways and Logan has joined in, but Cole is all for it.

The puppy yips for my attention.

"Someone wants pats," Natalie says, smiling at the dog. To me she says, "We can always use help at the bakery."

"That sounds fun."

"Come by anytime. We open at six."

I'm a night owl, not an early bird, and I fake choke at the hour, making everyone laugh.

"Well," I say, "I'd better get going. Things to do, people to see..." A life to build. Secrets to hide.

Tucker and Logan walk me toward the engine bay, and when Tucker veers toward the stairs with talk about changing for a run, Logan stops on the sidewalk, the pup easily cradled in one arm and squirming to get out of his hold.

"Sure you don't want to hold him?" Logan asks. "Because he really wants you to."

"Boys don't always get what they want," I tell the puppy. "The sooner you learn that, the better." To Logan, I say, "I guess I'll see you when you get back."

"Will you?" he asks, making me stop and look at him.

"What?"

"Be there?" His expression is serious, and there are nuances there I can't define. "Or did I just give you get-out-of-town cash?"

"Ouch." That dig was a little too close to home. "I guess you'll find out."

He pulls his key ring from his pocket and juggles the dog while working a key loose and offers it to me. "To the apartment, in case you want to use the shower."

"Thanks."

"If you don't stay," he says, "just leave it on the counter."

He turns and disappears into the engine bay, and I'm left feeling like I've abandoned him again, before I'm even gone.

7

Isabel

I finally feel like I'm caught up on my sleep. The rain outside is just short of snow, making a slushy mess and creating perfect cleaning weather.

I've done all I can in my room—picked up and installed two-inch wood blinds, captured the mouse family, and rehomed them in the neighboring woods, placed traps in my room, then caulked every possible hole they, or others, could return through. I've also cleaned the place to within an inch of its life and added a shower curtain.

It has turned out to be a very livable space, but then, I'm not exactly picky. In my ten years in New York, I've never been able to afford a place of my own; I've always had to share with rodent and critter roommates. Oh, and human ones too.

I'm finishing up a light clean in Logan's apartment with thoughts of grabbing fast food for dinner and curling under a blanket to work in my sketchbook—a little brainstorm on the next steps in my life, some more sketching the motel's room configuration. I can't seem to keep my mind from coming up with potential changes that will add value to the motel. But then, I've spent nearly half of my life creating settings that are irresistible to buyers. Here, I'm setting a stage to sell an experience instead of a product.

I rinse the mop and replace it in a utility closet. For a guy, he's pretty clean.

A phone rings, and I freeze, puzzled. It's not the cell in my pocket. I turn toward the sound and scan the room. "He has a landline? Didn't those go out with the eighties?"

But then I remember him telling me about power outages and how I get spotty cell reception here, so I guess it makes sense.

I finish up my work while the phone rings and I'm about to walk out the door when an answering machine picks up. An *answering machine*. It's like the Dark Ages around here.

"Hey, Logan, it's me."

The female voice makes me turn and step back into the apartment. He says he's not hooking up in his place, but that doesn't mean he's not hooking up, period. And I'm...curious.

"I tried your cell, the firehouse, and the bar," she says. "You must be on a call."

There's something about her voice that sounds familiar, but I can't place it.

"I'm between shows in San Francisco and came up to visit a few girlfriends in Portland. Thought I'd swing by to see you."

Between shows?

The information and the voice connect, and my stomach chills. Maya. Logan's sister and my BFF once upon a time. I wasn't prepared for this. Don't think I'd ever be prepared for this.

"But my rental got a flat," she continues, "and the roadside service is backed up because of the weather. I'm about twenty minutes away. Don't worry, I'm fine. It'll only be a couple of hours, and the heater is working. Hopefully, I'll see you before you get this message. Have Tucker make up the sofa for me. Oh, and I've got some juicy gossip about a high school friend of ours. Love you."

The line disconnects.

"Oh my God. No, no, no." My heartbeat kicks up, and panic crawls along my spine. "*Shit.*"

My mind is spinning. I *so* didn't see this coming. Maya lives in New York. She's got an apartment I'd kill for. She's the well-respected fashion designer I always wanted to be. She's successful and beautiful and smart and talented—despite my majorly selfish act all those years ago.

I close my eyes and press my hand to my forehead. "Why am I such a fuckup?"

As if I needed confirmation, Aiden calls. I send it to voice-mail and pace the apartment, trying to think of all the ramifications of Maya coming while I'm here.

I stop at the window and watch the slush build into snow. "I think karma just delivered a long overdue gut punch."

I can't let her just sit out there in this weather. And it wouldn't hurt to learn what she knows about me and my fabricated world before she spills it to Logan. To everyone. Self-loathing is one thing. Being exposed as an epic failure and a liar after ten years of study and work...

My shoulders drop. It was inevitable. I just hadn't thought it would happen so soon. Wasn't prepared to deal with the most regretted mistake of my life in front of everyone who means something to me.

I take a deep breath, go to the landline, and call her back.

"There you are," she answers, obviously thinking it's Logan. "I was sure you were on some awful call—"

"Hi." Silence stretches for the length of time it takes for me to suck in a breath so I can continue. "I'll come help you with the tire."

"Who is this?"

"It's awful weather, and it's dangerous for you to be on the side of the road like that in the dark. I'll be there in twenty minutes. Bye."

I disconnect before I have to answer that question, because if she knew it was me, she probably would tell me not to come. And I wouldn't blame her.

Instead of digging in my car for my snow gear, I borrow a pair of Logan's snow boots and grab a parka. The drive isn't long, but it's messy and dark. Even if she still hates me—which would be totally justified—I'd still go to help her out.

I've followed her life on social media, watched her succeed and climb the industry ladder. It's alleviated my guilt to some degree, but I don't think I'll ever get completely over the regret of betraying her.

I catch sight of her SUV on the opposite side of the road, on the shoulder, emergency lights flashing, and my stomach jumps into my throat. Confrontation really isn't my thing, but with us both in town, both sisters to best friends, I have to do it sometime.

This is turning out to be the opposite of the fresh start I need.

I pull up behind her, leave my headlights on so we can see what we're doing, and turn on my emergency lights as well. It's still sleeting, but not as heavily as it was when I left the motel.

"This is going to suck so hard," I mutter before getting out.

Maya opens the driver's-side door and stands from the car. "Hi, thanks for coming."

She approaches me, pulling her long down jacket around her. I instantly recognize it as a Brunello Cucinelli taffeta down puffer coat retailing for seven grand. I don't doubt her boots are a three-thousand-dollar pair of Loro Pianas.

Those expensive boots stop five feet away, and when I meet Maya's gaze, hers is shocked. Damn, she's even more beautiful than she was as a kid, and she was always a showstopper. Her features have refined over the years. She's got Logan's jet-black hair and green eyes, but hers are a quieter shade, leaning toward hazel. Part of me was sure she'd get to New York and become a model instead of a fashion designer. She has the looks, the height, the body, the savvy. She may have come from hell on earth, but she's always looked like an angel fallen from heaven. A lot of people have underestimated her based on her beauty. I always enjoyed watching her set them straight.

"Isabel?"

"Hey. Can you pop the trunk so I can get the spare out?"

She doesn't seem to notice the freezing rain. "What are you doing here? Logan didn't say—"

"That's because I just got here. The day before yesterday, in fact." I take a couple more steps and put my hand on the trunk. "Open it, please. It's freezing out here."

She pulls the key from her pocket, presses a button, and the trunk pops open. Inside, there are suitcases, and I have to pull those out to get to the spare.

"Isabel, *what* are you doing here?" Maya asks again.

"Last time I looked, it's still a free country. Get back in the car."

"Not until you tell me why you're here. And why you were answering Logan's phone."

"You're still as stubborn as ever." I'd forgotten about that. In my memories, all I saw was the best friend and all our good times together. "I'm taking a break between seasons, and Logan's letting me stay in one of the rooms at the motel."

She leans in to grab a suitcase, but I slide my hand beneath the handle. "Good God, stop. Getting that Cucinelli dirty would be a crime, and it's not happening on my watch." I hoist her luggage from the car and drop it to the asphalt with a huff of laughter and a shake of my head. "I see you still travel light."

Maya laughs, creating a crack in the ice between us. A wave of emotion hits me out of nowhere. I loved her so much, for so long. Then I went and fucked it all up. I've never had a friend like her since. Which serves me right.

"You couldn't get a flat tire on a beautiful fall night, huh?" I say. "Had to do it in this mess?"

"I definitely should have consulted the weather service before getting a flat."

"Now we're on the same page."

I lift the trunk liner, take out the lug wrench and the jack, then hoist the spare from the trunk. My fingers are already numb, and I'm wishing I'd grabbed gloves. I take everything to the other side of the car, grateful I don't have to do this in the roadway.

Maya follows, standing beside me. "Can I help?"

"Not in a ten-thousand-dollar outfit you can't."

"Fifteen, actually. I'm also wearing a silk Saint Laurent blouse and leathers, not to mention a Gucci bra and panties set."

"You still suck at math. That would add up to about twenty grand."

"I got the Cucinelli on sale."

I laugh—hard—my hands braced on the edge of the open trunk. The stupid conversation, the icy rain, seeing her after ten long years, it cracks something inside me that's both bitter and sweet.

I'm soaked to the bone, and more than just my fingers have gone numb. My hair is wet, and icy water streams into my face. I place the end of the jack over each lug nut and use my heel to loosen them all before lying down on the frozen pavement to set the jack. It all feels like it takes forever because I can't feel anything with my numb fingers, making me clumsy.

"If I get frostbite," I tell her, "you'll have to watch me get my fingers and toes amputated."

"I'll sue you for emotional trauma."

I smile, remembering how she loved any sarcastic phrase

involving an attorney—"So sue me" or "Don't make me lawyer up" or "I take the fifth" or "I bill by the minute."

"Oh, for Christ's sake," I say, "by all means, let's bring the sharks into this."

Maya laughs.

In high school, Maya toyed with the idea of becoming a lawyer, even though she loved fashion. She believed that being a lawyer would bring her the respect and recognition she craved and end the bullying she despised. Eventually, she came around to the idea that there was nothing wrong with doing something she loved instead of something that would bring her money and revenge. And once she came over to the dark side, we made plans. So many silly, unrealistic, high-school-type plans.

We would get into the same college and room together in the dorms. Then move out together into an apartment. We'd go on double dates, join the same sorority, work as a team on all our school projects. We would each be the maid of honor for the other and godparents for each other's kids.

God, we had so many dreams.

I don't realize silence has fallen between us until Maya speaks again. "So, how are you?"

"I'm just peachy." I get the jack into place, roll to my knees, and start cranking the jack to lift the car. "Nothing says 'good times' like a workout on the side of the road in icy rain."

My back and shoulders hurt from all the cleaning I did today, and now they're burning.

"So, what are you doing nowadays?" Maya asks.

That's a broad question I don't know how to answer. Running, hiding, scrounging for money, coming back to the closest thing I have to a home to lick my wounds, all come to mind, but I decide not to answer. This is supposed to be a fresh start after all.

"Logan told me you're still in New York," Maya says. "I'm there too. Where are you working?"

Damn. I'm back on the tightrope and piranhas have joined the fun.

"Rutherford," I say. It's only one job among many, but I'm not in the mood to extrapolate.

"Didn't they merge with Concord Holdings last year?"

"They did. Maya, get in the car. You're shivering."

"If you're out here, I'm out here."

That hits me like a punch to the throat. Tears rush my eyes so fast, I can't hold them back. Luckily, my face is already wet. I'm reminded of how completely we had each other's backs all through high school. How did I ever let her go?

"I was designing for Bellencourt when Klein bought them out," she says. "It got messy, so I moved to Holland." She says it as if it isn't one *major* fucking achievement. Not just working for Bellencourt, Klein, and Holland, but the ability to switch companies, holding her status as a designer. Only the top— tippy, tippy-top—designers have that luxury. I did well in school, graduated in the top ten percent of my class, but I evidently didn't have the "it factor" and could never get picked up as a designer.

I, of course, already know about Maya's life—or as much as I can glean from social media. And we all know how "realistic" social media is. I follow her life as a sort of penance. Stupid and selfish, but her success makes me feel less guilty for taking her scholarship. And I've paid the price. Maya has the glamorous life we dreamed about as kids. She travels all over the world to consult with other designers, chat with buyers from top-tier department stores and high-end boutiques, search for fabrics, attend fashion shows and photo shoots.

Maya is the real deal.

She also doesn't seem to realize my social media is more smoke and mirrors than reality. Who am I kidding? She's probably never even thought about checking on my social media. A successful designer living the jet-set life hardly has time to reminisce about high school bullshit.

And that's good for me, because that means the juicy gossip she mentioned on the message to Logan probably isn't about me. Which means Maya won't be exposing my lies to everyone who matters—Tucker, Cole, and Logan. At least not now.

But now that we've seen each other again, now that I'm back on her radar, my fake life is in jeopardy, because I know just how many contacts she has. A few directed questions and Maya could uncover my lies and blow my life apart. And I'm ashamed to say she'd be justified. I feel the truth tugging at the threads of the falsely woven tapestry that appears to be my life, when the reality isn't even close.

This meetup makes it clear that whether I stay here a week or the rest of my life, I'm going to have to come clean at some point. Dammit, I just wanted to leave all that bullshit behind.

"How did you learn to change a tire?" Maya asks. "I didn't realize it's something I never learned until this tire popped. And I feel pretty stupid standing on the side of the road like a damsel in distress."

"You've never had a fiber of damsel in you. I didn't know how to do it either until I had one. YouTube is very helpful."

"Only if you have internet."

"Fair point." There are a lot of dead spots in the mountains.

I need to talk to her about the elephant between us. We didn't both come from New York to end up here, on the side of the road, in freezing rain to change a freak flat tire by accident.

By leaving New York with no intention of going back, I took the first step toward ending all the bullshit in my life.

Up until about five years ago, I believed that when you take initiative toward a goal, the universe jumps in to lend support. Only, for the last five years, I've made effort after effort after effort, and I keep ending up in the gutter.

Evidently, the universe does *not* like me much. Can't say I like myself very much either.

"Come on, Maya, get in the car and turn on the heater. Your teeth are chattering."

"How much longer?"

"Not long."

"I'll wait."

"God, you're stubborn."

"Right back at you."

I don't know how long this whole process takes, only that over half of my body is numb by the time I wrench the flat tire into the trunk, then replace her luggage. I shut the hatch, and for a long moment, Maya and I just stare at each other. We're both drenched, rain running down our faces.

"Can we talk—" I start.

"Why don't you get in and—"

We speak at the same time. Maya nods, acknowledging we want the same thing, and points to her SUV. She starts the engine and fiddles with the knobs as I settle in the passenger's seat and put my hands in front of the air vents pumping out warmth.

For a few long moments, neither of us says anything. I consider asking if she wants to get coffee, but I think it's better to just get this over with.

"I should have done this a long time ago. It was..." Emotion rises up and tightens my throat. "It was wrong of me to take that scholarship. Selfish and mean-spirited."

She sighs. "It's stupid how we hold on to things that don't matter anymore." There's no anger in her voice, just matter-of-fact stoicism. "But for the record, I know me losing it wasn't your fault."

"I should have come forward and told the scholarship board Briann lied."

I'm reminded of just how tentative that scholarship had

been for Maya, hinging on the verification of hours worked at a nonprofit where Briann and I also volunteered. Briann was pissed about Maya getting the scholarship, and when the scholarship board called to verify Maya's hours, Briann lied. It took weeks to straighten out the facts, by which time, the scholarship had been offered to me. If I hadn't taken it, the money wouldn't have been awarded to anyone that year.

On the one hand, no matter what happened, Maya lost out on the scholarship because of Briann's lies, something I had nothing to do with. But on the other, a truly selfless friend would have turned down the scholarship out of loyalty. I didn't.

She's staring out the wet windshield, somber. "They wouldn't have believed you."

"Why would you say that? I had all the motive in the world *not* to tell them since I was second in line. That's the very reason I would have been credible."

Her gaze lowers to the console between us, and her smooth forehead is pulled tight enough for a vertical line to appear between her brows. She runs her fingernail along the stitching in the seat.

"That all happened so long ago, it really doesn't matter. Besides, Briann was getting back at me for talking shit about her after she stole my boyfriend. I can't even remember how it all got so out of hand."

"I believe it was a series of relentless pranks."

"Ah, yeah." She smiles softly.

"If I remember correctly, the glue in her ChapStick container might not have been the worst prank, but it was the last straw."

"Yeah. That was a good one."

We go quiet, and the sleet turns to rain again, pounding on the roof.

"Anyway," she says, serious again, "you needed to get out of Portland worse than I did."

My stomach grows heavy. "Why do you say that?"

"That boyfriend of your mom's, Derik something. Tucker told Logan. Logan told me."

Shame throws a shadow across my soul. "Should have known those guys couldn't keep their mouths shut."

My life was never smooth, but it went to complete shit over the span of twelve hours that early June night. The night before my graduation.

I can remember the events like they happened yesterday. Maya had learned her scholarship had been revoked and offered to me. She was livid with the situation and didn't want to see or talk to me. It was the third day we hadn't talked, and I was hoping to patch things up at graduation.

But life had other plans. That night, when my mom was at work, waitressing the dinner shift at a local café, her boyfriend Derik came home falling-down drunk. He came on to me, and when he wouldn't take no for an answer, I kneed him in the balls.

He was rolling around on the floor by the time Tucker came home. Derik's mistake was to get up and try to fight Tucker. My mom came home in the middle of it all and instantly took Derik's side. She called the police and had Tucker arrested. She also kicked me out for lying, all while Derik was saying shit to me like "This ain't over " and "Payback's a bitch, just like you."

My account to the police got Tucker released, but with nowhere to go and Derik on the warpath, Tucker thought it would be better for me to get out of town. I accepted the scholarship that wasn't truly mine, pooled money from Tucker's and my odd jobs, and left for New York.

I haven't spoken to my mother since, nor do I care to.

"You know what was harder than losing the scholarship?" Maya asks. When she looks up, I shake my head. "Losing you."

Well, fuck. My shoulders slump, and tears burn my eyes.

"I didn't think you'd want to talk to me after what I'd done. I couldn't even forgive myself. I sure didn't think you would."

She lifts a shoulder. "Logan also told me you two had sex before you left."

"For Christ's sake, why do men blab so much? It wasn't a thing. It was just a stupid pact we made so we weren't virgins when we went off to college."

She looks at me. "And now?"

"Now nothing. I told you, I just got here. I'm taking some time to decide what direction I want to go next, that's all."

"How long will you be here?"

"Maybe a week or two."

We fall quiet again. A car passes us, the driver honking his horn because we're stopped on the side of the road.

"We should probably get going," I say. "Logan's working, so you've got the apartment to yourself."

"No," she says, melancholic, "I think I'll head to a girl-friend's house in Portland."

"Are you sure? Logan would love to see you."

"Yeah, it's fine. I'll be here a few weeks, I'll come by before I leave."

I should be relieved, but I'm just hurt. Something I can't blame on anyone but myself.

"Sure, okay." I pull the door handle. "It was good to see you. Congrats on getting all you wanted out of life."

"Thanks, you too."

I step out of the car and make my way to my driver's door. Before I even get in, Maya has turned around and is headed back toward Portland. I get into my car and sit there for long, quiet moments while my mind floods with all the coulda, woulda, shouldas I missed out on.

8

Logan

The kid is screaming in my ear. *Right* in my ear as I secure a splint on his left leg.

It's way too fucking early for this.

Six a.m. and I haven't had coffee yet, after a busy night. It might be October, but we're still getting a steady stream of vacationers taking long weekends to pack in a little more fun before the season turns cold—in this case, a group of teenagers who came up from Portland to mountain bike along the forest trails after dark. While it's been raining all night. In nearly freezing temperatures.

Every year I'm in this job, my belief in Darwin's Law increases. "We're getting you some pain meds, Justin. Hang in there."

Bobby drops to one knee on the other side of the backboard, meds in hand. "They couldn't have done this in better weather?"

"Teenage boys aren't known for their brilliance."

"Ain't that the truth."

"When you're done there, can you get me the REEL or hold tension so I can get it?" I ask, referencing a splint that will stabilize the whole leg, and the one I prefer to use on femur fractures.

Bobby and I are equals, both paramedics with roughly the same amount of experience, but I've been with Hood River Fire and Rescue for eight years, he's only been with us for going on two. While I'm better at backwoods medicine because of my time in the mountains and recreational areas, Bobby's better with split-second triage and managing a dozen things at once. He also kicks ass in big buildings, but we don't have many of those in Hood River.

Bobby finishes drawing up morphine, looks at me, then at the kid's leg. There's no obvious break, as in, his femur isn't sticking out of his skin, but I'm pretty good at telling real pain from fake pain and judging the severity of an injury based on pain level.

"You think?" Bobby looks at the kid, then back at me. "Nah, man, he's just freaked out."

"Twenty bucks."

"You're on."

"What are we betting on?" Cole comes up to us and bends to look at the kid's leg.

"He thinks the kid broke his femur," Bobby says as he pushes morphine.

Cole glances at the still-screaming kid, then at Bobby. "I'm not betting against Logan on this one."

"Cap, hand me that REEL," I say, referencing the metal-and-Velcro splint I prefer for femur breaks. One Bobby hates for no reason at all.

"Dude," Bobby says. "Don't use it just because you brought it."

"Don't *not* use it just to make yourself look right."

With morphine flowing through his veins, Justin quiets and goes glassy-eyed.

"My eardrums, man," I say. "They're still ringing."

"We sent the other kids ahead to meet us on the main road," Cole says, then calls to Tucker and Carter.

We each take a corner of the backboard, while Carter hitches the equipment and supply bags across his back and over his shoulders and follows. "How did I become the pack mule? We should have drawn straws."

"Sure," Tucker says, cutting a grin at me. "Next time, kid."

We use "kid" as a nickname for guys with less experience, not necessarily fewer years on the planet.

We slip and slide down the steep terrain and muddy ground, but manage to keep Justin stable until we reach the road where we put him on the gurney inside the rescue. Mud turns the white sheet brown and drips on the floor of the rig.

"Jesus," I say, looking down at myself. "We're going to need to clean up with fire hoses."

"I happen to know where we can get a few," Cole says. "We'll stop and pick up coffee and donuts from Nat. See you back at the house."

"Royal, can you get the pup?" I call to him.

"Got him."

Royal rounds the front of the rescue with Bobby, and as soon as the doors open, I hear Bobby say, "What the... Jesus Christ."

"What happened?" I call.

"Your dog got into my water. It's all over the fucking place."

"You won't melt," I tell him.

Royal comes around the back of the unit holding Lucky and grinning.

"Jesus," I say to the dog, running my hand over his wet head. "What did you do? Swim in it?"

"Looks like he picked up the cup and shook it," Royal says with a laugh. "The whole cabin is wet."

I sigh and shake my head, and Royal heads to the engine.

With Bobby driving, I brace the gurney so Justin is jostled as little as possible, and when we reach a main road, out of the mountains, my phone pings with texts and voicemails.

My first thought is of Isabel and the motel. Once we're on better terrain, I release the gurney and sit back. Justin is passed out from the morphine. I press my fingers to his wrist to make sure he hasn't tanked due to something going on internally—like a fragmented bone slicing the femoral artery—and use my other hand to pull my phone from my pocket.

When I find the kid's pulse steady and strong, I relax and look at my messages. They're from Maya, not Isabel. And they were sent last night. They either came in while I was on a call and didn't hear them or they came while I was passed out in the scant amount of time I had to sleep, or they were delayed getting to my phone, something that happens relatively often in the mountains with shoddy reception.

Last week, she told me she'd be in San Francisco for some kind of work thing and that she'd try to stop by to see me. I immediately think of the long-standing rift between Isabel and Maya, and I *so* don't have the patience for that drama right now.

Her texts don't say much other than "Hey, you around?" and "Was going to come by." So I listen to her voicemails and learn she had a flat and was sitting on the side of the road, in the sleet, at night, alone.

"Fuck." I drop my head back and close my eyes. The three people she would call for help are working—me, Tucker, and Cole.

Her last message says not to worry, she'll call AAA. A little tension ebbs from my shoulders.

We arrive at the hospital before I have time to call her back. Bobby and I get Justin into the ER, and I head right back outside to start cleaning up on the rig. I check the cab, sure Bobby and Royal were exaggerating the water situation, but nope—everything is wet. Water soaked the seats and splashed everywhere.

"What in holy hell?" I pull out the thirty-two-ounce cup Bobby always fills with ice water. Not only is it empty, but there are teeth marks in the plastic. I find the top, which is chewed to shreds, the straw missing. "Good Lord, dog."

I imagine the pup getting hold of the cup's edge and shaking it like he does the stuffed toy I picked up for him, and I can't help but laugh.

I dry things off, soaking up as much water as possible, then work on the back where mud covers the floor. Bobby is still inside, and I have no doubt one of the half dozen super-sexy nurses that work in the ER is on duty and he's chatting her up.

While I wait, I sit on the rear step of the rescue and call Maya.

She answers, "Hey, you."

She sounds sleepy, but it's good to hear her voice. "Hey, sorry, I was on a call in the mountains. Shitty reception. You okay?"

"I figured. Yeah, fine."

"Still need help? Did AAA come?"

"No and no."

I smile at the image of Maya in all her designer glory changing a tire in this weather. "Don't tell me you changed it. I'd pay dearly for that video."

"Nope, Isabel did."

A thick silence falls over the line. When I can't make sense of it, I say, "*What?*"

"She was in your apartment when I left a message and came herself, because AAA was backed up a few hours."

I shouldn't be surprised—Isabel always has been the kind

of person who would give the shirt off her back to someone in need. I guess it feels nice that's still part of her personality.

They were as tight as tight could be back in high school, but the scholarship fiasco and the Derik fiasco ripped them apart. They never spoke again. Until last night, obviously. "How did that go?"

She sighs heavily. "I'm not completely sure."

"Did you fight?"

"No."

"Did you make up?"

"No."

I close my eyes, my patience on edge. "Maya."

"We bickered like we used to." There's a melancholy in her voice. "And we talked about the scholarship thing. She apologized, and it was sincere."

"That all sounds good."

"Yeah."

"Then why do you sound, I don't know, off?"

"Long-standing pain doesn't just evaporate. Seeing her again, talking about all that bullshit just brought it all back. I decided to stay with Delia until Isabel goes back to New York. I've been working my ass off, and I don't have the energy or the interest in patching things up."

"I get it." Silence falls over the line, and it feels tense on Maya's side. "What?"

"I don't know. There's just something...off about her. I can't put my finger on it."

I'm guessing that has to do with all the turmoil Isabel's been through lately.

"Anyway," Maya says, "if you're going to date her or whatever, just, I don't know. Just be careful."

"What does that mean?"

"This is going to sound stupid because I haven't seen her in forever, but it feels like she's hiding something, and I know how you feel about lies. "

I hate lies. And liars. But my mind returns to the day Isabel came into the firehouse and had my back. No one's said one smartass or derogatory thing about the motel or the dog since. The guys have started looking at me differently too, like I'm smart, not the dumbass who bought a money pit. And it really feels good for a woman to have my back for a change.

That doesn't change how I feel about lies. Isabel is definitely keeping things hidden, and for that reason, Maya's advice is good advice.

"There's nothing going on with us," I tell Maya. "I'm just giving her a place to stay."

Maya promises to call me later in the week, and I disconnect, wondering again about the money I gave Isabel, and whether or not she'll be there when I get home.

Bobby comes around the back of the rescue, sullen. "You suck. Broken fucking femur."

I punch the air above me with both fists. "Knew it." Then I hold out my hand. "Twenty bucks, dude."

"You're a fuckin' shark, just like Isabel." Bobby pulls out his wallet and lays a twenty in my hand. I tuck it away, happy to have a supplement to my civil servant's pay.

And maybe a start toward collecting the stupid money I gave Isabel.

9

Logan

I turn into the motel's driveway, and the first thing I see is Isabel's Jeep—gone.

"Goddammit." I hit the steering wheel with my palm.

I park and sit there a minute, getting my shit together. The puppy, who fell off the seat and has been wandering around the passenger's footwell, puts his paws on the seat, trying to get up. When he can't, he barks at me. Okay, it's more of a yip than a bark.

I reach down, draw him into my lap, and tell him, "I'm so fucking stupid."

She told me she wasn't staying. Whatever issues she has with her ex are her problems. I can't solve them. Her circus, her monkeys.

But that doesn't make me feel any better. I still have to pay back the money I borrowed from the guys. Maybe she's trying to avoid seeing Maya again. Maybe she patched things up with Cocksucker and she's headed back to New York. I sure as hell saw my mother go right back to my father no matter how abusive he became. It ultimately cost her everything.

"Some people just get their wires crossed," I tell the puppy. "Sometimes they just can't break that nasty cycle."

I'm disappointed and annoyed Isabel is one of them. She seems so, I don't know, sassy and independent. She acts like she's her own person, not like a woman who's been beaten into submission.

I climb from the truck and set the pup on the ground. He follows me to the office, where I grab the keys inside the door and head toward room seven. Between the office and Isabel's room, the puppy conks out and lies down. He's had as busy a night as me, up every time I was.

"Dude, the ground's cold." I go back, pick him up, and stuff him into the front pocket of my hoodie. "We've got to get you a winter jacket."

At the door, I push the key into the lock, but stop and stare at the window. There are blinds covering the glass. Two-inch wooden blinds. The nice kind you can get cut to size at big-box stores like Home Depot.

My heart thumps with an extra beat, and I push the door open to find the room neatly organized, all of Isabel's clothes still here, folded into piles, bed made, another set of blinds over the second window. And it smells clean. Like lemon-and-pine clean.

In the bathroom, I find a slew of cleaning supplies lined up against the wall between the toilet and the shower, which now has a shower curtain, and a smallish makeup bag on the counter. She's put one of those over-the-door hooks on the bathroom door, and a towel hangs there. I touch it and find it's still wet.

All the air seeps from my lungs, and my muscles relax. I know I shouldn't care whether she goes or stays. This is just a wake-up call. A reminder *not* to get into her. She may have been up front about not staying, but she's not telling me the truth about what's going on with her. I have to catch pieces of the problem by overhearing phone calls.

As I return to the apartment, I look into the windows of other units. Some look the same, but some have clearly had work done.

Just as I open the apartment door and get another whiff of lemon and pine, her Jeep pulls into the lot.

She hops out and looks at me warily, like she's expecting something bad. "Hey."

"Hey."

After a second, she saunters toward me carrying a pink bakery box. "How was your shift?"

I drop the pup inside the office where it's warm and close the door. He instantly starts a what-the-fuck whine. "Busy. Looks like you worked at Natalie's this morning."

"I don't know if *working* is the right word. More like making a mess and slowing down the process." She offers me the box. "She did send me home with these for you, though. Chocolate croissants."

"You weren't planning on giving them to me, were you? You were just going to sneak them into your room and eat them all yourself."

"Truth be told, I was going to eat every damn one." She pushes the box toward me again. "Save me from myself."

"Don't have to ask me twice." I take the box and set it on the hood of my truck.

She's wearing torn jeans and a hoodie with the Fashion Institute of Technology logo on the front. Her dark hair is twisted into something that resembles a crazy-ass bun, and she doesn't have one stitch of makeup on. She's fucking gorgeous.

But that doesn't mean I'm into her. Because I'm totally not.

I lift my chin toward her room. "Looks like you've been busy around here."

She shrugs. "Doing what I can." She tilts her head and squints at me, reading me in a way only she can. "Oh, man. That 'getaway money' comment at the fire station wasn't a joke. You really thought I'd bail."

I shove my free hand into my pockets and open my mouth to thank her for helping Maya out, but she shakes her hair away from her face and says, "I've got to go. I'm helping Mike out today. His daughter's got some emergency dental thing."

Mike is the head cook at the Cockloft, and his daughter, Tori, often comes in after school to hang with him in the kitchen. "How in the heck did you get corralled into that? I can go. Cole and Tucker are headed home too."

"I guess it was an early appointment, because he came into Natalie's just after she opened to try to let you know he was going to be in late. Natalie says that when you're unreachable, it's because you're involved in a call or in a remote area where there's no cell service. He wasn't sure how long the appointment would take because she had to be sedated, but he told me what needs to get done, and I can totally handle it." She pulls the paper from her back pocket and waves it at me. "See? Look how short this list is. Pffft, cake."

I make a grab for it, but she pulls it out of reach. "I'll take care of it."

"Isabel." I go after it again, and she turns away.

"Hands off," she says, laughing. "I made the promise, I'll follow through."

"You've already worked this morning."

"So have you. It's no big deal. It'll give me something to do."

"Maybe you should use that time to sleep."

"I could say the same to you."

She keeps turning in circles so I can't reach the paper, and it becomes a contact sport when I wrap both arms around her to keep her still. But she's holding the note at arm's length, which I can't quite reach, even with my front side very intimately up against her backside. The feel of her makes me forget all about what we're fighting for. All my mind can register is the round-ness of her ass against the front of my jeans. The fresh straw-berry scent of her shampoo. The way she fits me.

"Oh my God." I keep my hands on her arms, even though she drops them. While my little head is awake and ready to party, my big head has floated back through the years. "You still use that shampoo?"

She glances over her shoulder, and she's not fighting me anymore. Her breath is quick, and her body relaxes against mine, increasing pressure in all the right places. A gnawing sensation I haven't felt in a long time sinks into my stomach, my pelvis, between my legs.

"What?" she asks.

I stare at her questioning look, completely unable to remember what she's asking about or how we got in this posi-tion. A position where I could just lower my head to have my mouth on hers. "What, what?"

"What did you say about my shampoo?"

Oh, right. "You used to use something strawberry." I don't want to let her go. I really, really don't. I'm even wondering if dropping my mouth to her neck to see if she still tastes familiar would be as bad as kissing her mouth. Then her phone rings, and she doesn't reach to answer it.

It's a reminder of all that's happening with her, everything she won't talk about, and there's no telling how long she'll be here before she's gone again.

I force myself to unwrap my arms and step back. "Thanks for helping Maya last night. I can't imagine what a mess it was to change a tire in that weather."

She turns, facing me. "I've been in that situation, and it's no fun. It also didn't seem like a safe place for her to be stranded for any length of time. No big deal."

"How did that go, exactly?" I have no idea how once-inseparable best friends turned mortal enemies who haven't seen or spoken to each other in a decade would look.

"Better than expected." She seems as surprised by her answer as I am. "We fell back into our smart-ass bickering like no time had passed. I finally took the opportunity to apologize for the whole scholarship debacle. But in the end, she didn't want to be here while I was here, so she went to Portland to see friends."

There's no mistaking the hurt in her voice, but I don't have time to say anything because she suddenly comes forward and pokes me in the chest. "You told her about us. We had a deal. A pact."

I tilt my head. "I don't remember telling her anything about us. I mean, what's to tell? It was just—"

"A pact," she says.

"Right."

"You're full of shit."

"Maybe. Quite possibly."

She sighs dramatically, shaking her head. "Men. God. So glad I'm not into guys anymore."

My brows shoot skyward. "You're not into guys anymore?"

"Get that dirty thought of me and some other hot woman out of your head. I'm off men—as in taking a total and complete sabbatical from your species."

"We're more of a gender, not a species."

She drops her head back and stares at the sky. "This. This is only one of the many reasons I've taken several giant steps away from your *gender*." She gestures toward me with Mike's list. "I'm done with men until further notice, which will never come, by the way."

"Then you really don't need this anymore." I pluck the paper from her hand, but she's so damn quick, she snatches it right back.

Then she does something totally unexpected—she shoves the paper into her mouth, a determined look on her face.

"What the—"

She mutters something to the effect of "Top secret...my eyes only."

I bark a laugh while she chews on the paper, her expression silly, but pleased with herself. I laugh so hard, I have to brace my hands on my knees. And I can't. Stop. Laughing.

"Stop it," she grumbles. "I've got a top-secret assignment here. You're so rude."

I laugh and laugh and laugh. Tears flow from my eyes, and I can't catch my breath. I'm doubled over, an arm across my belly.

"This ain't half bad," she says around the mouthful. "I can see why goats like this stuff. Mmm, fiber. Maybe I've got a goat gene in my family. That would explain a lot."

I fight to catch my breath. "Jesus Christ, stop."

"Come on, am I right?"

Still trying to catch my breath, still bent at the waist, I look up at her. "You're probably going to get lead poisoning from the pencil."

Her eyes go wide, she turns her head, and spits it out, and I'm laughing again, my back braced against the grill of my truck.

"What in the hell is wrong with you?" she says, mock mad. "Laughing as I infect myself with lead, and you call yourself a healer, or a savior, or whatever the hell."

"I'm kidding. Everyone knows there's no real lead in pencils." I grab her hand and pull her into me, where I wrap her tight, which elicits a round of pretend choking. "Damn, it's good to see you."

She wraps her arms around my middle, but still acts like she can't breathe. "You're not exactly a string bean anymore, and you're crushing my lungs."

I let her go and catch my breath, wipe my eyes. "I was never a string bean."

"If you say so."

"Okay, if you're determined to go to the bar—"

"I am."

"—I'll catch a few hours of sleep, then come in and help."

She makes a face. "That might not work out well. I'm pretty possessive in the kitchen." Her voice shifts into a mad scientist. "And there are rolling pins and meat tenderizers and knives. Shiny, *shiny* knives—"

"Then, I'm sure we'll have lots of fun." I put my hand against her forehead and give her a gentle push the way I did when we were kids. "We've got a scrimmage against the cops tonight. You should come. You can watch the puppy."

"I don't do puppies." Her mood shifts into something I can't quite read. "And why are you playing a game on a Monday night?"

"Because it's the day most of the team could get off. And I've never met a woman who doesn't melt at the sight of a puppy."

"You have now."

That's...curious. "Then Tucker's going to get an earful, because he said a firefighter with a puppy would draw women like moths to a flame."

"A: why would you ever listen to Tucker? And B: I doubt you have much trouble drawing women."

I'm not going there. "You should come. The guys and their wives or girlfriends will be there. Lots of people to talk to, and you said you want to get to know people in town."

Over the course of those few sentences, I realize I want her to come so she can see how fun it would be to live here. Somewhere deep in my psyche, I must want her to stay. I have no fucking idea why. I've never felt anything more for her than friendship. And, okay, lust. So whatever the hell just went on in my head, I can't explain.

"Never mind," I say, wishing I could pull the offer back. "You don't have to come. I don't even know why I suggested it."

"Because you're a good guy and you like to see other people happy." Her assessment is somber, but sweet. "We'll see. No promises. Now, go get some sleep while I seize, convulse, and froth at the mouth from lead poisoning."

10

Isabel

I haven't been to an ice-skating rink since I was a kid, and this one isn't at all what I remember.

It's new, built in just the last couple of years and way nicer than any rink I've ever seen. The lobby is well stocked with merchandise, from water and candy to hoodies and scarves. The floor has nice black rubbery mats and bright red lockers for skaters.

Inside the rink, the roof is high, with lots of natural light coming in from skylights, and the metal trusses creating the roof are painted white, the bleachers all around the rink painted gray.

All in all, very clean and modern.

There are about fifty or sixty people here, half dressed in blue, half in red, sitting behind the team benches, clustered behind the team they're rooting for. It's clear the blue team supports the cops, the red, firefighters. A skater sweeps toward me and makes a sideways stop just in front of the boards.

"Didn't think you'd come." Logan's face is flushed with

color. His already gorgeous green eyes are on fire, and his dark hair clings to his sweaty skin.

Damn him to hell and back, I honestly can't name one man prettier than him.

"I'm here to see Tucker," I tell him. "Don't fall all over yourself."

He laughs, and it feels good to find someone who gets my sense of humor and takes things lightly. New York was a mecca of uptight, insanely busy, competitive, and downright angry assholes. I've only been here a few days, and the stress from everyday life in New York has faded, something I didn't even know I needed. But there were a lot of things I loved about city life.

"Natalie and Tina are up there." He lifts his chin toward the benches.

Nice to know there will be friendly faces and I don't have to look like a pathetic loner, but I got over that a long time ago.

A whistle blows, and Logan looks toward center ice, then back at me. "I don't suppose I could get a good-luck kiss."

"Keep dreaming."

He's grinning when he pushes off the wall and glides toward center ice, where he joins his teammates in a line, including Tucker, Carter, Cole, and Bobby.

I wander toward the bleachers, passing the collection of blue fans to reach the red fans. My gaze travels lightly over the crowd, holding on a woman who is very deliberately watching me. She'd be pretty if she got rid of the resting bitch face.

Intuition tells me that look has something to do with Logan, but she's rooting for the cops, not the firefighters, so who knows? Women get wound up by the most asinine things.

Natalie waves at me from halfway up the stands. "Isabel."

I climb the bleachers in large steps and sit beside her. Her mother and Tina are sitting on the other side. I see a couple of the employees from the Cockloft around me and a whole lot of the volunteers I met at the firehouse and lift my hand to say hello, then lean forward to say hello to Tina and Betsy.

Tina's holding a toddler. He looks about three, but what do I know about kids? He is also clearly biracial like Tina. And if he is, in fact, Tina's son, she must have had him extremely young. She barely looks eighteen as it is.

"This your kid?" I ask.

She smiles like a proud mama, and I can see how much she loves him in one glance. "All mine."

"He'd do well in New York. Those big blue eyes and that mocha skin, they'd eat him up. If you ever want to try him in modeling, I can give you a few reputable agents to contact. Could pay for his college tuition."

"Really? Interesting. I'll think about it. Thanks for the offer. Hey, take your jacket off for a second. That shirt is so cute."

I slide out of my jacket and look down at myself. I'm wearing one of my long-sleeved boho designs with straps criss-crossing in a fun pattern across the chest and back.

"Oh my God, that *is* cute," Natalie says. "Did you design that?"

"Thanks. Yeah, it's mine."

"I need one," Tina says, looking at the shirt with stars in her eyes, which makes me laugh. "Like *need*."

"I have some with me. I'll hunt in my stuff and pull one out. Are you a small or extra small?" I ask, sliding back into my jacket.

"Small. Wait, is that a tattoo?"

I look toward my upper left chest near my shoulder. "Yeah, just a small one."

"Can I see it?"

I slide my arm from the jacket and tug my shirt down to expose most of the tattoo—a quote that got me through some really dark times among flowering vines.

"Wow, that's beautiful. Did you design it?"

"Yeah. I've had it about four years. Looks like I need a color touch-up." I push my arm into my jacket and pull it tight around me. "Do you have any?"

"No, but I've wanted one representing Trevor since he was born. I just haven't jumped because I'm not sure what design I want and I'd really like to have it on my shoulder, but I've seen a few tats on the shoulder that look weird. Guess it's a tricky area because of the dips and curves."

"I'd be happy to sketch a few designs for you. I spent an entire year of school haunted by shoulders."

"That would be amazing. I'll pay you," she's quick to add.

I laugh. Sure, I need money, but there's no way on earth I'd take it from the women who've made me feel so at home here. "What color top do you want? They're jewel tones—garnet, emerald, sapphire."

"How much are they?" she asks. My expression must have given away the fact that I wouldn't charge her because she gets a determined look and says, "I *want* to pay you for it. I mean, unless it's like five hundred bucks. That would wipe out my clothing allowance for a year."

I laugh. "We'll talk. And I think sapphire would be amazing on you. What about you, Nat? I won't be offended if you say no."

"Couldn't pay me to say no. I'd love an emerald one in small."

"Good choice."

Tina claps, excited. "Thank you."

"My pleasure." I scan the rink. "Who's who down there?"

"Tucker is nine," Natalie says. "Cole is thirty-five, Bobby is sixteen, and Logan is twenty-two. Don't try to remember them all, they go on and off the ice so fast, I can't keep track of any of them."

"Sounds like good advice."

"How's your burn, sweetheart?" Betsy asks me.

I've almost forgotten about the singed skin of my forearm where I touched the oven wall while removing muffins this morning.

I look at Betsy and smile with my finger to my lips and whisper, "No one's supposed to know. If the guys find out, they'll tease me about it forever. But it's fine, thanks."

Betsy laughs. I'm told she has some type of dementia, but I have yet to see her forget anything. Then again, I've only been in town a few days.

As the teams fly to the other end of the rink, my gaze moves with them. They don't look like a bunch of cops and firefighters playing on the ice like kids. They're good. Really good.

My gaze catches on bitch face again, and I hold her fuck-the-world stare until she looks away, then let my gaze follow the guys down to this end again.

"Looks like you're on Emily's radar," Natalie says.

"Who's Emily?"

"Logan's ex."

"Ah. The looks make sense now."

"Best just to steer clear of her," Tina says. "That bitch face is earned."

"*Pffft,* she's cotton candy compared to the women I work with in New York. They tried to eat me alive. Guess I didn't taste too good. They kept spitting me out."

That brings laughter from several people I didn't realize were listening, and I return their smiles when they look over at me.

I lower my voice and ask, "Was it long-term?"

"He says they were just hooking up," Natalie says. "She says they were a thing. When he tried to call it off, she got nasty."

I wince, but I'm curious about how that all came about.

"Do you really think that motel will be a moneymaker?" Natalie asks. "For Logan's sake, I hope so."

"No doubt about it. He's renovated that apartment with all

quality materials and craftsmanship, and he's got an eye for design, albeit a bit on the masculine side. That place has real potential."

Two of the guys collide on the ice and end up on the ground.

I suck air through my teeth. "Ouch."

Within seconds, they're both up, pulling at each other's jerseys and throwing punches.

"Good Lord," I say. "Do they realize how ridiculous they look? Fighting with puffy gloves. Pussies."

Natalie laughs. "Tucker doesn't mind looking ridiculous."

"Ah, I should have known it would be Tucker causing trouble and looking like a pussy."

Tina laughs. "That man has a little too much testosterone, if you ask me."

"Don't they all?" I ask.

"Thanks for spotting Mike in the kitchen this morning," Natalie says.

"Not a problem. Happy to help. Just remember, if someone asks about a button in the potato salad that almost choked them, I'm in no way responsible."

"So that's where it came from." An older guy turns from a few rows down, grinning. "I was wondering if it was a Cockloft conspiracy to get rid of me."

"Nope, just me and my loose buttons. Glad you didn't choke."

"Sweetheart, give Mike your recipe," he says. "I haven't had potato salad that good since I was a boy."

"Aw, thank you." Guess that moonlighting job with a caterer paid off in unexpected ways. When the man faces forward again, I smile at Natalie. "This sure is a friendly place."

"Small town. We're like one big dysfunctional family."

Play continues on the ice, but my gaze blurs. I'm running on fumes. My mind swerves to my most pressing problem: money.

To get a fresh start, I'd need first, last, and a deposit for a place to live—no matter where I end up. I'd need a job that could pay the bills. This may not be New York, but it's also not Mexico. And, hell, who says I want to stay here? I highly doubt there's any need for my fashion skills here, but I've developed all kinds of other proficiencies in all kinds of jobs over the years. A girl has to keep her head above water. Dealing cards, for example. But, again, not a skill transferable to this small town.

"What did you do today?" Natalie asks. "I mean after you worked at the bakery and the bar?"

"Did a little job hunting, tossed out a few résumés."

"Where?" Tina asks.

"San Francisco and LA."

"Oh," she says, part disappointment, part whine. "I was hoping you'd stay closer, like Portland."

"That's sweet. I had planned on looking there too."

"Not going back to New York?" Natalie asks.

To be honest, I hadn't been one hundred and ten percent sure I wouldn't go back, but after being here a few days, yeah, I'm sure. "Nope. If I never see New York again, it will be too soon."

"Score one for us." Natalie gives Tina a high five.

It's silly for me to feel so good about the friendship of these people I just met, right?

The thought barely registers when the phone rings in my pocket. Leave it to me to get ahead of myself. How am I supposed to settle anywhere else with this whole Aiden-rifle bullshit hanging over my head?

I pull out my phone with a sigh. Before answering his call, I tap into my bank account. Still overdrawn. I shake my head and send the call to voicemail. One which I will delete later without listening to. There's only one thing I want to hear from him, and that doesn't include verbal abuse. So I send him a text instead.

It's looking like I'm going to have to sell the gun. I really don't want to, I just want to trade it for the money you owe me, but I'll do what I have to do. It's your choice.

I want to walk away from all my failures over the last five years, standing on my own two feet, not begging for a loan from Tucker or Logan or Cole. One I'd struggle to pay back.

"Everything okay?" Natalie asks.

I shove the phone back in my pocket. "Yeah, just an ex who enjoys harassing me. Similar to bitch face over there, I suppose."

I'm considering the information of her relationship with Logan. About how they were hooking up and that's all Logan wanted. Now that's something I could get onboard with—the sextastic Logan 2.0.

I should probably at least pretend to be interested in the game, but it's about as exciting as football, Ping-Pong, or backgammon. "Where's his dog?"

"On the bench with the other guys."

I look that direction but see no sign of the puppy, just another bunch of guys sitting on the bench, cheering on their team. "Isn't it cold down there?"

"There are rubber mats," Natalie says, "and he's wearing a jacket."

"A what?"

"A doggie jacket," Natalie says.

"Doggie," Trevor repeats.

"You know, the coverings made for dogs to keep them warm?"

"They didn't have those when I was a kid." Or maybe we were just the kind of white trash who didn't concern ourselves with something as meaningless as a dog's comfort. I return my gaze to the bench with a strange desire to actually put my eyes on the puppy. "They're pretty big. They could squish him if they aren't paying attention."

"They may not look like they're paying attention," Natalie says, "but I can guarantee you every one of them knows exactly where that dog is. They are all born caretakers."

Interesting turn of phrase. I wonder if they see themselves as caretakers. More likely, saviors. I wonder if I'm mistaking the zing I feel whenever he's around. Maybe Logan's sending out compassionate vibes, not sexual ones.

My mind zips right back to this morning, playing keep-away with Mike's note. I can easily bring back the big, strong, warm feel of him all along my back from shoulders to ass. Definitely lickable. And damn that scent of his. Just remembering makes me light-headed.

I recognize Royal as he windmills over the half wall separating the bench from the ice and another guy bursts into the game in Royal's place. Someone picks up the dog from the ground and the guys pass him toward Royal, one by one. They each kiss the pup on his way past.

Natalie smirks at me. "Told ya. Big bunch of softies down there."

"He's also become their mascot and good luck charm," Tina says, "which is why they're all kissing him."

"I don't suppose I could get a good-luck kiss."

Logan's words pull back the image of him, grinning, stubble on the hard angle of his jaw. Lips a girl would want all over her body.

"So, have you planned the wedding?" I ask Natalie.

"She's fussing over a dress," Betsy says.

"Oh yeah? Moms sometimes hand down their dresses, don't they? Betsy, do you still have your dress?"

"She wore it in her wedding to Evan and thinks it's bad luck to wear it when she marries Cole."

"Not bad luck," Natalie says, "just..."

"Bad form?" I supply.

"Yes, that." She sighs. "But I do love that dress."

"Have you thought about having it altered? Restyled?"

"I asked a couple of places, but it was as expensive as buying a new dress."

"And she can't find anything she likes," Tina says with an eye roll. "Rows and rows and rows and *rows* of dresses along with a perfect figure to fit them, and she can't find one she wants."

"I'd be happy to work on Betsy's dress," I tell her, excited by the idea. I miss sewing and drawing and designing. I may only have done it all for myself and my Instagram followers, but it's fun and creative, and yeah, I miss it. "See if I could come up with something you like."

"Really?"

The look on her face makes me laugh. "Sure."

"That's a lot of work," she says. "Will you be here that long?"

Good question. "I'm looking ahead one day at a time right now, but I promise I won't start and leave you stranded. Besides, it's fun for me. Let's get together this week, look at the dress, and talk alterations. Because really, Evan wasn't the only person who got married that day, you did too. So, wearing that dress on your second wedding day could be part you, the changes, part Cole."

"I like the sound of that. Thank you."

A buzzer sounds, and everyone in the stands shoots to their feet, screaming, clapping, whistling, and making my heart jump. It isn't until I stand that I see the people in red are the only ones celebrating.

"What happened?" I raise my voice to be heard over the crowd.

"They won," Natalie says, grinning. She's a beautiful strawberry blonde. I remember thinking the same thing when Evan sent me a picture of their wedding I couldn't afford to attend. I decide right then and there, I won't miss her wedding to Cole.

As the teams line up to tap gloves in a show of sportsman-
ship, spectators start emptying the stands.

"Coming to the bar?" Natalie asks.

"What? Why?"

"After-party. Come, it will be fun."

I'm undecided, pretty worn out from the long day, when I
look at the rink and spot Logan's jersey. He's holding his helmet
in one arm, the puppy in the other. God, he's ridiculous. Just
when I'm about to focus on the bleachers so I don't tumble
down head over ass, Logan looks up into the stands. His gaze
focuses right on me, his smile electric.

Yeah. I'm definitely going to the bar.

11

Logan

I'm still high from the blood-pumping, adrenaline-induced scrimmage against the cops, and the killer win, of course.

I grabbed a shower before I left the rink because I knew I'd be busy once everyone got to the Cockloft. We see the cops often enough on calls that we all know each other for the most part, and we work well together, so we've got a bar full of family and friends along with all the cops and all the firefighters. Our rivalry is as old as time.

I fill the last of three pitchers and place them on a tray. Before I can pick it up, Isabel is there, grabbing it. "Are these for Zach's table?"

"Would you chill?" I say. "You're not working."

"Have you opened your eyes lately? This place is packed. I can't just stand around bullshitting when you guys are working your tails off."

Most everyone else seems to be able to do just that. I'm reminded of what an incredible heart she had as a kid. It's good to see that hasn't changed.

She picks up the tray with the kind of smooth balance that exposes her experience waiting tables.

"How is it that you can be so good at so many things?" I didn't think of the question before it came out of my mouth, but I realize it's something that's been nudging me subconsciously.

She turns, a swivel so smooth, the liquid in the pitchers on the tray barely sways. "What do you mean?"

I gesture to the tray. "You've definitely waited tables before. You also play poker like a shark, sub for a prep chef like a pro, and lend a hand at the bakery. You certainly aren't taking that break you came here for."

I don't mention the way she can also live in an awful motel without whining or how she can hold what looks like everything she owns in a Jeep. Nor do I point out how easily she melds into a crowd or how instantly she makes friends, though that's just as curious.

"It's just life, isn't it?" she asks. "I mean, you're a great example of how someone can manage more than one job at a time."

That sounds to me like she's been juggling multiple jobs, only that doesn't jive with what I know about her life in New York. The truth is, I have no idea what's going on with Isabel, but I do know some of her puzzle pieces are clearly not fitting as they should based on what I know of her life through social media and Tucker.

I guess what's driving me crazy is that I don't trust myself now. And I don't trust women.

Before I can bring up the discrepancies, Isabel gives me a conspiratorial look and lowers her voice to say, "Incoming."

Then she turns away right as Emily slides onto a barstool in front of me—which means Isabel heard about the mess between me and Emily in the not so distant past.

"Hey," she says, sweet, innocent, as if she won't turn into a man-eating shark the moment things don't go her way. Great reminder of why I'm single and why I want to stay that way.

All my walls go up, making me stiff and edgy. "Hey. What do you need?"

"You."

"Not on the menu."

"Then I'll settle for a lemon drop. No one makes them like you do."

I start on the drink, my gaze flicking toward Zach's table and the way Isabel melts right into the group. She definitely flirts while she's working, but she's a subtle flirt, giving almost intangible signals—the way she holds her body, the way she smiles and laughs, lots of eye contact, leaning in, subtly sliding her fingers against the skin in the open neckline of her sweater.

I don't blame her. We all know it brings in tips. But I wonder if I see Isabel's brand of flirting as sweet and open because I want to see it that way. Then again, maybe it just seems sweet and open compared to the woman sitting in front of me now, who is far more like a barracuda than a kitten.

"How's work been?" Emily asks. "I heard you got a rough call yesterday."

One of the problems with Emily—among many—is that she's an EMT for a local ambulance company, so we cross paths far too often for my taste. That'll teach me to screw around with someone so close to my second home—the firehouse.

"Yeah." I think of the twenty-something rafting the Columbia River, just trying to have some fun in the sun. He caught an eddy wrong, flipped, hit his head on a rock, and drowned. I worked on him for forty-five minutes before I gave in to the failure. Pisses me off that I couldn't get him back. "Tragic."

I slide her drink across the bar, and when she reaches for it, she bypasses the drink and takes my hand instead. I immediately pull away, annoyed, creeped out. She's got issues. Issues I didn't see until after we'd hooked up a few times.

I ended things at the beginning of the summer, and she's dating one of the cops who played in the game today, who also happens to be standing nearby, talking with friends.

"Classy," I say. "Dalton is twenty feet away."

"I'd drop him in a heartbeat for a second chance with you."

When I look at her, all I see is the awful lie that put me through the wringer, only to discover the depth of her manipulation.

"Forget it." I walk away before I say something I shouldn't.

"Where's your puppy?" she asks.

Instead of answering, I take another drink order and get back to work.

"What did you name it?" She's just trying to elicit conversation, but I know exactly where that will lead.

Eventually, Dalton comes over and kisses Emily's neck. But Emily is still looking at me. She's so messed up. It's like she wants me to be mean to her. I'm reminded of the way my mother wanted my father to be mean to her. Without the abuse, my mom didn't believe my dad loved her. They were so fucking twisted.

I should be—probably am—as fucked up as Emily, even while hoping to God I'm not.

She moves on with Dalton, and Isabel returns to the bar with the tray. "Can I get three cosmos, two mules, and two drafts?"

I reach for glasses and start mixing.

"You okay?" she asks. "She giving you a hard time?"

I cut a glance at her, assessing. "Who told you?"

"She did in a way. Gave me the stink eye from the moment I walked into the rink. When I asked Natalie what her problem was, Nat told me you two dated and she didn't take the breakup well."

I'm relieved Nat didn't get into the whole pregnancy scare. "Then you know the story."

"Not the whole story."

"When you want to share the whole story about Cock-sucker, I'll tell you the whole story about Emily."

"Why is that still bothering you?"

I stop what I'm doing, plant my hands flat on the bar, and meet her gaze directly, defiantly. "Because he hurt you."

She doesn't turn away or try to bluff. No stories, no excuses. Just bold, direct eye contact. "You're angry with Emily, and I'm pretty damned sure that's why you're acting like a dick to me, which is totally unfair, by the way. And I'd tell you what happened, but you wouldn't believe me. Which is fine. You don't have to believe me. It doesn't matter to me one way or the other. That's your issue, not mine. If you want to worry about some nonexistent abuse you made up in your mind, so be it. Just don't act pissy with me over something you don't know anything about or because you're really mad at her."

She just took me out at the knees. She's right on every damned point. How fucking annoying is that?

Her phone rings. She yanks the cell from her pocket and looks at the screen. "Fucking men." She answers with a terse "What?"

Then she turns away, starts toward the back door, and heads outside, and I'm left staring at the closed door for a long time. What in the hell am I doing? I don't want to be into her.

I'm not. I'm *not* into her, goddammit.

A tap on my legs signals the pup is awake. I look at Tim, another firefighter helping out behind the bar. "You got this? I've got to take the dog out."

"Give him a name, for God's sake."

I scoop him up from the floor at my feet. I already think of him as Lucky, but I've never called him by the name. There's still a chance someone will claim him, and I already know that won't go over well with me.

His blue eyes are sleepy, and he yawns, his pink tongue curling before returning inside his mouth. Why do I like this guy so much? Why do I feel the need to rescue everyone? I'm sick of the bullshit. I need some serious boundaries.

I take the pup out the back door and find Isabel standing near the fence that encloses the dumpster. She hammers a button on the phone—Disconnect, I'm assuming—and bites out, "Fucking moron."

She doesn't startle when she sees me, just watches me set the pup down, then follows his path until he pees on a strip of grass near the back door.

"He's potty trained already?" Isabel asks. "Doesn't that usually take, I don't know, months?"

"Not if you're diligent about it. They're smart. They pick things up fast." When the pup is done, he wanders into the surrounding brush, roots around, and returns walking backward dragging a tree limb five times his size with him, then plops down across one of my feet and chews on the wood.

Isabel laughs. "Hope you weren't planning on going anywhere soon."

"I could use a break."

Isabel presses her shoulder against the fence. "Yeah, a break would be nice."

"When do you head back to New York?"

She shrugs her free shoulder. "I don't know."

"Are you even going back to New York? Nat said you put in some résumés on the West Coast."

"I'm leaving my options open."

She can't even pick a city to live in—a reminder she's already got one foot out of town.

"What about him?" she says, indicating the puppy. "You keeping him? Seems like it would be hard to take care of a puppy with your schedule."

"Fess up. What have you got against puppies?"

"Nothing. They just..." Her gaze rests on the dog, and her expression clearly registers discomfort. "They just remind me of a dog I had when I was a kid."

"I don't remember you and Tucker having a dog."

"We didn't. I picked her up from a box in front of the grocery store one day, and she was gone three days later."

"What happened?"

"Derik Merlin happened."

"Your mom's boyfriend? The one who—"

"Yes, that one." She cuts me off before I can remind her of how sleazy he was by coming on to her. "He hated everyone and everything, including my dog. I came home from school one day, and she was gone. Just gone. And Derik was very pleased with himself." She presses her fingers to closed lids. "I've had countless nightmares about what he did to her."

"Maybe he just gave her to someone else."

She opens her eyes and meets mine. "You didn't know him."

The darkly edged certainty in her voice sends a tingle across the back of my neck. "Your mom really picked from the bottom of the barrel, didn't she?"

"My mom *scraped* the bottom of the barrel."

"You never told me about that when we were hanging out together in high school. About the dog, I mean."

"It's not the kind of thing I wanted to talk about. I tried my damnedest to forget, and when I couldn't forget, I thought of her in doggy heaven, playing with all the other dogs." She shrugs. "So, yeah, I guess I have an aversion to puppies. Besides, they require commitment, and that's not in the cards for me."

Reminder after reminder after reminder. Eventually, it should stick.

"He doesn't require anything of you," I say, looking down at the pup, who's curled into a ball with his head on my foot. "At the moment, he doesn't require much of anything from anyone."

"No point in getting attached if you're just going to lose them."

The tone of her voice makes me think that's her outlook on life, not just pets. "Are we still talking about puppies?"

She shrugs again. "Puppies, relationships, whatever. That was your MO with Emily, wasn't it?"

"I didn't have an MO, and we didn't have a relationship." I'm annoyed, and my voice carries the emotion. "I was very clear every time I saw her that all we were doing was hooking up. It was mutual. I wasn't using her."

Isabel lifts her hands, palms out. "Chill. I'm just wondering if that's where you're at in life right now or if it was specific to Emily."

I think about the question for a minute, then tilt my head. "Why does it matter?"

"Don't look at me like that."

"Like what?"

"Like, like..." She gestures toward me, suddenly flustered, her face gaining color. "Like I'm into you. 'Cause I'm not."

My mood turns around, and I grin at her. "Yeah, you are," I say, half joking, half hoping. "You're *totally* into me."

"*Pffft.* You're dreaming again. When did you get so full of yourself?"

"Probably during those first couple of years after you left. Had to build up my sexual esteem after you bailed."

She laughs, drops her arms, and turns toward the bar. "I'm gonna grab my stuff and go—"

But I'm not ready for this to end. I like the intimacy of it. I reach out, and my hand lands on her biceps. She flinches and turns to release my grip instead of jerking away. The sight of those finger-shaped bruises on her skin fill my head.

"Sorry," I say. "I didn't mean to hurt you."

"I know." She rubs her arm. "Bet you would have held on tighter if I was about to fall down a flight of stairs. Even tighter if I was trying to get away from you, with the stairs behind me."

Those images rise up in my mind, and she's right. That's exactly what I'd do, bruises be damned. "Is that what happened with Cocksucker?"

"As far as the bruises go, yeah, that's how I got them. Only, I did get away, and I did fall. Not all the way down the steps, but far enough to leave bruises in a few places."

It's a legit story, and I do my best to take it at face value. But the truth is, I don't think I can tell when a woman is lying and when she's not anymore.

"Are you keeping him?" she asks, looking at the puppy.

"I don't know. No one's come forward."

"Tucker says nobody will."

There's something about the way she says it that's challenging. Snarky, sassy, sexy. She's getting under my skin.

I reach down and separate the pup from his tree limb, then face her again. I let my gaze skim her beautiful face, her long, dark silky hair. Her breasts stretch the fabric of her shirt, the crisscrossing straps exposing the smooth skin of her chest, hiding the tattoo I really want to see. Her posture speaks of an underlying attitude she's probably oblivious to.

"You should really just decide if you're going to keep him or not and get off the fence," she says. "Name him or something."

"The only thing I'm on the fence about is you."

She gets a confused look on her face, opens her mouth to say something, but only exhales.

I take it as tacit permission to cross the line I've been too aware of from the day she showed up, and in one step, I close the distance between us. "Guess I better just get off the fence altogether."

With my free hand, I cup her jaw and press my lips against hers. They're soft and warm, and I know instantly, one kiss will never be enough.

When she doesn't pull away, I angle my head a little more and kiss her again, this time catching her lower lip between both of mine.

She sighs, so I slide my tongue across the flesh.

She moans, and I don't have to do anything else. She steps into me, pressing her body against mine. Then she slides her hand around the back of my neck and pulls my head down. Her kiss isn't the least bit tentative. It's an I-want-you-right-fucking-now kiss. Fire licks through my veins. I slide one arm around her waist and pull her against me, holding the puppy out of the way so we don't squish him.

She tastes me in a bold, sexy move, and I'm on fire from the roots of my hair to the soles of my feet. I groan into her mouth and wish I had somewhere to put the dog so I could get both my hands on her. The next best thing is walking her backward until she's against the building. Until I can press into all her sweet curves and devour her hot mouth. Pressure builds between my legs, and I rock my hips against hers.

The sound that comes from her throat matches the all-in way she kisses me, and I'm trying to think of how to take the next step, but with the pup, I can't do much of anything. And I have no doubt that if we let even a sliver of reality in, this will be over with no guarantees of ever happening again.

Right on cue, the puppy whines. I reposition him, but that only gets him close enough to press his cold nose against my neck. The final blow is the puppy leaning in and licking Isabel's cheek.

When she pulls out of the kiss, she sighs and looks at the dog. "Thanks for the reality check, buddy."

But she's still leaning into me, and I swear she's got to feel the beat of my heart in my dick pressed against her pelvis.

Her gaze returns to mine, lowers to my mouth, and she strokes her thumb across it. "You always were an incredible kisser."

"I was?"

"Mmm-hmm."

"You know," I say, going for light. "I've been told I'm pretty good at more than kissing."

She laughs. And laughs. And laughs, dropping her forehead to my chest.

"It's a good thing my ego has fully, *robustly* recovered."

She pushes me back a few inches. "Don't read anything into this. I'm off men. *All* men."

"Uh-huh."

"I mean it."

"Uh-huh."

"For real. I can't do"—she makes a circle with her hand, gesturing to me—"this." Then amends, scanning my body. "I mean I could *do* this, boy oh boy could I *do* this." Then her hand moves between us, and her gaze meets mine again. "But not this."

"Yeah, I can't do *this* either."

"So, we understand each other."

"We can *do* this," I repeat her gestures. "But not this."

"What? No, no, no. Because *this* would lead to *this* and I can't do *this*."

I grin. "I'm officially confused as hell."

She puts a hand against her head. "So am I."

I laugh. I love the vibe between us. Kinda fun, kinda serious, really sexy.

I don't want to let her think too long, so I slide my arm around her waist again and pull her in for another series of white-hot kisses.

The sound of the knob on the back door makes me take one giant step back before the door opens. I shift the puppy in front of me, just to make the possibility of Isabel and me kissing that much slimmer.

It's Tucker. He looks between us. "You two gonna work or get a room?"

"Shut up," Isabel says to him. "Like you're one to talk."

"Be right in," I tell him.

When the door closes again, I smile at Isabel. "I vote for the room."

She groans. "Yeah, no. This would get really messy, really fast."

"Right, right." I nod and rub my eyes with my free hand. "You're so right."

When I drop my hand, she holds my gaze and pushes off the wall. "I'm going to head back to the motel. If I stay here too long, *that* is going to happen again."

She turns for the door, and I use the back of her shirt to tug her into me again. She's laughing when I kiss her, but as soon as my mouth is on hers, her laugh turns to a moan.

I pull away to catch my breath. "What's wrong with this? I can't remember." I kiss her again. "And you *did* just call me an incredible kisser."

As if the reminder makes her hungry, she groans, opens, and leans into me, her breasts pillowing against my chest, her hands sliding up my back. I can't help but want more. Lots more. We're flash fire together.

"I changed my mind," I say between kisses. "You're not right. *This* is right."

Lucky yips and whines, and I growl as Isabel breaks the kiss.

She slides her hand over Lucky's head. "I think he's smarter than both of us."

"You mean individually?" I ask. "Or combined?"

She laughs and turns for the door, dodging my attempt to grab her again. And in the end, I'm left with nothing but a hard-on, the taste of her on my tongue, and a high-maintenance puppy.

12

Isabel

Five-Alarm Confections is a really cute place. A combination of café and bakery, heavy on the bakery. The kitchen takes up half the space, the display units, stuffed with baked goods, another twenty percent, and the dining room with small tables, the remaining thirty percent. All they serve here is pastry and coffee, but they're always busy.

I've learned that a good chunk of Natalie's business comes from the community in the form of special events, stocking local stores, and supplying local restaurants with desserts for their menu. I also know she's quite successful, but more importantly, she loves what she does. It's given me the incentive to search for a place and a job that work for me, not one I contort myself to fit into. But I still have no idea what that could be. Or where.

Once the last tray of leftover croissants has been bagged for delivery to one of the local nursing homes and Tina has locked the front door and turned over the Closed sign, I dust off my hands and say, "Dress. I've been waiting all morning for the dress."

Natalie bounces on her toes before turning and disappearing into the bathroom. Tina sweeps the floor and sets a stool out, and I grab my sketchbook, where I've loosely drawn some styles that would showcase Natalie's figure best.

"Can't wait to see it," Tina says, her eyes bright.

"Didn't you see it at her wedding with Evan?"

"No, we didn't meet until after Evan died."

Remembering Evan is gone still hurts my heart. But that evaporates the second Natalie comes out of the bathroom, holding the bodice to herself while her mother buttons up the back.

An excitement I can only describe as giddiness fills me. The realization that fashion still thrills me is bittersweet. The thought of giving up on it haunts me with bone-deep, esteem-crushing failure. But life has a way of shoving reality in your face every chance it gets.

As Natalie stands on the stool and I make a slow three-sixty around her, Tina and Betsy smile ear to ear, oohing and ahhing over the way Natalie looks in the dress, a royal crepe A-line. And rightfully so. The dress is beautiful, and Natalie is gorgeous in it.

I'm already deep into alterations in my mind by the time Natalie asks, "What do you think?"

"I think it's amazing."

She looks down at the dress and slides her hands across the pristine fabric, which is bare satin except for the dozens and dozens of crystal buttons from the nape of her neck to the hem of the train. The sleeves are three-quarter, the neckline square, the skirt flaring from the high waist.

"The simplicity is incredible, and it fits you perfectly. That's pretty hard to beat."

"I know." Some of the excitement fades from her voice. "I

should probably just keep looking for a new one. Maybe I'll get lucky and have a daughter who could wear this."

"Oh, no. No, no, no. I'm always up for a creative challenge."

I pick up my sketch pad and sit to put pencil to paper, then lose myself in possible alterations. As I toss out questions like *Do you like lace? How about bling? What about the sleeves? How do you feel about showing some skin?* I sketch, alternating my gaze from Natalie to the sketch pad.

"That's amazing." Tina is watching me over my shoulder. "Damn, girl, you're talented."

Not talented enough is the first thought that fills my mind. Immediately followed by the reminder that I've dragged my mess of a life and all my lies across the country with me.

"It's incredible," Tina says. "Nat, come see this."

Natalie steps off the stool and holds the dress's skirt up as she comes toward me. I turn the book around and point to areas with my pencil as I explain the suggested changes. "We take off the sleeves and leave narrow straps. We bring the neckline down and the bust up. Then taper the A-line into a modified fit-and-flare to show off your sexy body, but by no means are we touching that incredible train."

"Oh my God." Natalie glances over her shoulder. "Mom, look at this."

I turn the sketch pad toward Betsy. She pulls in a sharp breath and puts a hand over her heart as tears glisten in her eyes.

I hold my breath, unsure if those are happy tears or disappointed tears. "We could tone down the moderations if you think it's too much."

"No," Betsy says with an adamant shake of her head. "No, it's gorgeous." She reaches out and wraps her hand around Natalie's. "Honey, you're going to look stunning."

Natalie and Betsy and Tina laugh and twitter about the changes, but my gaze is stuck on the sight of Natalie and Betsy holding hands. It opens a stream of loss inside me. My biological mother was just that, a mother by DNA, but she was never a mother in the true sense of the word. And that empty part of me throbs now, seeing a healthy mother-daughter relationship. I push the loss aside and refocus on the sketch. "A little lace here and here? Maybe a few pearls and crystals all in here? And along here?"

"*Yes.*" Natalie pushes the word out on a breath, hand over her heart. "Yes, it's perfect."

"Well done, sweetheart." Betsy gives my hand a squeeze and leans in to kiss my cheek. "You're so talented."

These snippets of praise eclipse every grade, every competition, every kudo I ever received in fashion school.

Maybe feeling successful doesn't have to be an arduous fight. Maybe it can be as simple as a few sketches that change someone's perception for the better. Maybe not every success in life requires a war to attain.

"I'll set up my sewing machine."

13

Logan

I'm sitting on a workout bench in the engine bay, waiting for Bobby, our other paramedic, to get here so I can head home. Lucky has discovered Master and Bates, the two black-and-white cats the house adopted when they were left on our doorstep as kittens.

I can't tell if the cats find him amusing or annoying. Probably both. Master is hiding on the front tire of the rescue, swatting at Lucky's tail every time he passes. The dog has yet to figure out what's happening, just swivels and barks at nothing. It's almost as entertaining as the way he chases his tail, spinning round and round and round, until he's stumbling sideways like a drunk before plopping on the ground. That had us all laughing our asses off last night.

I'm officially off the fence—at least about Lucky. If anyone thinks they're taking him from me now, they'll be in for one hell of a fight. As far as Isabel is concerned, I'm in a tug-of-war between my mind and my body.

I'm scrolling through Isabel's Instagram feed, something

I've only checked out a couple of times over the years when I wondered how she was doing. But this research is for an entirely different reason. I'm detecting something off about her story. I don't want to have this suspicion, but it's ingrained.

As a kid, I had to have a constant finger on the pulse of my parents' moods. Had to learn to read body language and voice inflections. Had to know where Maya was at all times so I could get her out of harm's way if my dad was on the warpath.

I don't want to get involved in whatever mess Isabel is caught up in, but my protective instincts don't shut down just because I want them to.

From the first day of college at the Academy of Art in San Francisco, Maya worked her ass off. She never had time for any extracurricular activities, including the everyday stuff, like a job or learning how to change her own tire. Yet Isabel went to an equally challenging school and ultimately learned to multitask in ways that speak of everyday life skills. Isabel is a jack-of-all-trades, where Maya is all but helpless outside the fashion industry.

They were equally good students, equally industrious, equally well liked. So why does Isabel seem to have more everyday talents? Why doesn't she talk about her jobs—either the one she left or the one she wants? Maya can't *stop* talking about her work when she's here. And why isn't Isabel in any hurry to get back to New York?

Her Instagram feed is filled with artistic shots of the city, selfies of her in front of racks of designer clothing, with runway models behind the scenes at a fashion show, in front of department store window displays.

Cocksucker isn't in any photos, though she could have deleted them after they broke up.

"Hey." Tucker wanders into the engine bay and opens his locker to put his things away. "Why aren't you gone?"

"Waiting for Bobby."

"He's here. Inside, talking to Sorenson."

I close Instagram, hike the strap of my duffel over my shoulder, and turn toward Tucker. "Are we good?"

"About Isabel? You're both adults. As long as you don't fuck her over, we're fine."

Lucky has finally caught on, locating Master where he's hiding in the wheel well. He jumps up, putting his paws against the tire, barking. Master reaches down and swats at Lucky, making him jump back and bark even harder.

I lean my shoulder against the lockers and watch Bates jump up on the rescue's hood and stalk toward us, clearly trying to stay hidden from Lucky.

"You get any sense that something's going on with her?" I ask.

Tucker shuts the locker and turns toward me. "What do you mean?"

"Can't put my finger on it."

Bates crouches, his gaze intent on Lucky, his tail swishing.

"Her last boyfriend was a douchebag." Now Tucker's watching Lucky and the cats too. He crosses his arms and shakes his head at Lucky. "Dude, watch your back."

The words are barely out of Tucker's mouth when Bates launches from the hood of the rescue, flying at Lucky like a hawk, talons out. Lucky scampers to get out of reach, but Bates still catches his tail. Lucky yelps and hightails it to the safety of my legs while Tucker and I laugh.

"He's going to turn out to be a great source of comic relief," Tucker says, then turns the conversation back to Isabel. "We worked the bar together last night, and she was fine. Seemed in good spirits. We had a great time," he says, grinning. "Bickering and laughing all night, entertaining the customers. I didn't realize how much I missed her. Sure feels good having her back. I'm not looking forward to having her leave again. She and Natalie hit it off. She's working on Nat's wedding dress."

"She is?" That seems like a big project. "Is she going to stay long enough for that?"

He shrugs. "Unless a job offer comes in and she has to leave, I guess."

Right. An annoying reminder. After that kiss, I haven't been able to think about anything but getting more.

"How many times do I have to tell you to stop trying to figure them out?" Tucker says. "Women are puzzles we were never intended to understand."

Guess I should have expected this take from Tucker. He never stays with one woman long enough to even try to understand them.

"Tantor dropped a shitload of product at the bar late last night." Tucker says. "We didn't get it all put away."

"I'll get it." I scoop Lucky up, but before I can leave, Sorenson belts out my name in a very annoyed tone.

"*Roberts.*"

I wince and turn just as Sorenson comes through the door to the engine bay. He's holding one of his work boots and throws it at me. I instinctively turn to shield Lucky and catch the boot with my other hand.

"You owe me a pair of boots," he says, hands on hips. "And if that dog decides to cut his teeth on anything else I own, he's out. Do you hear me?"

Shit. "Yes, sir."

When Sorenson disappears into the station, Tucker grins at me. "I have a feeling Lucky may not live up to his name. In fact, he may even rival Bandit for the bullshit you have to go through to keep him."

I inspect the chunk out of the leather and wonder when in the hell Lucky had time to do that. He was with me the whole time. Then my mind strays to how quiet he got while we were watching a movie in the rec room. I thought Lucky was asleep, but now realize he was chomping on Sorenson's boot.

"Probably wouldn't go over well if I told Sorenson that if he kept his boots where they belong, they wouldn't get chewed up."

"Only if you want a demotion." He slams the locker and heads inside, saying, "Last I checked, those Red Wings jumped to nearly three hundred bucks."

I sigh out a long breath and look at Lucky. His eyes are bright, his tail wagging. "It's a good thing you're cute."

I keep the boot so I can buy the right size and style, and on my way to my truck, my thoughts turn toward Isabel.

I think she worked at the bakery this morning, so I don't know if she'll be at the motel or not, and I've got mixed feelings about seeing her. Because I want her. And I shouldn't. I try to rationalize that whether she leaves or not is no big deal—I'm not looking for anything heavy. And if she's leaving anyway, her lies don't matter either. I guess I just have to keep my expectations in check.

When I pull into the driveway of the motel, I'm confused by the sight of a dumpster, until I remember telling her she could order one. I just didn't expect it to be here so fast.

Isabel's Jeep is open, as is the door to room seven. By the time I shut down the truck, Isabel is in the parking lot. A definite zing of interest lights me up on the inside. I should see that as a warning sign, but I take one look at that smile, that ponytail, the fit of those jeans, and...I don't see a warning sign anywhere.

She lifts a box from the back of her Jeep, and I step in to take it from her.

"Thanks." Lucky goes straight toward her, jumping to put his front paws on her leg, begging to be picked up. "Why do they always go right to the person who doesn't want them?"

"Maybe he knows you really *do* want him, you just don't want to show it. What's all this?" I ask on the way into the room.

I place the box in a corner, and Lucky roams around sniffing everything. "You decide to stay a while?"

"I don't know. I'm just breaking out my sewing machine to help Natalie with her wedding dress."

"Tucker said you're making it?"

"No, just altering the dress she wore at her wedding to Evan."

"You've got a lot on your plate."

She shrugs and smiles like it doesn't matter. "I always have a lot on my plate. Hey, I want to show you something."

I rest my hands at my hips and look around. "I hope it's not another mouse family infestation."

"Not in my room, but I have rented out other rooms." She's smiling as she takes my hand and drags me from the room and around the side of the building. "We've got a new mouse family on vacation in room six, a pair of newlywed rats in one, and the cockroaches in room four are looking for a long-term lease, but I vote no, because they keep sneaking into room nine, which is pissing off the momma racoon and her babies. Luckily, the snake couple in room five promised to take care of all of them —except the racoons. We're on our own there."

She's pulling me around the back of the building.

"Are you for real?" She certainly doesn't seem fazed by the rodents, serpents, or insects. Maya won't even stay in my apartment, and she doesn't know about the infestations. "You're kidding about the critters, right?"

"Oh, no. And none of them like me disturbing their peace. I decided to start excavating in room twelve, waaaaay down the other end of the motel. You're going to need a hard-core exterminator to get all the creepy-crawly woodland creatures out."

I'm suddenly overwhelmed by this news. I stop and drop her hand to look around. "What are we doing? And why are you still smiling? You're a very peculiar woman."

"You aren't the first to say so." She points west. "See the marked trees?"

I frown and look closer. Small reflective squares catch the sun on several trees. I wander closer and see the squares are different colors.

"What in holy hell?" I look at her and gesture to the trees. "You used my condoms to mark the trees?"

"You had an industrial box of them. You won't miss a few. Oh, but make sure these don't get mixed up with those, because, ya know, these all have holes in them now. Anyhoo," she says, ignoring my what-the-fuck stare, "if you take down the trees marked in green—green-apple flavored—rooms eleven and twelve will have views of the river and mountains, and room ten will have a partial view."

"How can you tell?"

"I went up on the roof. But don't go up there, because you need a new one the entire length of the motel, and there are a number of places you could fall through, just take my word for it."

"I spend a quarter of my life on unsafe roofs."

"Fair point. Now check out the trees marked in purple— grape flavored and my personal favorite. If you take those down, you'll give rooms six through nine a view. The ones marked in red—which should have been cinnamon flavored but are strawberry, blech—will give rooms two through five a view. And last but not least, the silver—unflavored and micro thin, all in the impressive size of extra-large, I might add—will give your apartment a view."

There's still a ladder leaning against the wall. I grab the rungs and climb it to the very top, where I get a glimpse of the view she's talking about. One I didn't even realize was hidden behind the trees. The previous owner must not have known either, because he let this place go dirt cheap. I mean, sure it's a dump, but the property alone...

I look down at her. "You know this raises the value like... I don't even know how much."

She's wearing a big, satisfied grin. "Try five hundred grand, in about a year or two."

"*What?*"

"I did a little research on the property value increases in the past couple of years, a few property comparisons, and looked at the forecasted rise in value."

I'm coming down the ladder, shocked, when she says, "Even if it's only half that, it's still a lot. Who did you buy it from?"

"A guy we used to make a lot of runs to. He lived here, had emphysema, and was on death's doorstep. Said he wanted to leave the money for this place to his kids, but he didn't have anywhere to go until he died, so he couldn't sell it and hated the idea of giving this headache to his kids. I got an appraisal, we agreed on a price, and I let him live here until he passed away."

"Oh, man." Her shoulders soften along with her voice. "You're the real deal. You can't just be hot as hell or sexy AF, you save puppies and help old men die happy too. I'm feeling quite unworthy of standing in your shadow at the moment."

That assessment embarrasses me, and I turn the conversation around. "How do you know all this stuff? About the property?"

"It's called the Internet. It's cool. You should look into it." She walks backward, smiling at me. "Make sure you toss those condoms when you take them off the trees, and you need a permit to cut those trees down, but I gave the planning department your address, and they said removing some trees shouldn't be a problem. They'd make great firewood too."

Then she's gone, disappearing around the edge of the building, and I'm left spinning. "What in the fuck?"

I look around and find Lucky trying to pick up a stick ten times his size.

"Ambitious," I say, tapping my thigh. "Come on."

Lucky starts toward me, all off-balance because of the stick, and we follow Isabel's path. She's getting more boxes from the car, so I grab a few to help out, while Lucky lies down and chomps on the branch. Better than Sorenson's boots. I'll have to take a stick into work with me every day.

"Isabel, I'm serious," I say, walking alongside her. "How do you know everything you know? The property, the bar, changing a tire on a snowy roadside. Maya never knows what's happening outside the fashion world."

"I guess I just get out more."

She's lying. I know it. I can feel it under my skin. "Come on." I set down the box in the room and look at her. "You can trust me."

"Logan, there's nothing to tell." She opens her sketchbook and drops it on the well-made bed. "I worked up a few more images based on how things could look when you take the trees down and get the place renovated." Before she walks out of the room again, she says, "And in answer to your unasked question, I learnt the whole sketching thing in college."

"Smartass."

She steps outside, and her phone rings. For the first time, she smiles when she answers. "Hey. Oh, yeah, sure. Nope, won't be a problem. You bet. Bye."

"Who was that?" I've picked up a long wooden box from the Jeep, and I'm checking out the detailed workmanship.

"Just Nat. She asked if I could—" She turns and gasps, shoves her phone into her pocket, and rushes to take the box from my hands.

"Oh, shit. You have to be really careful with this."

"Why? What is it?"

"Never mind." She faces me. "Thanks for your help, but I've got everything I need from the car."

I don't like the feeling of getting brushed off. "What's going on with you?"

"Nothing. Everything is fine."

"Everything is *not* fine."

"You're pushing again. Not everyone wants to talk about everything, and I don't like to be pushed."

"It seems like that's the only way you *really* talk to me."

"You don't want me to lie, yet you're demanding answers I don't want to give."

"I'm not *demanding* them."

"You're putting me in an impossible position. I talk about something I don't want to talk about and something that's, frankly, none of your business, or I say something that will placate you, something you want to hear so you'll drop it."

"Are you saying *I* make you lie?"

She lifts both hands and gives me an if-it-fits look.

"Why won't you tell me what's in the box?"

She slaps a hand against her forehead. "Didn't we *just* have this conversation? Like thirty seconds ago?"

"You're right, never mind." I'm done. She can keep her lies, but I want nothing to do with them. "I'll give you all the privacy you want. Come on, Lucky."

I turn and head toward my apartment, and I'm at the door before I realize Lucky isn't behind me. I turn and find him sitting on Isabel's foot. I call to him, but he just looks up at Isabel, comically massive stick still in his mouth.

"Jesus Christ." Rejected by my damned dog. I stalk back to Lucky, sweep him up with a scowl for Isabel, who just lifts her hands like don't look at me, and I stalk back to my apartment.

I'm angry, but resigned to the fact that I can't change her or even help her if she isn't willing. And a woman who keeps secrets is not the woman for me.

14

Isabel

When I get back to the motel after my shift at the bar, the lights in Logan's apartment are still on.

I learned a long time ago not to take responsibility for someone else's anger, but there's still a knot in my stomach from our earlier argument.

I don't owe him an explanation. I'm pitching in around here to pay him back for letting me stay. He has no right to be angry, but I know he's acting this way because he cares.

Telling him what's in that box is a powder keg, but I want this stress to end. I want to leave the past in the past and start the next phase of my life—one which is still a complete mystery—with a clean slate.

I've got to get rid of this fucking gun and cut all ties with Aiden.

I pull out my phone, take a deep breath, and call Aiden. I'm surprised when I get his voicemail. After how he's been hounding me, I expected him to pick up. Then again, it is late on the East Coast.

"Look, I'm over this mess," I tell his voicemail. "I just want to end it. Tell me how to get the gun back to you."

I disconnect, sick to my stomach over the loss of five grand. May as well have been a million. That's how important it was to me. But Logan is even more important. Everyone I've met in this small mountain town is more important to me, which is a huge wakeup call. There was no one and nothing for me in New York. I need to figure my shit out so I can find myself a new place to start over.

I don't see any movement in Logan's apartment, which means I'm going to have to make the herculean effort to apologize. For the record, I suck at apologizing. It always feels like defeat. Apologizing makes me feel small and weak, but I've gotta do what I've gotta do.

At Logan's apartment, I raise my hand to knock, but he opens the door before I can. "What's up?"

"Can we talk?"

"I don't want to fight." The resignation in his eyes shows me the wall he's erected between us. "It's your life. You can live it however you want."

He starts to close the door, and the words "It's a gun" tumble out of my mouth. His gaze laser sharpens on me again, but he doesn't say anything, which pushes me to add, "In the box. It's a rifle."

"You took a rifle from an abusive ex? And you expect him to leave you alone?"

"Let's get one thing straight." I don't try to hide my anger with his assumptions. "He was an arrogant narcissist, but he was not physically abusive. Mentally and emotionally, sure, and as soon as I saw it, I broke things off. You don't have to believe me, but you don't get to treat me like a liar when you have no proof what I'm saying isn't true."

Instead of closing the door in my face, he walks away, leaving the door open. Not exactly much of an invitation, but

Lucky appears in the doorway, jumping to put his front paws against my leg, wagging his tail, and I swear he's smiling.

God, he's so trusting, but I don't want to like him or get attached—my same goal with his dad. "Hi, Lucky."

I pat his head, step into the apartment, and close the door at my back, leaning against it, hands behind me. Lucky's still standing beside me, tail wagging. When I don't pet him again, he wanders toward a small dog bed and lies down.

Logan sits on the arm of the sofa, his attention focused on me. "I'm listening."

Here we go.

"We only dated a few weeks before I realized what a bastard he was. I never even slept with him."

As soon as I say it, I'm not sure why I did. Maybe so Logan won't think I'm as big a fuckup as I feel like I am.

"The gun came from an auction," I go on. "I thought we were just there to watch, but he bid on the damn thing and won, then didn't have any money on him to pay for it."

The sour feeling of being naive collects in the back of my throat and I look at the wood under my feet.

"I feel so stupid about the whole thing. When I look back, I realize he knew exactly what he was doing. He knew I had my rent money on me. I was going to pay it at the office later that day when I got home."

I leave out the part about how I could only pay my rent in cash because of how many rent checks I bounced.

"So I paid for the gun at the auction. He kept stalling on paying me back, which put me in hot water with my landlord. And when I demanded the money, he said I should just move in with him."

"How did you buy a gun on the fly like that? Don't you need a license or something?"

"Not for antiques, evidently. If it was manufactured before 1899, current gun laws don't apply." I close my eyes on a sigh and rub at the sting. Talking about this makes me feel about an inch tall. "Anyway, I had to pull money from my savings for the rent, which is when I discovered he'd siphoned all the money from my accounts. Every goddamned dime."

"You had joint accounts?" Logan asks, his voice softer now.

"No. He used my password—which is the same as all my passwords, shame on me—to get into my online bill pay and sent himself a check for everything I had." I sigh out a ton of self-disgust. "So I used his code for the keyless lock on his back door and took the rifle. I thought he'd pay me back right away, but he knew I didn't want the gun, and he thought if I got evicted, I'd come to him. So, when I did get evicted, I drove across the country instead."

I leave out the part about the whole job issue. That's just too big a can of worms to open right now. In fact, I hope I never have to open it.

Logan looks at the floor and shakes his head. "My dad used to do that to my mom. Gaslight her. Made her feel small. Tried to convince her she was nothing without him."

I close my eyes for a second, trying to hold on to the rising anger—at him, at myself. "*Please* don't compare me to your mother."

He meets my gaze, apologetic, but I still see fire in his eyes. "You're right, I'm sorry. It's just...a bad habit. I'll stop."

I take a breath and continue. "I used the last of the cash I had stashed away in my apartment to get here. I keep telling him I'll give the gun back if he repays me the money he stole and the price of the rifle. I could pawn it, but I'll get next to nothing. Right now, it's my only leverage."

The little things you learn about someone in just a few weeks—it all has the ability to blow your world apart when things go south.

Tears are choking me, but I refuse to cry. Not for that fucktard.

"Shit." Logan's voice holds sympathy, but also disgusted anger. This time, I know it's for Aiden, not me, but it still pushes the tears I've been trying to hold back over my lashes, and I wipe them away.

"It's no big deal. Live and learn, right?" I can't look Logan in the eye. "I just left him a message. Told him I'm done with it, and I'll give him the gun back. If he doesn't respond, I'll just head down to Portland when I'm free and get rid of it. Minimize my loss."

Telling Logan this ugly story crushes what little self-esteem I have left. If it was only this instance, I wouldn't feel so bad. People cross other people every day. But Aiden is a far more complicated thread woven into my life. Like an invasive vine, he slithered in and took over. I didn't see it until it was too late, and I can't face telling Logan all the dirt.

"It *is* a big deal," Logan says. "Does Tucker know this?"

"Oh, God no. I have enough trouble. Nobody knows."

"What about the police?"

"I looked into it. Even went to the station in person and told them the story, and they said there's no way to prove I wasn't the one who sent him the check from my account. Even if they traced the login to his computer, we were dating. There's nothing to say it wasn't me who logged in from his place. That's when I took the gun."

"Guns and controlling men don't mix well. Are you sure he doesn't know where you are? I don't like this situation at all."

"All he knows is that I'm from Portland and that Tucker is a firefighter somewhere in the state. Besides, he couldn't fire a gun if his life depended on it. Seriously. He's a collector, not a shooter. He's all about using his money to collect pretty things and put them in pretty cases to show them off."

"Like you."

I huff a laugh. "Well, yeah. I mean, he's got good taste."

That makes Logan laugh. I sag against the door, suddenly

exhausted. This has all been weighing on me so heavily. It feels good to tell someone. Only now I feel vulnerable. As in, exposed and waiting to be filleted. I also feel shittier than shit about myself and need space.

"Okay, good talk." I turn, grab the door handle, and pull the door open.

Logan is at my back before I can slip out, using a palm above my head to close the door again.

His arms wind around my middle, and he pulls me back against his body. His scent curls around me, woodsy with leathery notes. Damn, that is a serious aphrodisiac. He's warm, and all his hard planes feel perfect against my curves.

It feels so good to have someone care about me. Something I didn't realize I was missing until I came here and found everyone caring about me.

His lips touch my neck, followed by "I'm sorry that happened to you."

The sweetness of the moment melts all my rough edges.

He kisses me again. "Thank you for telling me."

Emotion curls inside me—relief, gratitude, affection, need. So much need.

I lay my head against his shoulder, reach back, and drive my fingers into his hair, and by the time his lips make it around to mine, I'm ravenous. As soon as he kisses me, I open and taste him, loving the feel of his tongue against mine.

His growl is a mix of lust and pleasure, and a rush of desire sinks low in my body. The sound of him, the feel of him, the smell of him, he floods my senses until I don't know where I end and he begins.

As soon as I turn in his arms, he lifts me off the floor and presses me against the door, sinking his hips between my thighs at the same time that he sinks his tongue into my mouth.

We spark into flames, and I cross my ankles at his back as he carries me into the bedroom. Before we reach the bed, I've got his shirt off, the button of his jeans undone. This need feels wild and deep. Out of my control.

"This isn't a thing, right?" I'm compelled to get him to agree this isn't going anywhere outside this bedroom. "We agreed."

"Right." He lays me on the bed, pulls my shirt up, and kisses a path toward my breasts as he drags the tee off over my head. My jeans, then his. My bra and panties, then his boxer briefs. He briefly takes in my tattoo, running his fingers across the ink on my skin, but we're both too focused to talk about it.

Everything happens so fast, yet not fast enough. He's all hard hills and planes of muscle. I want to slow down and savor, but my body won't have it. I love the way his hands and mouth move over me, with strength, passion, and reverence. Like he wants all of me, all at once.

I don't think I've ever felt this wild desire on both sides at the same time. There may have been a drunk hookup or two over the years that felt passionate, but this is different. This is deeper. This should scare the shit out of me, but this is also Logan. I've never been afraid of Logan.

He reaches toward the nightstand and, while he's still kissing me, pulls out a condom. In seconds, it's rolled on. Then his hand is between my thighs, his fingers stroking, the head of his cock pushing into me. Then the shaft. His power makes me arch. He fills me, stretches me, pushing me toward oblivion.

Then he stills. Or mostly stills. His muscles are twitching, his body trembling with need. It's humbling, witnessing all this strength tamed, feeling the white-hot passion between us, controlled by his will.

He's breathing heavily, his bright eyes searching mine. I can read everything going on inside his head. I see a revelation crossing his face. One of those this-got-out-of-hand-fast thoughts.

"Don't stop." My words are breathy, coming between pants.

I lift my hips, and his eyes flash with lust, then glimmer with stars. "Logan, don't stop."

That's all it takes to get him moving again. And damn, he's got moves. Bracing his hands on the mattress, he drives his hips between my thighs, slow and deep. Consistent. Relentless. His gaze on mine.

"You feel *so* fucking good," he says from behind clenched teeth.

I can't speak. My orgasm comes at light speed, taking over and slicing through me. My nails dig into his biceps. I arch and shudder. And, yeah, maybe I scream. I'm not sure. My body suddenly has a mind of its own.

Logan stills again. Sweat slides down his cheek, his chin, and drips on my chest. "Fuck, you just got really juicy for me."

A whine comes from somewhere in the room. Lucky. I close my eyes, not wanting either of us to move.

"Shhhh," Logan tells the dog in a sweet, soft sound. "You're okay."

That quiets the dog immediately, and Logan eases to his forearms so our bodies meet hips to chests. He lowers his head and kisses me. His hands slide into my hair. "Tell me about the tattoo." He looks at it again, sliding his thumb across the skin as he reads the words. "The best view comes after the hardest climb."

"It's just something that helps me get through the hard times."

"It's crazy sexy." His gaze meets mine again, and I see all kinds of emotions there. "You should call in sick to the bakery tomorrow."

I feel like I've lost time. Like I've missed part of the conversation. "What?"

"We're both going to need to call in sick." His voice is deep and rough. "Because we're going to be right here, in my bed, all day tomorrow."

"That's... You..." I'm having a hard time thinking, hard time talking. "This isn't a thing. Calling in sick would make this a thing."

"No, it doesn't. A thing doesn't become a thing just because we stay in bed longer."

"Logan—" The warning is pushed out of my mouth when he's making another one of those plunges that fill me until I moan, and I can't untangle words or meanings. All I can do is grip his hips and sink my nails into his sweat-slicked flesh as he thrusts again.

Logan slides one arm under my thigh, draws my leg up and out, giving his hips more room. So he can fuck me deeper, make my back arch, elicit moans. I might or might not have begged. All I know is he's driving me toward that peak again like it's his damn job. And I shatter again like that's my damn job.

And while I float back to earth and feel him still hard inside me, I'm seriously considering a career change. I love this damn job.

15

Isabel

The man is true to his word. We spent all night in bed. Truly a sex marathon. Every time I tried to leave, he tempted me back and did beautifully wicked things to my body until I didn't have the energy to stand.

It's almost 4:00 a.m. I have to work at the bakery in a couple of hours, and I'm sandwiched between Logan and Lucky. Logan is behind me, his naked body stretched along mine, his arm over my waist, holding me tight. Lucky is curled into a ball on the other side, leaning against me, and both boys are in a deep sleep.

I allow myself to pet Lucky, slide my hand over his sleek fur, play with his soft ears, press my face against his head and breathe in his puppy scent. God, there's nothing like the smell of a puppy. But I force myself to pull away because the memory of the pain I suffered when I lost my pup all those years ago makes that scar on my heart throb.

I need to leave. I don't want to wake up with Logan. I don't want to deal with the whole morning-after thing. And I'm starting to feel those telltale bubbles of panic deep in my gut. Panic over becoming attached. Panic over hurting Logan. Panic over being trapped in this small town. Panic over being nudged into a role I'm not ready for or interested in.

Hood River is beautiful, and the people are great, but outside of that, there's nothing here for me, not unless I want to spend the rest of my life working two and three jobs. Not unless I want to officially give up my first love—fashion. And I'm not ready to make that heart-wrenching decision, even if it is obviously coming. Besides, if my past history with men is any indication of how my future will turn out, I need to save both Logan and myself the headache. Possibly, the heartache.

I roll to my back. As expected, Logan stirs. His big warm hand slides across my belly, up my torso, cups my breast. He presses a kiss to my neck. By the time he goes still again, my body is thrumming for more of what he's already delivered. The man can turn me on in his sleep—literally.

Not a thing. This is not a thing. We both agreed this was not a thing—at least four or five times—over the last six hours. But the way he's been holding on to me all night, I'm not sure how committed either of us is to living by that rule.

I really need to get out of here. I've already stayed way too long.

Lucky is sleeping on top of the covers, so there's no way to move them off me without waking both him and Logan. I decide to slide underneath the covers to exit at the foot of the bed. At least I don't have to worry about untucking the sheets. They became a tangled mess the minute we hit them.

I decide inching straight toward the foot of the bed is the best way to escape my predicament without waking either of them. If Logan catches me, he'll kiss his way back into my body. If Lucky catches me, he'll rouse Logan.

Those bubbles of panic just doubled in size. I should have left hours ago. But, God, the way this man can make my body sing is incredible. I'm pretty damned sure I'm ruined, because I can't think of one man who's ever been as amazing in—or out of—bed.

I move excruciatingly slow. At this rate, I might be late for work. An inch at a time, I move toward the bottom of the bed. When I get my head under the covers, Lucky groans and rolls, stretching out to the space I'd been filling. I freeze, hoping he doesn't wake Logan.

I'm completely covered by the blanket, looking at the fabric over my face, and the absurdity of this situation hits me. My panic turns to humor, and I have to bite my lip to keep from laughing. I'm such an idiot sometimes.

A little more, a little more, a little more. My butt is almost at the footboard. Another foot and I can get out from beneath the covers. It's hard to breathe under here. I finally sit up, my legs over the footboard. I look over my shoulder and find both boys still sleeping, and sigh.

Then I'm trailing through the apartment, grabbing my clothes and pulling them on along the way. I finally open the door and slip out of the apartment, and when I close the door behind me, I pause and sigh. But I don't feel relieved. I feel a strange sense of loss.

I shake it off, return to my room, and catch an hour of sleep before I shower and head to the bakery.

Still, I feel half-asleep when I arrive. But I find a second wind when Natalie says I can make cinnamon rolls. We stand at the counters facing each other, and while she whips out loaves, baguettes, and sandwich rolls, she instructs me every step of the way. They're easier than I expected, but then she did have the dough already made when I arrived. All I really have to do is butter it up, add the cinnamon-sugar mix, roll, and cut. Still, it's fun.

But I'm distracted by the fact that Aiden hasn't returned my call. Not one text or voicemail in the last twenty-four hours.

Maybe he's over it and doesn't want the gun back. Or maybe he found another woman to manipulate and forgot all about me, but something tells me I'm not that lucky. Whatever the reason, it's making me uneasy after Logan's "guns and control freaks don't mix well."

"Everything okay?" Natalie asks as I sprinkle cinnamon sugar with walnuts and raisins on the buttery dough. I didn't think I'd like raisins in a cinnamon roll, but then I tasted Natalie's, and, any way you slice them, they're amazing.

When I look at her, I realize she's talking about my interest in the phone.

"I was just expecting a call that hasn't come yet."

"For a job?"

"No, I haven't heard back from anyone."

"You will," she says with a certainty I wish I possessed. "It will be so nice to have you on the West Coast."

She's right, it will be nice. Closer to Tucker and the people I've met here. Closer to Logan. But still too far away for a relationship. Yeah, I'm glad I left before he woke up.

I finish a log of cinnamon rolls, laying the cut pinwheels onto parchment paper covering a large tray, and grab another mound of dough to roll out and start the process again, this time with no raisins.

Tina gets off the phone and comes to Natalie with a piece of paper she tacks to a bulletin board. "Pumpkin spice and banana walnut muffins for Kayla's Kafé."

Then she picks up a pot of coffee and wanders around the dining room filling cups and chatting with locals.

Betsy is filling orders with loaves and pastries that Natalie finished before I arrived. When Natalie told me the bakery opens at 6:00 a.m., she meant that's the time they open their doors to the public. Natalie gets here at about 4:00 a.m. to start baking. Betsy comes in at five to package orders put in by local restaurants, delis, cafés, and stores. Tina comes in at six to run the register and the small dining room, and Blake Tudor, a nice guy in his sixties, comes in at seven to start deliveries.

This place is a well-oiled machine, and a very popular hub of Hood River. One of the unique and fun elements of the café is the way Natalie designed the space, with no walls separating the customers from the baking. They can watch everything being prepared, baked, shelved, and packaged. Natalie says she likes the way it brings customers into the process and allows her to be available to chat with locals.

Can't argue with the success of the place. There's a line of people waiting when the doors open and usually a handful of people still hanging out when it closes at 2:00 p.m. Everything is baked fresh daily, and the shelves are mostly bare by the time the shop closes. Any leftovers are donated to various facilities in the area, from homeless shelters to convalescent homes.

When Natalie turns away to check the ovens, I check my phone. She turns back and catches me. We both laugh.

"You don't have to tell me anything," she says. "It's not my business. But if you want to talk, I'm here."

I sigh as I roll out the dough. In the background, people place orders with Tina, and I look around before I speak. "It's an ex who's being an ass. I really just want a fresh start, you know? But there's a lot of bad blood between us. I'm trying to give something back to him, but he's being a dick about it."

"Mmm," she says, shaping dough into loafs as she nods. "I know all too well how you have to put the past behind you before you can start fresh. Cole and I both had to deal with that before our relationship would work. He had to let go of the guilt he felt over Evan's death and of loving me. I had to let go of caring about what others thought of me, even the guilt about going on and being happy when Evan would never get that chance."

She drops the loaves into baking tins. "But the past definitely needs to be settled before you can move forward without problems. My suggestion: make the tough decisions, give the difficult apologies, clean up whatever mess you made in the past, learn from it all, and move on, a better person."

I nod as I roll the dough into a buttery, sugary log of yum. "Yeah. Good advice."

But judging by Aiden's games, having me apologize takes all the fun out of his manipulation. I'll keep that advice in mind for another situation, but I don't see that happening with Aiden.

16

Logan

I pull into the parking lot of Station 21 with a smile on my face. A big smile. I wasn't thrilled when I woke up and found Isabel gone, but I'm surprised I got her to stay as long as she did.

It might very well have been the best fucking night of my life.

As soon as I park, Lucky climbs into the passenger's seat from the footwell and props his paws on the door, looking out the window, tail wagging. He jumps out with me and runs into the firehouse, where he's greeted with enthusiasm.

"Luckiest dog on the planet," I mutter to myself, smiling.

I skip my run—Isabel gave me a real workout last night—and check in with Bobby, whose shift is ending. After we exchange information about the prior shift and the functionality of all the equipment, I tell him he can head home early, and I start my own morning routine, rechecking equipment and supplies.

Lucky trots out of the house and sniffs around the engine

bay. He's become so animated since I've had him. Bold and opinionated. I know that's because he feels safe to be himself, and I love that I've given him the security he needs to express himself.

I stop what I'm doing as that thought hits me square in the forehead. Maybe if I was more accepting of Isabel, she would feel safe to tell me all she's not telling me.

A series of bangs echoes through the bay. I shoot to my feet and spin toward the noise. Lucky's got ahold of a pair of suspenders on turnout pants hanging on the wall, tugging with all his might. His jerking and tugging knocked over a SCBA tank, which started a domino reaction. The noise of the metal hitting the cement is still reverberating around the engine bay when all the guys appear in the doorway, serious until they figure out what happened, then they're all laughing their asses off. Lucky manages to pull the turnout pants off the hook and proudly trots to me with a bright red suspender in his mouth.

"Kid," I tell him, prying the suspender from his teeth. "You're killing me."

Once I clean up Lucky's mess and the rescue is fully stocked, I bring the box holding Sorenson's new boots into the house and drop them on the table in front of him, sick over how much they cost me. My savings feel like they're draining out my feet. He smirks up at me. "Bet you won't make that mistake again."

I join the guys at the kitchen table with a big cup of coffee. Like Gigantor big. I listen to the guys' tales of the prior shift with one ear, but my head's still in the clouds, remembering Isabel sitting on my lap, hand fisted in my hair, riding me. And damn, can that girl move. She gave one of the grape condoms a thorough taste test, one I didn't ever want to end.

I expected it to be good. I wouldn't have been surprised if it was great. But she fucking blew me apart. I sure as shit hope that's not the one and only time we hook up while she's here.

The fact that she left my bed before I was awake leads me to believe she may be difficult to lure in again.

"Roberts."

I instantly drill into my memory for what the guys have been discussing, but still have no idea. "Yep?"

"Where's your head at?" Tucker asks.

In bed, with your sister. "Just thinking about renovations on the motel."

"I thought Isabel was helping," he says.

"She is. She gets a lot done on the days I'm working. She's almost filled up an entire dumpster with shit from the rooms."

"She's not too much trouble? Because I can get her to come stay at the loft."

Over my dead body. "No trouble."

The house phone rings, and Sorenson gets up to answer it. "Station 21."

He crosses his free arm. "Uh-huh."

I know that look, so I chug as much caffeine as I can before we have to leave. Calls like this are either too ridiculous for the airwaves or a favor the asker would rather keep quiet.

"Right." Sorenson lets out a heavy sigh and rubs his forehead. "Yeah, sure. Later."

"Are we headed out to a bullshit call?" Tucker asks.

"Parrot in a tree."

"A bird in a tree?" Royal says. "What's next? A fish in water?"

The guys laugh.

"It's an African Gray, that costs over two grand," Sorenson says.

"Jesus," Carter says.

"It's been loose forty-eight hours, and the owner is afraid it will die because it was raised from a baby in a cage. We'll take the ladder truck."

Sorenson turns toward the engine bay with the rest of us following, and we all step into our gear. Lucky's figured out that getting into our gear precedes something fun, and he's spinning in circles, barking at us to hurry up.

"How tall is the tree?" I ask.

"Guesstimate is seventy or eighty feet." Sorenson is the first one dressed and climbing into the truck. The man is in his forties, but he moves like a twenty-year-old.

"Too bad Bobby's not here." Tucker grabs the rail and climbs into the truck. "He kicks ass at those heights."

"I'll do it," Royal says, climbing in behind Tucker.

Sorenson calls out the window. "Sixteen-fifty-nine Whippoorwill, gentlemen."

And the truck heads out.

I put Lucky on the driver's seat of the rescue, and he moves to the console between the seats. He loves looking out the window while we drive, and he's really good about staying in the rig without complaint while we're at an incident—as long as he has a toy to play with and everything else is locked down. Now that I've had him several days, I don't know how I ever lived without him.

Carter and I follow in the rescue and head toward the location in a mountainous area of town.

"Isn't that Harry Stucco's address?" Carter asks.

"Sure is."

"Didn't he just get out of prison?"

"Sure did." He's a lawyer who got in too deep with the lowlife drug dealers he defended.

"He must have had a lot of money stashed away if he's got a two-thousand-dollar bird."

"I'm betting it's a trade."

Carter looks at me sideways. I meet and hold his stare.

"Ooh," Carter finally draws out. "A drug trade."

We're quiet for a few minutes, and when we stop at a light —since this is no way an emergency—Carter says, "So, Isabel. What's she like?"

Just the sound of her name kicks off sparks in my gut. "Strong, independent...a little mysterious."

"Mysterious? I didn't expect that."

"Neither did I." And when the mysterious part of her deals with exes with a grudge, I'd skip mysterious.

"Damn she's hot. She say how long's she staying?"

I cut a smirk at him. "Why are you asking? Aren't you still seeing Carly?"

"Yeah, but it's casual. I could totally date someone else, but I'm not asking for me. I heard you two had a thing way back."

"It wasn't a thing, and it was *way* back."

"Are you working on her?"

Or she's working on me. I'm not sure which. "Doesn't matter. She's not staying."

"Oh no?"

"No. She's a fashion designer in New York. That's her version of The Show," I tell him, using the term baseball players use when they're rising from the minors to the majors.

"Right. Makes sense."

I knew this all along, only it's hitting me in a different way today. Never thought I'd wish I *didn't* have nuclear chemistry with such an amazing woman. Just the thought of last night's steam makes me shift in the driver's seat. But in the end, I have to open my eyes to the truth. "There's nothing for her here."

I feel heavier now that I've acknowledged that despite what happens between us, I only have Isabel for a short time. I tell myself it's okay, that I'm not up for anything but sex. When she leaves, it will be no big deal.

"She's going back to New York, then?"

"I don't think she knows yet."

"Does she know your sister? Isn't Maya a fashion designer in New York too?"

"They knew each other in high school, but haven't kept in touch."

"So you think you and Isabel will have some short-term fun?"

"Why are you so interested in what I'm doing?"

He shrugs. "Someone ought to be getting in on that action."

I'd been planning on getting as much of that action as she'll give me, but talk of her leaving has made me a little edgy.

I turn my attention to the forest as we climb into the mountains. Carter looks through the windshield and up at the trees. "These look taller than eighty feet."

"Yeah, they do."

"If Cap sends Royal up there, he's gonna shit himself."

That makes me laugh.

The engine stops in the street in front of a home on at least a couple of acres and we pull in behind. Sorenson is the first one out of the truck and starts toward the door. A man in his sixties comes out of the house before Sorenson gets there. He's dressed in a suit and tie, his graying hair cut well, his stubble-beard more gray than brown.

"He looks pretty legit for a disbarred lawyer," Tucker mutters. "But he's got the mouth of a convict."

I look up at the treetops. Only the outer edge of the forest is illuminated; everything inside is dark and muted. "Pretty hard to spot a gray bird in there."

Tucker, Carter, and I are looking up at the trees, hands on hips, when Harry and Sorenson come over, and we move a few dozen feet off the road, into the trees.

"There she is." He points to a tree. "The little cunt."

"Whoa," Sorenson says. "No need for that kind of language, Mr. Stucco."

"I got her from a motherfucking cocksucker, so I shouldn't be surprised she's just as deranged."

Motherfucking cocksucker makes my mind turn back to Isabel. I take another look at Harry. Sure, he's a lot older than

Isabel's ex—at least I assume so—but he's giving off that royal-asshole vibe I imagine her ex did.

"If you hate her so much," I say, "why did you call us to come get her? Why not just let her go?"

"Because she's worth a lot of money." He doesn't have to end that comment with "dumbshit." It's clear in his tone.

We back the truck into the space and raise the ladder, but don't put it against the tree yet. We move in slow motion because we don't want to scare her to another spot, or we could seriously be here all day.

She squawks some but doesn't fly away. In fact, she looks interested in what we're doing.

"Who wants to go up for her?" Sorenson asks.

"I'll go," Royal says.

"Dumbshit." This comes in perfect but strangely pitched English from the top of the tree and makes us all laugh. Everyone except Harry.

"This is going to be fun," I say.

"Not," Tucker adds.

"Hold on." I turn toward Harry. "Can you bring out a treat?"

"I don't have time for this shit." He starts toward the house.

"What's her name?" I call after him.

He turns to spit out, "Dolly."

Tucker grabs a lightweight rescue blanket from the truck. "Prison clearly taught him some manners."

He lays the blanket over Royal's shoulder. When everyone looks at him like he's got two heads, he says, "What? I googled how to catch birds on the way over."

"Too bad Google couldn't get its lazy ass over here and catch the thing," Sorenson says.

Harry returns with a treat. It's the size of a cigar and covered in seeds, which Royal takes.

"I can't stand around while you all have your thumbs up

your asses," Harry bitches. "Just bring her in when you catch her."

We watch Harry stalk back into his house.

"Prick." This comes from Dolly, speaking what we are all thinking.

I look up at the bird. "I like you, Dolly."

She makes a laughing sound, walking one way on the branch, then the other.

"That's eerily human," Royal says. "She might be freaking me out a little."

"Make sure she knows the difference between your finger and the treat," Tucker says. "Her beak is strong enough to amputate a couple of digits."

Royal's face drops, eyes go wide. "*What?*"

I elbow Tucker. "Stop messing with him. He's going to have enough trouble with the height. Have you ever been that high, kid? You know the term nosebleed section? There's a reason for that."

Tucker laughs at the way I mess with Royal right after telling Tucker to stop.

"Maybe I shouldn't be the one to do it," Royal says.

"Maybe you ought to stop being so gullible," Sorenson tells him. "They don't know what in the hell they're talking about. Think of this as getting a scared cat to come to you. Move slow, talk softly to her, offer the treat."

"That's also good advice for getting a woman into bed," Tucker says, slapping Sorenson on the back. "Great tips, boss."

Sorenson smirks at Tucker. "Don't go for the blanket until you're close enough to be sure you'll toss it over her."

"Yeah, okay." Royal's a good sport. He dutifully takes the treat and the blanket and starts the long climb.

"Get the fuck out," Dolly says, making Royal stop and look back at us.

"Are you sure this is the best way?"

"No other way I know of," Sorenson says.

Royal starts up again. He's moving painfully slow, but Dolly doesn't like this at all. She's all but dancing on the branch, wings extended, feet restlessly scooting back and forth.

"Motherfucker," Dolly says, followed by laughter that sounds like it comes straight out of a horror flick. "Get the fuck out, get the fuck out, get the fuck out."

"Jesus," I mutter. "He's never going to get her."

"I'd bet twenty on that," Tucker says.

"Do you know how to do anything without betting on it?"

"Just a healthy dose of competitive spirit. You taking the bet or not?"

"I'll go in for twenty." Sorenson rarely jumps in on the bets, but he's looking up at the tree, grinning. "He's gonna get her. He's got the patience of Job."

"I'm saving my money for the renovation. Isabel is kicking ass, and I anticipate her asking for more cash to keep going."

I wonder if I could keep her here with the renovation.

The thought pops into my mind from nowhere, confusing me. I have no idea why I would think she'd stay to do someone else's work for free. Besides, she's not a contractor. She's not exactly skilled enough to do more than what she's doing: cleanup.

"Has she mentioned how long she plans to stay?" I ask Tucker.

"Not a word."

Just as Royal reaches the top of the ladder, a gentle gust of wind comes through, making the ladder sway.

Royal grips the ladder, muttering, "Holy fuck."

"Holy fuck," Dolly answers. "*Squawk.* Holy fuck."

Tucker and I are laughing, and even Sorenson is grinning.

"One of you might need to go up there for moral support," Sorenson says.

"Get the fuck out," Dolly says, followed by crazy laughter

and dancing on the branch. "Piece of shit, *squawk*, get the fuck out."

"Guys," Royal says. "I think she's possessed. I'm *not* kidding. She just turned her head all the way around."

"Prick is coming, prick is coming," Dolly says. "Get the fuck out, *squawk*."

We all glance at the house and find Harry standing in the driveway, arms crossed, scowling.

"I think I'm starting to understand why she flew away," I say under my breath.

"Hi, Dolly," Royal says, "I'm Royal, your friendly neighborhood hero."

"Royal hero, *squawk*, Royal hero."

"Hey, did you hear that?" Royal smiles down at us.

"Yeah," Sorenson says, "you're a goddamned hero."

"Look what I've got for you, Dolly."

She sidesteps toward Royal. He's holding out the treat, his fingers on the very end, presumably so Dolly doesn't bite his fingers off.

Dolly quiets and checks out the treat. But instead of just taking it from him and staying in the tree, she walks right off the branch and onto Royal's shoulder.

Royal makes all kinds of terrified noises, punctuated by "Holy fuck. Don't eat me. What do I do now?"

While Tucker, Sorenson, and I are laughing, Dolly solves the problem, by taking the treat from his hand and happily chomps away.

"Try coming down the ladder," Sorenson says when he catches his breath. "See if she'll stay with you."

On the slow descent, Dolly demolishes the treat, and when Royal touches down, Dolly is snuggled up into the crook between Royal's head and neck. Royal, on the other hand, is stiff and awkward.

"I'm afraid she's going to take a chunk out of my ear."

Dolly makes a strange chortling, purring noise that sounds like contentment and deliberately rubs her head against Royal's cheek.

"I think the only thing you're going to have to worry about," I say, "is leaving without her."

She turns her head and softly chatters, "Royal hero, Royal hero" in his ear, cuddled against Royal's neck.

"Someone's got a crush," Sorensen says.

Harry comes forward.

"*Squawk*, prick is coming, prick is coming," and she turns on Royal's shoulder to give Harry her back. "Get the fuck out."

Harry approaches, reaching toward Dolly with both hands, like he's going to grab her and throw her back in a cage. Royal puts a hand out and turns so Harry can't reach the bird. I can't say I've ever seen this intense look on Royal's young face.

"Where did you get Dolly?" Royal asks with an authority that's ten years older.

"None of your goddamned business," Harry says. "Give me the fucking bird."

"Prick, prick, prick," Dolly says, her tone softer, like she's trying to whisper. "Get the fuck out."

"As an employee of the state," Royal says, "I'm bound to report any signs of abuse. Would you like the ASPCA coming out to your house and asking you questions about where and how you got her? Would you want them looking around your house to make sure there aren't other abused pets on the premises? Who knows what else they'd find, am I right?"

Harry pulls his hands back and raises his hackles, but it's obvious that idea spooks him. "I don't abuse her."

"Prick," Dolly says.

"Law enforcement may take one listen to her and think differently."

"Royal." Sorenson's voice says the same thing I'm thinking: *what are you doing, kid?*

"Just take her," Harry says, gesturing to Royal and Dolly. "She's nothing but a noisy shit pot of trouble anyway."

Sorenson cuts in. "That won't be necessary—"

"Crapping all over my furniture," Harry says. "Waking me up at all hours. You were right," he says to me. "I should just have let her stay out here and die. Take her."

As soon as Harry turns and stalks back toward the house, Dolly turns forward again, hunches into a comfy spot on Royal's shoulder, and makes sounds of contentment.

When Harry's front door shuts, Sorenson throws up his hands. "What in the fuck?"

"What in the fuck?" Dolly mimics.

"He doesn't deserve to own animals," Royal says.

"Twenty minutes ago, you thought she was going to eat you," Tucker says. "Now you two look tight enough to plan a fucking wedding."

"It wasn't right," Royal insists, "the way he treats her."

"We don't actually know how he treats her," Sorenson says, hands on hips and clearly not happy about this. "All we know is she got loose and he called us to get her."

Royal is brooding now, petting the feathers of Dolly's chest with one finger. "You let Logan have two cats *and* a dog."

"We're not building a fucking menagerie." Sorenson shakes his head while looking at the sky before turning and heading toward the truck. "You're not keeping it. We're dropping it off at the Humane Society on our way back to the house. Now get that ladder down and let's go."

As soon as Sorenson's in the truck, I knock Royal's shoulder. "Kid, don't fuck with my animals. You're the one who pointed out he was a Dalmatian and we should keep him."

"As if you weren't thinking it already." Royal looks at Dolly. "Guess I'll just have to make a parrot petition."

Tucker laughs. "The kid's getting sassy. I kinda like it."

"Rescue one." The dispatcher comes over the radio. "Report

of a woman down, Eight forty-five Singleton Street. Young children reported in residence."

Sorenson picks up the call. "Rescue one responding. Engine one to follow. Eight forty-five Singleton."

Carter climbs into the rescue with me, chuckling. "We're building a fucking menagerie whether Sorenson likes it or not. He's one of those people, you know? The kind that says 'no pets,' then amends to 'I'm not taking care of them,' only to find him asleep in a recliner with a puppy on his chest, a cat tucked beside him, and a bird perched on the back of his chair. Just watch, it'll happen."

I laugh. "Can't wait to see that. Make sure we get pictures."

I'm feeling good as we turn the corner onto Singleton, until I spot a cop car in front of the house. It's a nice neighborhood of large homes and manicured lawns. Corbett Sosa, a local cop about my age, is crouched on the front porch, easing a toddler into an older boy's arms before returning to the house. Another police car rounds the corner behind us.

"Shit." My mood tanks. "This doesn't look good."

"Is that baby covered in blood?"

The younger kid has a rescue blanket around his shoulders, but I can see his white T-shirt is drenched in something dark.

I pull up to the curb, trying to catch the color of whatever is all over the kid, but it could be anything—chocolate, juice, shit.

Carter and I get out and grab the ALS, or advanced life support, bags and head up the walk. As I near, I get a better sense of the situation, but it's not a good sense. The older kid, maybe nine or ten, is crying, his shoulders shaking with sobs as he tries to hold on to his wailing sibling.

"Check out these two," I tell Carter before entering the house.

It doesn't take me long to find Corbett and the victim, a woman in her midthirties on the floor, a knife still in her chest, blood everywhere. I've seen my share of tragedies, but the raw violence of this situation still shocks me.

Corbett pulls his hand away from the woman's neck and shakes his head. "She's gone."

My shoulders sink. There's no doing CPR with a knife in her chest. But my dread is for those kids, not her. She's already found peace, but those kids are in for a lifetime of hell.

"The father?" I ask.

"Probably. She was just granted a restraining order. Units are trying to track him down."

We both know restraining orders are a double-edged sword. Sometimes they get the guy to give up and go away. Sometimes they trigger the abuser into a rage.

When I go back outside, the engine is here. Royal is holding the youngest kid, and Sorenson is crouched in front of the older boy, who's sitting on the engine's bumper. With the boy's hands in his, Sorenson talks to the kid, who's wiping his tears on the shoulders of his shirt.

Carter comes up beside me and shakes his head. "We're so keeping that fucking bird. He's a marshmallow underneath all that gruff."

"That he is."

My heart is beating in my stomach, and my chest aches. Culture teaches boys they need to be strong. Told they're the "man of the house" when the father figure leaves. Told to protect the mother and siblings while Dad's gone. Age and ability don't matter, and emotions aren't always logical.

I was far older than that kid when my father killed my mother, but my earliest memories are of the abuse my father leveled on my mother and me. I never let him near Maya, which ultimately ended in more beatings for me. And I remember the crushing weight of failure every time he abused my mom.

As an adult, I know she had a thousand chances to leave

him but chose to stay. Chose to lie and lie and lie about what was going on. Isabel comes to mind, and the thrill that came to work with me has turned to concern. And frustration.

A CSI van pulls into the driveway and I make my way back to the rescue and put the bags away. Shortly after CSI gets here, social services shows up, and detectives are driving toward the house as I'm driving away.

Carter lets out a heavy sigh. "This day started out pretty good, but went downhill fast."

"Dropped like a fucking rock."

17

Isabel

I work longer than usual at the bakery again today. Trevor, Tina's son, has a fever, so I'm covering the dining room and pitching in with the baking when I can.

It's almost two o'clock, and I still have to do a dress fitting for Natalie and work a shift at the bar. I love helping these people out. They're so sweet and generous. But I also need time to figure out what's next for me.

When the last customer leaves and I lock the door after him, I sigh, turn, and slump against the door.

"We don't have to do the fitting today," Natalie says, putting pans in the industrial-size sink. "It's been busy, and we're short-handed. That always makes the day long."

"Oh, but I really want to."

I move into the kitchen and start on the dishes while she cleans counters and ovens and puts equipment and supplies away. Blake finished up local deliveries around noon, and Natalie sent her mom home around the same time, or they would have fought over Betsy wanting to do more than her injured arm should.

Apparently, her original café, right in this very spot, burned down some time ago, and she received second- and third-degree burns in the process. She's recovering well and has quite good range of motion, but it's clear she would run herself into the ground to help Natalie.

"It's like my reward," I tell her. "I've been looking forward to it."

"Only if you're sure."

"I'm two-hundred-percent sure."

We finish up the work, and I send Natalie to change into the dress. When she comes out, I have her stand on a stool. I pull out my measuring tape, pins, notebook, and fabric marking pen and get to work marking the dress with the changes we agreed on and jotting notes about the alterations.

"I'm getting the lace tomorrow," I tell her. "I'll bring it in to make sure it's what you want."

"You're such a natural at this. Your sketches are just gorgeous. Can I get copies of the ones you made for this? I'd love to frame them."

I smirk. "Really? You can have the originals if you like them that much."

"You really don't realize how talented you are, do you?"

I'm confused and uncomfortable. Am I talented? Based on the last five years of my life, I'd have to say a resounding *no*. I guess being a small fish trying to make my way in an ocean of sharks has made me forget all about any talent I may once have had. I can see how comparing myself to others for the last ten years—and always coming up short—has seriously damaged my self-esteem.

Maybe that's how Aiden slipped past my defenses. He made me believe in my abilities again. But it wasn't real. I'm beginning to wonder if anything in life is real.

"I guess I've been living in a jungle of competition for too long," I tell her. "It's impossible not to compare myself to other designers when we're all competing for a few select opportunities. This is probably my favorite part of the process. Well, no, I also love sewing and watching something from my mind become reality. And, yeah, I love dressing models and taking pictures." I laugh at myself. "So, I guess I love all of it."

"That's the same way I feel about baking."

I kneel and place pins for a hem all around the bottom, tapering it into the train. I can't get over the gorgeous buttons all down the back of the dress and the train. Such a simple but powerful design statement. "Damn, these buttons make my eyes glitter."

"Right? They're so..."

"Romantic."

"Yeah." She sighs. "Romantic."

A few beats of silence pass, and I'm struck at how comfortable I feel with this woman I met such a short time ago. In fact, everything about Hood River feels good to me, and that's not just my night with Logan talking either.

"So what do you think of Logan now?" Natalie asks. "Cole told me you two had a thing in high school."

"He's exaggerating. We were friends, and we made a pact to not go off to college virgins. That's it. Seriously."

"Oh," she sounds disappointed. "That's too bad. He deserves a good woman in his life."

"What happened with Emily? There seems to be bad blood between them."

"She fucked with his head. It was really—wrong."

I stay quiet, hoping she'll say more. I stand and start tucking the shoulders and the bodice to pin an outline of the new neckline.

"She was getting serious about him, but he wasn't serious

about her, so he broke it off. When she couldn't beg him back, she told him she was pregnant."

My hands freeze; my gaze darts to Natalie's. "Oh, jeez."

"Logan was pretty wigged out about it at first. Mostly because he didn't want to be tied to Emily. But he came around to the idea of being a dad pretty fast. Was even excited about it."

I continue pinning and adjusting. "What happened?"

"Turns out she was lying."

"*What?*" I'm incensed for Logan. "Who lies about that? A kid between two people doesn't keep them together."

"Exactly what I thought. I'm the one who overheard the truth in the bathroom at a fundraiser." Natalie grins. "Evidently, Logan's amazing in bed."

My brain explodes with mental images from last night. His hands in my hair, his gaze locked on mine because he loved watching me climax. His muscular body glowing with sweat, his muscles rippling. The sex wasn't just sex. It was an event. An all-inclusive, no-holds-barred, VIP, luxurious, unforgettable event.

"So how long do we have you before you head back to all the lights and glamour?" Natalie asks.

That fake persona keeps coming back to slap me in the face. The longer I'm here, the more fake I feel, and my heart sinks a little.

"Oh, I don't know. The break has been nice, but I need to get back to real life. I haven't heard anything from the jobs I applied for in LA and San Francisco, but I'll spread a wider net, see if I can get any bites."

I'm uncomfortable with the topic so I change it. "Now that I have a reason to get my sewing machine out, I may replenish my Etsy inventory to keep myself busy until the right job comes along."

"You have an Etsy store? What do you sell?"

"Boho workout clothes, a few dresses, tops, bags, whatever strikes my fancy, really."

"Like a clothing line?" Natalie asks, her face bright.

I laugh. "It's more of a way to keep idle hands busy, and a little fun cash doesn't hurt."

Fun, as in putting-food-in-my-belly fun. It's also work from my heart. Designs that are fun and frivolous and not meant to impress anyone except the buyer.

Now that I have my sewing machine out and set up, I'll unpack some of my fabric and play a little. It's only a fraction of the fabric I had in New York. When I could, I picked up leftovers from whatever company I was working for at the time, crashed industry wholesale events, even pulled a few bolts from the trash.

It killed me to throw most of it out, but I didn't have time to try to sell it or the room to bring it with me. Eviction is like that, and the New York City Marshals weren't exactly sympathetic. I don't blame them; they handle all the evictions throughout the city. I'm sure they've heard every sob story known to man and then some.

"Do you have the pieces with you?" Natalie asks. "Or are they back in New York?"

I've got absolutely nothing back in New York. "With me."

"It would be fun to have one of those rep sales parties at someone's house. Like Tupperware or Magic Chef, where you invite people over, hang out, eat, drink, talk, and shop." She shrugs. "Just a thought. You've been working so hard for everyone else while you've been here, it would be nice for us to do something for you."

I can't think of a time over the last five years when someone did something for me just because. "That's so sweet."

"I mean, I know a designer at your level doesn't need to do a small-town sale like this, and I imagine your designs are expensive, but there's quite a bit of sleepy money around here. It would be a great way for you to meet people too."

Do I want to meet more people? I know I said I did when I first got here, but I'm doing my damnedest to keep my past in the past, and meeting new people puts me in a really bad place where I have to either lie to keep the persona going or fess up to all the years of lying.

Coming here hasn't turned out to be much of a sanctuary after all.

"I'm sorry," Natalie says. "It was just a suggestion. We don't have to."

"No, it's okay. The truth is I'm at a crossroads. The fashion industry... It's not what I thought it would be. When I was in school, it seemed so glamorous, you know? Beautiful people, bright lights, accolades, validation. Later, I discovered it's also one hell of a lot of work, which is fine, I was on board for that. But I also realized the industry is only glittery on the outside. On the inside..." I give a one-shouldered shrug. "Gritty is the best way I can describe it."

"I could imagine. I was in culinary college when Evan hurt his back. I quit to take care of him. I wasn't there very long, but I saw both sides of it—the competition was fierce, the hours long and unrelenting. To be honest, the kitchen felt more like a battlefield. And you make shit for money."

Wow, someone who really gets it. "Exactly."

"I'm so much happier running my own place, but it really is a lot of work. After I finish here, I go home and plan out marketing with Tina. At night, I usually brainstorm new ideas and recipes. I work twice as much as I would at a regular job, but that doesn't seem as unbearable when you're working for yourself."

"I've never considered working for myself. I mean, you can't launch a line of clothes without investors unless you're independently wealthy, so there's that."

"Isn't what you already have, the beginnings of a line?" While I'm trying to form an answer, she adds, "And do you have to launch an entire line to be happy or feel successful? You could always skip an investor and grow slowly over time. I'm just throwing out options. Sometimes we get so caught up in that grind, we forget to stop and adjust our navigation. Maybe this is the perfect time and place to reevaluate. Take a few months, see what you miss and don't miss. When you're not in a meat grinder, you have time to think, make better decisions. But I also don't know the problems you'd face reentering the profession if you took time off, so I'm certainly no expert."

"I'm grateful for the suggestions." I smile at her. "You're all done. You can change."

She steps off the stool. "Even if you're not looking to make those kinds of changes in your life, a home party would be a great way to get a little cash and let your hair down."

"Thank you. Yeah, let's do it."

18

Isabel

My conversation with Natalie keeps replaying in my mind as I wipe down the bar.

The reasons I never considered working for myself are superficial. I was so focused on my ideal—the travel, bright lights, accolades for my work—that I missed other, quieter, and possibly more fulfilling opportunities.

I'm well aware my career failure is probably a well-deserved kick in my ass from karma. But I like the way Natalie made working for myself sound. I never made much money on Etsy because I never posted more than a few things at a time. I was too busy working three jobs to keep my head above water. I looked at my boho designs as an escape from the grind of life, a way to be creative and have fun, because, yeah, I really love designing, and no company hired me to do that.

What if Natalie's right? What if I don't have to grind to find happiness? Success, even. Giving up my dream is a big leap—more mental than physical, but still a leap. Across a pond of alligators. But, realistically, it's no closer or farther away than it was when I was in New York.

I check on the customers at the bar, then make my way around the empty tables, wiping them clean, refilling condiments. I pause to pull my phone from my pocket, checking for a message from Aiden, but there's nothing.

"What in the hell are you doing?" I mutter to my phone. This is either another controlling tactic, a true disinterest in getting the gun back, or he's dead.

I pause to consider if hoping for the latter makes me a bad person. In truth, I don't wish him harm. Okay, maybe just a little. My urge is to call him, to find a way to end this thing, but that's probably exactly what he wants. Why he's stopped communicating. Or he figured he'd never get it back and gave up.

No, Aiden never gives up.

Not knowing what's happening with him makes me crazy. Which is precisely why he's doing it. I'm beyond over the fucking head games. Only now, out of the situation, around real people, normal people, do I realize how stupid it was of me to take the gun—immature, self-righteous, and short-sighted, not to mention illegal, considering the whole breaking-and-entering thing.

I look up and find firefighters pouring in the back door, both paid and volunteer, and my heart lifts in anticipation of seeing Logan, but my focus veers into confusion when I see Royal with a parrot on his shoulder.

Logan's the last one in, wearing turnout pants and a navy-blue T-shirt with the Hood River Fire and Rescue logo on the upper left chest, Lucky trailing at his heels.

He scans the bar, spots me, and veers away from the table where the other guys sit to lean on the bar while I fill pitchers with water and soda for the guys.

"Hey." His eyes are soft, but the rest of him is tense and heavy.

"Hey. Let's hope no one complains to the health department of animals in your restaurant. What's with the bird?"

"Long story short, the bird got out, the guy who had her— it's not clear if he owned it or had taken it in lieu of payment for something—but he was an asshole, and Royal all but challenged the guy to a duel for the bird. All that comes out of her mouth are curses. Very colorful curses. And barking. She and Lucky have only been together a few hours, and she's already imitating him. The guys have started adding to her nasty vocabulary. All in all, she and Lucky are welcome comedic relief."

I laugh. "How entertaining."

"Not everyone think so." He looks over his shoulder. "See that scowl on Sorenson's face?"

"He doesn't find her entertaining," I say.

"The jury's still out, but there's no doubt Dolly took a real shine to Royal. He's gone from probie to birdman. She talks like a sailor, but treats Royal like her long-lost lover. His pitch is that because I got two cats and now have a dog, it's only fair he gets a pet too. But I think the deciding factor may be Royal training her to poop in one place. And, of course, not bite anyone. She's ornery with everyone but Royal. The only reason we still have her with us is because we've been running calls since we picked her up and haven't had time to drop her at the Humane Society."

Lucky finds his way back behind the bar, and once he spots me, his whole body wags and he jumps, his paws against my shin.

"Don't get any ideas, buddy," I tell the puppy. "Just because you weaseled your way into bed with me once doesn't mean I'm keeping you."

Logan smirks. "Is that a message for him or for me?"

I smile at him. "Maybe both."

"Maybe? So then *maybe* you'll come to the game Saturday night?"

"What game?"

"Hockey? Remember? It's a tie-breaker game. We're coming back here after."

He leans his forearms on the bar, and his smile finally appears. "I woke up alone, but I have a very vivid memory of going to bed with this sexy, dark-haired, mind-blowing beauty."

"Oh, yeah?"

"Oh, hell yeah. Can't stop thinking about her."

"Maybe you and Lucky ought to have a heart-to-heart."

"Was he stealing the covers?" He looks over the edge of the bar at the puppy, now lying at my feet. "Total bed hog. He looks small, but he takes manspread to a whole different level." Then he changes the subject. "Hear any more from Cocksucker?"

I shake my head. "He's got to be the king of head games. As soon as I want to make arrangements to return the damn gun, he goes dark. I'm so over it. Want to take a trip to Portland with me this weekend and browse pawnshops?"

"Excuse me, ma'am, did you just ask me out on a date?"

"I don't think pawnshop trolling counts as a date."

"Might we get food or drink while we're out?"

"We might."

"Then I believe it's a date."

I shrug. "Call it what you like."

"I might have to seal that offer with a kiss to take it seriously."

He's making all the right moves, saying all the right things for me to believe he's okay, but he's most certainly not okay.

I place the last pitcher on the tray and cover his hands with mine. "Want to talk about what happened today?"

"Can I get that kiss if I tell you?"

My brows shoot up. "Here? In front of your guys, who include my brother?"

"I talked to Tucker. He and I are good."

"How nice for you both."

He turns his hands over and slides his fingers through mine, his expression grim. "We had a fatal domestic call earlier today. It was...really awful."

Shit. Now it all makes sense—the pain in his eyes, the fatigue in his expression. "Those have got to be extra awful for you."

"I haven't been able to shake it." His gaze lifts to mine and scans my face with an intimacy that brings the night back in full force. "But a kiss would help."

"Relentless," I say, then pull my hands away and grab the tray. "Unisex bathroom in three."

A grin lights up his face. "You're on."

19

Logan

What I'm feeling for Isabel is in no way casual, and I didn't expect feelings this fierce. I've done casual, I've done serious, I've done everything in between, yet she slipped right under my skin without me noticing until it was too late.

Last night in bed, a huge shift happened. I couldn't say when or how, just that it did. I'm not on my game tonight at all. Since that domestic call, I've been edgy and anxious, my thoughts dark.

Isabel opens the bathroom door, slips in, closes it, and leans her back against the wood, smiling like she's got a secret. "Hey."

We meet in the middle of the bathroom, and I wrap my arms around her, pulling her body against mine in a bear hug. The relief uncoiling all my muscles is so incredible, I moan. She links her arms at my neck and pushes up on her toes so our bodies meet everywhere. All those amazing curves I explored last night are still here, confirming our night was not a figment of my vivid imagination.

I pull away just enough to lower my head and kiss her. Her

mouth is warm and sweet, and I want to drown in her. It's been a hell of a shift, and it's not even half over. I feel like I'm running on fumes and she's my fuel.

Breaking the kiss, she scans my face like she's looking for an answer to the unasked question, *Are you okay?*

I stroke her cheek and slide one hand into her luxurious, thick dark hair. "I've been thinking..."

She laughs. "I'm not sure anything good ever starts that way."

"Hear me out."

She steps back. "*Eesh.*"

"Why don't you let *me* call Cocksucker?" She's already shaking her head while I continue. "We can have a man-to-man talk about this. Set up a way to give the gun back."

"I appreciate the thought, I really do, and if I thought that would work, I'd be all for it. But he's not a normal guy. He's intensely competitive. I actually think having you call him would make things worse, not better."

She's probably right. "Okay, but can you just give me his name so I can have Sosa run a background on him? We could find out something that would be useful in resolving this. I can't stand the thought of a guy somewhere out there with a grudge against you."

"It's Aiden McBride."

I'm surprised at how willingly she gave his name. She must want this over as much as she says she does. "How old is he?"

"Thirty-two."

"Lives in Manhattan or...?"

"Yeah, Manhattan. I'll text you the address."

I nod, desperate for more answers to questions I've had floating around in my head since she arrived, but I don't want to push my luck either. I want to build on this trust until she's comfortable confiding in me.

A knock at the door makes her jump, and she presses her face against my chest to muffle her laughter.

"Logan." It's not a human voice coming through the door, but Dolly's. "Food's here. *Squawk,* food's here."

"Don't go getting creepy on me, Buchanan," I warn, only to hear Dolly's laughter fading as she and Royal move away from the door.

"Damn," Isabel says, smiling, "that's a little freaky."

I lift Isabel's face to mine and kiss her again. I swear I could never get tired of kissing her. "Hockey, Saturday night? And Portland sometime this weekend?"

She's grinning as she nods.

"And, while I'm on a roll, how about meeting in your room tomorrow morning? I'll bolt back to the motel if I know you're waiting for me."

"I just happen to have tomorrow off from the bakery." She kisses me one more time before she turns for the door and smiles over her shoulder. "I'll keep the bed warm for you."

I catch her for another kiss before she leaves the room. Then she's gone.

Back in the dining room, I sit down to a family-style meal with my team and watch Isabel as she continues serving people at the bar, then cleaning up and stocking when she's free. She's fluid, the movements automatic, like she's been here from the day we opened, four years ago. She must have bartended in college, but that sixth sense tingles across the back of my neck, the feeling that there's a lot about her I don't know.

Everyone is trying their best to put the morning behind them. Royal's feeding Dolly a snap pea from the plate of Google-approved foods Mike brought for the parrot, and the guys are trying to teach her new words or get on her good side.

Underneath the table, Lucky is systematically untying everyone's boot laces.

Isabel stops often to talk and refill drinks. She laughs at our stupid jokes and at Dolly, who gives her a catcall whistle every time Isabel passes the table.

On our way out, I pull Isabel aside for one more kiss, then head back to the station with the idea of calling Sosa and asking for a favor.

20

Logan

The air is crisp and scented with fireplace smoke. I'm hyped, but trying to keep my expectations in check as I head home. Isabel may have been up for sex when I saw her yesterday, but there's no telling how she'll feel about it today. Still, I'm hoping my morning wood will be good for something other than frustrating the shit out of me.

When I pull into the motel, I'm relieved to find her Jeep parked in front of her room. I take Lucky to the apartment and give him a treat, then start toward room seven. I see a sticky note on her door, and I deflate, sure it has to be a "maybe next time" type of note. But when I pluck the note from the door, it reads, "Come in."

As I reach for the doorknob, my cell rings with Corbett's number. My stomach tightens. "Hey," I answer. "Have you got anything?"

"He's basically a nuisance just waiting for the right moment to escalate into a legit problem," Corbett says of McBride. "He's had several run-ins with the law for minor offenses— a dozen speeding tickets, drunk in public, disorderly conduct, harassment, that kind of thing. He's fairly well off, owns a place in Manhattan, a couple of nice cars, a sailboat. He has several guns registered in his name, but they're all antique. Judging by their age, I'd question whether or not they'd actually fire, but he hasn't got any weapon offenses."

In one way, I'm relieved, but in another, I see him as an escalating problem, and I'm glad Isabel got away from him when she did.

I thank Corbett and refocus—on the beautiful woman waiting on the other side of this door from me. Of how strong she had to be to break away from such a manipulative man. Maybe she's as different from other women as she seems. Maybe she really is what she presents—exactly the kind of woman I've looked for, but never found.

I convince myself that McBride isn't as much of a problem as I thought. Once he gets the rifle back, he'll drop the harassment. A man like that will turn his lazy attention to an easier target. Besides, he's in New York, across the country from Isabel. My concern over McBride eases.

I open the door to her room, which is illuminated by the back window where the slats on the blinds cast a row of shadows across the floor. It's warm too, the heater humming in a corner.

Isabel is in bed, lying on her stomach, the sheets bunched at her waist, her very naked skin contrasting with the navy sheets.

I close the door and pull my arms from my jacket. The rustle drags her eyes open, and she gives me a sleepy smile that has to be the sexiest thing I've ever seen. Her hair is tousled, spilling over the pillow, falling in her face.

I sit on the edge of the mattress and reach out, brushing her hair out of her eyes. "Do you realize how fucking sexy you look right now?"

She laughs softly. "That's what I was going for, but I fell asleep waiting for you."

"I love that you were waiting for me."

"Get naked, mister, and stay within view. I wanna watch you unwrap the whole amazing package."

Flash fire flows through my veins. I stand, face the bed, and pull off my T-shirt. She stays on her stomach, head turned on the pillow, eyes dark and hot.

"Damn, you're delicious," she murmurs with a lazy lilt in her voice, but heat in her eyes.

I'm naked in thirty seconds, and I crawl onto the bed on hands and knees. I press kisses across her shoulder and down her spine, then get rid of the sheets and press the front of my body against the back of hers. My chest pressed against her back, my erection against her ass, our legs intertwined.

She jumps and laughs. "Oh my God, you're cold."

"Not for long." Our legs twine, and I press a kiss to her shoulder. "Skin." She's warm, curvy, soft, and she smells like strawberries. "You have no idea how badly I needed to be skin to skin with you."

"Mmm," she says, sliding her thighs against mine, lifting her hips to rub against my erection. "Show me."

With my lips pressed to her neck, I stroke one hand down her body, shoulder to thigh, and squeeze her ass cheek. "Damn, I love your body."

She reaches back and combs her fingers into my hair. "And I love the way you love my body."

She turns to her side, and I push up on my hands to let her turn over. Then she's smiling up at me, her hair fanned out on the pillow in a tangle, and my heart makes a slow roll in my chest, spreading emotion through my body. I rest on my forearms, her head in my hands. Her thighs wrap my hips, and her hands slide down my back.

"How long are you staying?" I know this is *not* a great time to bring it up, but I feel my heart opening for her. I can see us together in the future. I want this to go on and on and on, not end in a few days or weeks or even months. Which means I need to know so I can get my head in the right place and chop off my feelings for her at the knees if I need to. And if she's leaving, I need to.

One of her hands returns to my face. Her fingers brush my stubble, her thumb strokes along my bottom lip, and her gaze follows the path. "I've been thinking..."

"I'm not sure anything good ever starts that way." I echo her own words from the day before as a tease, but panic stings my breastbone. Until right this minute, I didn't realize how badly I want her to stay. This is a dangerous place for me. I have so few relationships with women that have been good, I can't believe I'm ready to trust another.

I lower my head and drop a few kisses on her lips to quell the nerves. My hard cock is snuggled against her sex, and our bellies are pressed together. I'm having a hard time concentrating.

"Let's revisit this conversation later." She sighs and slides her hand around the back of my neck. "Right now, let's focus on this."

She pulls my mouth to hers and kisses me in a way that makes it clear she's not interested in talking anymore. Who am I to argue? She rolls me to my back, and my body screams *hell yes*. She reaches into the drawer of the nightstand and pulls out a condom.

"You been in my stash again?" I slide my hands up her sides, cup her breasts, and ease my thumbs over her nipples. "Those aren't from the trees, right?"

She laughs. "A kid is the very last thing I need to add to my current situation."

She kisses her way down my abs, slides my cock deep into her mouth, and sucks. Lightning streaks up my spine, my head falls back on a moan, and stars burst beneath my eyelids, making my brain flare white-hot.

Instead of rolling the condom on, she works me longer. Until my vision blurs and my mind drops out. Until all I can focus on is the thick, soft strands of her hair between my fingers and the wet heat of her mouth surrounding me.

"Jesus Christ," I manage, "you're *so* goddamned good at that."

She strokes my length as she finally rolls on the condom, and I grit my teeth against another surge of need. I watch her rise on her knees, position me, and sink home with a moan.

I'm already breathing fast when my fingers dig into her hips. I hold her against me and roll until I'm wedged between her thighs, as deep as I can get. She crosses her feet at my back and lifts into me.

This is so goddamned good, I can already see the finish line, and as much as my body wants to sprint there, my heart needs more. I slide an arm between her body and the bed and hold her tight as I sit back.

The weight of her body pushes me even deeper, and we both moan. She cups my head as she kisses me, slow and deep. She unlocks her legs, presses her knees to the mattress, and uses her hips to rock my goddamned world.

"Fuck, you're amazing." I bite her jaw, kiss her neck, bend her backward so I can tease her breasts. I feel her climax rise inside her—hips moving quicker, hands fisting tighter, sounds rising from deep inside her. She comes with her arms locked around my neck, cheek against my head, her pleasure ringing in my ear.

And as I hold her steady until she floats back from the orgasm, I'm stunned by the realization that I've never been so happy in my entire goddamned life.

21

Isabel

I surprised myself with the number of pieces I have available to sell. I was building stock to put up online when the whole Aiden fiasco went south, then forgot about them in the mess of getting fired and leaving town.

Logan swapped shifts to work the bar during the party along with Tucker and Cole, which only increases my discomfort. I know they're being supportive, but it's hard enough to face potential failure as it is. I'd rather the three most important men in my life didn't witness it.

Only, as it turns out, my fears over tonight went unrealized. The women love my work. So much so that this all feels too good to be true, and I find myself waiting for the other shoe to drop. I keep reminding myself that if I look for bad, I'll see bad, so I keep pulling my focus back from the fear as I watch a dozen women comb through the racks holding everything I've made—tops and yoga pants and sports bras, and tables layered with bags and hair accessories and leather jewelry.

My stomach hasn't stopped skittering around in a circle

since Natalie organized this party. She's been keeping an eye on everything and helps women when I'm busy with others. Betsy is acting as if she's my sales rep, Tucker wanders by with sexy compliments for the women trying on my clothes, and Logan and Cole keep everyone's wineglass filled. Even Lucky makes the rounds, charming buyers.

I feel... I feel...

Loved.

I feel loved.

The realization hits me hard, and tears sting my eyes. I guess after feeling unloved for so long, basically since birth, I didn't realize how amazing it would feel to have people in my corner for nothing more than support. No ulterior motive. Okay, well, Logan has one.

I glance at the bar—out of fear or the need for reassurance, I'm not sure. But Logan's gaze is waiting. He smiles and nods, a silent *you've got this.* God, this man... I don't know what to think. I've never had a "normal" relationship. The men I pick all have some major flaw, and I mean major. Doug had a gambling addiction—I should have seen that coming, given I worked in the room where he gambled. Simon and Matthew both cheated on me—as if my self-esteem needed another kick in the ribs. Ty turned out to be married, which still haunts me. And of course, Aiden is a narcissistic prick.

But Logan is the real deal. Tucker and Cole would never have stayed friends with him if he wasn't. Honestly, I don't quite know what to do with him, or my feelings for him.

"Isabel, honey?" The question comes from one of the older women who owns a boutique in town. I pry my gaze from Logan's and smile at Helen. "Would it be possible to put in an order with you? Seems everything here is spoken for."

I glance at the rolling store displays Natalie borrowed from a local shop for the night, and I'm shocked to see them nearly empty. Women are chatting with garments slung over their arms in ownership.

"Hold on there, Helen." This comes from Amber, the owner of the only yoga studio in town. "Her pieces are more suited for my studio than your store."

"I can work with both of you," I tell them. "And I can tailor the pieces to fit your demographics so you'll both have exclusive designs."

"Oh," Helen says, beaming at me. "That sounds perfect."

I sit down and take an order from Helen, using my sketch pad to identify which styles she likes and how I might change them slightly to make them unique for her customers.

Once we identify the styles she likes, she puts in an order that staggers me. "You must have one busy shop."

"This is my slowest shop. I have two in Portland, one in Eugene, and one in Salem."

I'm taken aback. This is a fantastic turn of events. "Oh, wow."

She smiles. "I've done a lot of buying, been to a lot of merchandizing shows, and I know talent when I see it. You're gifted, sweetheart. But you already know that. This must be so different for you from New York."

"It is," I admit. "But it's for the better."

"Well, that's good to hear. I guess there's still hope we'll be able to order from you on a regular basis, then."

Holy shit. "That would be amazing."

"It would." She pushes to her feet. "Now I need to sample some of Natalie's desserts."

My phone dings with a message, and I wait for Helen to melt back into the group before I look.

Unisex bathroom, three minutes.

I smile and text back: *Make it one.*

He's still serving customers when I head toward the bathroom. Inside, I press cold water to my cheeks and study my reflection. I have color in my face and light in my eyes. Only now, seeing it, do I realize just how wrung out I felt and looked in New York.

Logan slips in the door and leans against it. His gaze travels over me. "You look incredible."

I pulled out a few of my few-but-coveted designer pieces to wear tonight, trying to give the impression I have more in my wardrobe than torn jeans and hoodies.

"You're on fire out there. Are you going to have anything left?"

I shake my head and laugh. "It's not looking like it. I've been trying to ballpark it, and I think I'm going to come out of tonight with close to five grand. Some of it I haven't earned yet, I have to fill some orders, but, God, I never thought that could happen from a small get-together in a small town."

"I love seeing you in your element. You're so charismatic. People are drawn to you."

I close the distance between us and press my body to his. "The only person I care to draw at the moment is you."

He lowers his head and kisses me.

"This is good, right?" I ask. "You and me?"

"It's really good."

I take a deep breath and push out the idea that puts me on the edge of a cliff. "What would you say to the idea of me staying?"

Something shifts in his gaze. Surprise? Wariness? I'm not sure what, but it doesn't exactly make my heart float.

He slides his arms from around my waist and takes a step back. "What about Los Angeles and San Francisco?"

This isn't how I thought this talk would go at all. "They're not going anywhere, and I kind of want to see how this unfolds."

"Us this or business this?"

"Both." I reach for his T-shirt and pull him to me, pushing up on my toes to kiss him again.

Only it doesn't change his serious expression, one that tamps down my mood.

"We need to talk," he says. "About everything. You can't keep things from me."

My heart dips, and annoyance tingles along my nerves. "I'm looking for a fresh start. I'd rather not dredge up the past when it doesn't matter anymore."

"I need honesty."

"You say that as if you expect me to lie. Why are you acting like telling the truth is going to be a stretch for me?"

"Because all you've given me since you got here are a lot of half-truths. Half-truths got my mom killed."

"I'm not lying to you, and I'm not in any danger. Why don't you trust me?"

"I *want* to trust you."

"Then do it. I know we both have baggage, but I'm not your mom. For that matter, I'm not Emily either."

A knock comes at the door, then Tucker's "Your dog got into the kitchen and dumped over the trash can. Shit's everywhere. Get out here and deal with him."

Logan rolls his eyes and slides his thumb across my cheek. "Can we talk more about this tonight?"

I cross my arms, feeling hurt and confused. "Not if this is the way you're going to act."

"Come on, you just sprang that on me. We've been locked into this is not a thing from day one."

"I wasn't even considering staying until today." God, this really took a wrong turn, and I'm both hurt and a little surprised he's pulling back. I obviously read him wrong. "Look, if you want to keep this casual, that's fine. It doesn't have to be a big deal. Going back to being friends is always an option. We know how to do that, so—"

He silences me with a kiss. A kiss that melts my frustration.

When he pulls away, he says, "I'm not saying I want to end this thing that's not a thing."

That makes me laugh. He wraps me tight, and I'm filled with the oddest feeling of both loss and love. In a way, I feel bruised inside. After all the bullshit I've been through, I guess that shouldn't be a surprise. I guess I was always too worried about surviving in New York to pay any attention to how I felt.

I press my face to his neck, close my eyes, and breathe him in.

"Tonight?" he says. "After this? We can talk about it?"

I exhale, drop back, and step away. "Yeah, okay."

But I'm not looking forward to this conversation.

22

Logan

I let Isabel leave the bathroom first, then brace my hands on
the sink and stare at myself in the mirror.

Her *"What would you say to the idea of me staying?"* triggered
something inside me. Unlocked a door of some kind, letting an
old, dark fear emerge. One I don't even fully understand.

If she stays, I'll be a goner, no question. Without her
impending move, I have no reason to keep up my walls.
Without my walls, I'll fall head over ass for her, and if she lies...

I push off the sink and shove all ten fingers through my hair.
I want to jump. I want to go all in and drown myself in her. I
just don't want to be screwed over again. Especially not by
someone I care about as much as I care about her.

I exit the bathroom with a million mixed feelings. It's
closing in on 10:00 p.m. and the customers are thinning out,
Isabel's party is breaking up, and she's closing out sales and
saying goodbye.

I keep myself busy by cleaning up Lucky's mess in the
kitchen, restocking the bar, helping with the tables.

When I return to the bar, Cole has shut down the register and is counting the money.

"Stop looking for trouble," Cole says without looking up.

"Huh?"

Cole wraps a rubber band around a stack of cash, scribbles a number on a tally sheet, then looks at me. "She went into the bathroom looking a lot happier than when she came out."

I glance at Isabel. She's subdued now, and I hate that I tugged her happiness down a notch. I feel a little like Scrooge, looking through a window at my possible future. And like Scrooge, if I don't change, I'll lose that future.

"She's thinking about staying," I tell him, "but she's still not being completely honest with me. I don't feel like I can trust her."

Cole puts the money in a banker's bag. "You know at her core, she's a good person. She's always had a heart of gold, and that clearly hasn't changed. These are issues you've *got* to get over, because no one is perfect, and no one tells one hundred percent of the truth, one hundred percent of the time. Nobody. Trust is *your* issue, not hers."

Cole takes the banker's bag and heads toward the office. As he passes, he delivers this parting shot: "She's also the best woman you've ever been with."

I war with my demons on the way home. Isabel may be behind me somewhere, but I'm not sure. I don't see her headlights, and she clearly didn't want to address this problem.

My headlights sweep across the property as I turn in, over the dumpster she's filled, over the walk she's swept, over the windows of the rooms she's cleaned—without being asked and without one complaint.

My logical mind is telling me Cole's right. I'm making too much out of nothing. But that pit in my stomach is still there.

Lucky lifts his head from the passenger's seat and rises into a wobbly sit.

"Tired, bud? You've been a busy pup." I pick him up and step out of the truck just as Isabel's Jeep turns onto the property. My heart lifts into my throat. The happiness that floods me when I see her is nothing I've ever felt before.

She climbs from the Jeep, and I collect Lucky in one arm. We stand beside our vehicles for a moment that seems to expand with the silent night.

"Still want to talk?" she says.

"Yeah." *Sort of, not really.* "Come in. I'll get Lucky settled."

Inside my apartment, I fill Lucky's bowls with food and water, but he bypasses the dishes for his dog bed. Isabel curls into one corner of the sofa, legs crossed.

I love the look of her in my apartment. I love the way the space seems to warm up with her in it. I love the way the same thing happens to me when I'm with her.

Instead of sitting on the sofa, I drop into a crouch in front of her and stroke her jean-clad thighs with both hands. I need the contact. Need to feel close to her, even when something deep inside me is trying to rip me away.

"You scare the shit out of me," I admit. "You know?"

Her expression is as surprised and confused as I feel. Those words tumbled out without my permission. "No, I don't know. What does that mean?"

"I really care about you. More than any other woman I've been with. And I've just been through so much shit, it's hard for me to see anything going right for me."

She exhales and uncrosses her legs. I slide my hands under her knees, part her legs, and pull her toward me, sliding her to the edge of the sofa, just short of my lap. She combs her fingers into my hair, her nails scoring my scalp. It feels so good, I groan. Tingles of relief flow down my tight neck and stiff shoulders, easing my tension.

"Maybe that's because you're always looking for the bad," she says. "Always waiting for the worst to happen. When you look for bad, you find bad. I'm certainly no Pollyanna, but I really do try to look for the good in everything and everyone, and even though I know that backfired on me with Cocksucker, it's also brought a lot of good into my life just when I needed it most. You, for example. When you look for good, you find good."

I think of all she's done since she's been here, all the loyalty and dedication she's shown—to Tucker and Cole, to Natalie and Tina, to the employees at the bar. To me.

I lift my hand to her face and slide my thumb over her cheek. "There sure is a lot of good to see in you."

That gets a smile from her, and the sight twists something at the center of my chest. I kiss her and she wraps her arms around my neck. Her kiss floods me with relief and joy, and I know in that instant I want her to stay. Yet at the same time, I don't fully trust her to stay.

I pull away and slide my hands over her thighs. "What made you think about staying?" I smirk. "I mean, besides me, of course."

She laughs, then goes serious again. "Natalie made a really compelling case for working independently. It's something I want to check out."

"Independently? Like your own business?"

"Yeah. She could work for a bakery or a restaurant or a catering company, but she's working for herself."

"She did create a pretty great gig."

"Right?" Her gaze drifts away again. "I don't know, I just started thinking about it. Our industries are totally different, and I don't know how well it would work for me, but I did great at the party tonight, got a couple of ongoing contracts with two stores."

"Would you be happy with that?" I ask. "I mean, you've already seen how opposite life here is compared to New York. I'm having a hard time seeing you leaving the city or being satisfied here, long term. This seems like more of a sabbatical for you."

Something passes through her eyes, and she looks away. Guilt. She's lying again. But I hear Cole in my head and check myself.

"I can't afford a sabbatical, so no, I don't see this as that. What I do know is that I'm not going back to New York."

The surety of her tone makes me feel grounded in that respect. "And San Francisco and LA?"

She sighs heavily. "I don't have my entire life figured out. Not all of us can be as accomplished as Maya or as secure in a career as you and Tucker and Cole. I'd have to see how it all works out. I don't have a crystal ball. I can't promise anything right now except that I love being with you, and I'm growing to love it here too."

Is that enough for me? Logically, I know now is all anyone has, yet I find myself desperate for reassurance.

"I'd have to have more parties, approach more stores to carry my work, develop an online presence. That would take time. A lot of time, given I don't have a wealthy investor just sitting around waiting to throw money at me." She shrugs. "But I think I want to give it a try, and I want to know what you think."

"I have no frame of reference for this kind of thing. That's Maya's wheelhouse."

"But on a personal level," she says with an eye roll in her tone, "what do you think about me staying? About changing this not a thing into a real thing?"

My perception of our relationship shifts instantly, and I see us more as one than two. I see us working together toward the same goals. I see having her in my life every day, and I swear a swarm of butterflies fills my chest.

"Honestly," I say, then pause, thinking about what I'm going to say before I say it. Isabel's gaze is eager and open, making this so much easier to say. "I love that idea."

"Really?" she says, expression shifting to surprise and hope.

"Really." And yeah, it really does feel right. Sure, I still have concerns and insecurities, but I push them away, because Cole's right—if I don't, I'm going to lose the best thing I've ever had in my life. "I love the idea of you staying. Of us being a thing."

I kiss her, and she eases into my lap, where I wrap her tight and slide my hands under her T-shirt, along her warm, smooth skin. I moan at the feel of her, at the way she dives in and gives all of herself. But I'm ravenous for more.

I unbutton her jeans with one hand and push the zipper down, then move my hands beneath the fabric and between her legs.

She gasps at the unexpected touch and breaks the kiss. Her gaze meets mine, heavy lidded and lusty. I stroke her, then sink two fingers as deep as they'll go and watch her lids flutter close, watch her head fall back, hear the purr deep in her throat, feel her hips rock into my touch.

"Damn," I murmur, "you're so fucking sexy."

She's hot, wet, and soft, lost somewhere in lust, her eyes glazed with pleasure. I love making her come. Love watching her shatter. I have to admit, I also love having a little control over when and how that happens, but this is the first opportunity I've had because Isabel is assertive in the bedroom. She goes after what she wants.

But right now, I want her to want me longer. Harder. I want her to want me with an intensity that marks her heart.

I work her deep, filling her up, rubbing her walls. Pressing my palm to her mound and grinding, only to pull away and stroke her clit with my thumb in a featherlight touch that makes her writhe.

In minutes, her clit is swollen and ripe. Isabel's on the verge of begging me to make her come. But I need her under my mouth, where I have even more control.

I pull my hand from her body and set her on the edge of the sofa, then peel her jeans and panties off her legs. I ease my shoulders under her thighs and push my fingers through her wet folds. Her scent fills my head, intoxicating.

Isabel swears and fists the sofa cushion.

I easily isolate the dime-sized swollen flesh, spread her folds, and take it in my mouth. But I go for overall heat and pressure and lick her.

"Logan," she says, her voice tight, her tone needy.

"Hmm?" I purposely let the sound vibrate over her.

"Oh my God." She lifts her hips, and I slide my fingers deep inside her again, then move my tongue to her clit. Barely, barely, barely touch her. Barely slide the tip of my tongue over the flesh.

She moans. "Yes, yes, yes."

I move slow. Excruciatingly slow, giving her a deep thorough finger fuck. A methodical taste of her clit.

She's impatient. Slides her hand around the back of my head and pulls me in, lifting her hips. I pull back, circle both wrists, and ease them not just back to the sofa, but behind her, where I hold both wrists with one hand and use the other to start that maddening sex play all over again. And, damn, I love having control. I love diving deep into her, exploring and finding every hot spot both inside and out.

Until I can't hold back anymore. Until I cover her with my mouth and stroke and suck until she shatters. Until her hips buck and her body shakes, and she screams with the intensity of the orgasm and melts into the sofa, panting.

Then I stand, scoop her up from the sofa, and head into the bedroom for another night of insanely amazing sex, and maybe, hopefully, a bridge in the chasm I created between us.

23

Isabel

After another intensely intimate night with Logan, I'm surer than ever that I really do want what I proposed to him yesterday—to stay and see where things between us go. Between Natalie's example and the success from my first sale, I'm beginning to believe I could be happy without getting to the pinnacle of fashion like I always dreamed. It feels like the right time to reframe success and take steps toward a career of my own making.

I spent all day working on the new designs for Helen and Amber and took breaks to pull shit out of rooms to add to the dumpster while Logan was at a training gig.

I walk into the rink at halftime, or whatever they call the break between periods. The guys are in a loose huddle, and I take the time to look around. Natalie, Betsy, and Tina wave me over, but the huddle breaks, and Logan comes toward me. I'm keenly aware of the daggers Emily's throwing my way, but they miss their target.

He stops at the wall, smiling. "Hey."

"Hey yourself."

"Get a lot done today?"

"I did. Guess it helps not to have a sexy man luring me into bed."

He grins and swings his legs over the wall and walks me backward, then we're hidden behind the bleachers.

I'm laughing, something to the effect of "How very high schoolish of you," when he kisses me, and I have to eat my words. This man isn't any more the guy I knew in high school than I am the woman he knew. Yet we still fit like puzzle pieces, and instead of scaring me, it thrills me.

"I missed you today," he says.

"Yeah, I missed having you to boss me around and tell me I'm doing it all wrong."

He laughs and kisses me again. When a buzzer sounds, he breaks the kiss. "Cockloft after this, right?"

"Absolutely."

Logan makes his way back to the ice, and I watch him return to his team with the deepest sense of acceptance and belonging and love I've ever felt.

I start toward the bleachers when my phone rings, and I stop to answer, tapping the green circle on my screen, putting the phone to one ear and plugging the other. "Hello?"

"Hello, is this Isabel Medina?"

The formal tone drags my stomach to my feet. Yeah, I know the voice of a bill collector. I close my eyes. "Yes."

"Sorry to call so late. This is Mary Stout. I'm in HR with Threadbare. I received your résumé, and we'd like you to come in for an interview. We can fly you in from New York, put you up in a hotel for a couple of days, or, if your schedule doesn't allow, we could set up a panel of interviews on Zoom. How does your schedule look?"

My mouth is hanging open. Threadbare is a wildly successful fashion company, and the position I applied for is senior designer. I applied more as a tongue-in-cheek whim than a serious interest. I knew they'd put my résumé at the bottom of the stack based on my previous job titles.

Only they didn't.

For a minute, I forget where I am. I forget the life changes I'm considering. I even forget I'm crazy about an amazing man, right here, and "I'm available" pops out of my mouth. "I'm actually in Oregon right now, visiting family."

Guilt floods me, and my face flashes with heat. I've given the same "I'm available" answer dozens of times during the last five years. The answer is automatic, only this time, instead of feeling excited, I feel sick. Confused. Caught between worlds. Didn't I just agree to go all in with Logan? Didn't I just set up contracts for boutiques in Oregon?

Instead of looking like a total flake and backpedaling on my immediate answer, I let Mary tell me about the arrangements she'll make and she says that she'll contact me again tomorrow. Which is when I'll tell her I've changed my mind and cancel altogether.

And, wow, that decision sends a sizzle of fear all through my chest.

I've committed to stay in one place. In this tiny town where this kind of job offer will never be extended to me.

I head toward Natalie, and Trevor yells, "Is-bell" from Tina's lap. I tap his nose and greet him with "Hello there, handsome," before sitting beside Natalie.

"Looks like things with Logan are heating up," she says, grinning.

I force a smile, but I feel guilty as shit over the phone call I just took.

"Does this mean we get to keep you?" Tina asks.

Get to keep me? Has anyone ever actually *wanted* to keep me? God, this is all happening so fast. Big changes in a short amount of time, when I've spent most of my life getting small changes over an extended period of time.

"I'm letting things unfold to see what happens next," I say.

"That's fantastic."

"Thank you. And thank you—all of you—for setting up and helping at that party. I made good money and really got my groove back."

"Always happy to participate in a girl getting her groove back," Natalie says.

"They're talking you up all over town," Tina says. "Overheard Devon McCluskey and Brenda Tyson raving about you at the bakery today."

"Really?" I can't lie, that makes a tingle run through my stomach.

"Hold your path, sweetie," Betsy says. "Good things are coming for you."

Hold my path. That's as sage advice as I've ever heard.

These women have become the sisters and mother I never had, and I'm struck by how easily I found them. Effortless, even. In New York City, no one knows their neighbor, even in the same apartment building. Everyone stays to themselves with an occasional "Good morning" in the elevator. No one looks at each other on the subway, drowning in their EarPods and cell phones. I already have more people I'd call friends here than I ever had in New York.

I check out the bench and find the puppy always in someone's lap, getting kissed and passed among the guys. "Where's Royal's bird?"

"He and his sister are sharing her, so Dolly stays at his sister's house when he's on duty. I hear she got to Sorenson's dinner plate once too often. She was also a jealous bitch when it came to Lucky, and of course, Logan has seniority."

I'm smiling over that information when my phone pings with a message. Guilt over accepting the job interview returns full force. Mary is probably texting to confirm the agreement for an interview. As soon as I get home to my computer, I'm going to cancel by email. I can't wait until tomorrow.

That decision takes some weight off my shoulders.

But when I pull my phone from my pocket, I find a message from Aiden, not Threadbare.

Jesus. I am looking *so* forward to getting him and everything associated with him out of my life.

The message reads *Does the new guy know about all your smoke and mirrors?*

An icy sensation curls in my gut. New guy? How could he possibly know...

I have to read it twice more before I realize Aiden has to be here, has to have seen me kiss Logan. I look up, my breath coming quicker, panic jumbling my brain.

Aiden stands in the ice rink's lobby, staring through the glass between the lobby and the rink, smiling. And it's not a nice smile. It's a got-you-bitch smile, and my stomach free-falls.

This problem between me and Aiden has to be more complicated than I thought, or he wouldn't have spent the time and money to track me down himself. And it has to be about him and me, or he would just have taken me up on my offer to ship the rifle back to him and given me my money back. But I've always known this wasn't about money, at least not for him. The damn thing cost less than his monthly wardrobe allowance. No, for him this is about control.

Logan may think Aiden's dangerous, but that couldn't be further from the truth. Aiden is a coward. He likes nothing better than a good mind fuck, and I'm *so* done with those games.

"I'll be back," I tell the women. By the time I stand, Aiden is gone from view.

I hurry down the bleachers and push into the lobby only to find it empty. I make my way toward the exit and scan the parking lot. He's nowhere. If the text wasn't still on my phone, I would believe I'd imagined seeing him.

I call him and put the phone to my ear, but I get his voicemail. I hang up and text him. *Chickenshit. You come all the way here to find me, then run and hide?*

When I get no answer: *I told you I'd give the gun back, you wasted your time and money tracking me down.*

Still nothing. I growl and shove my phone into my pocket.

I'm going to have to come clean with Logan. Much cleaner than I expected. I really did want to leave my mess behind, but Aiden knows too much. Before we were dating, when he was upper management, and I was just an errand girl, he asked about my Instagram profile. Because he was in the industry and could find out the truth with one phone call, I had to tell him that I was the window display designer, not the designer of the clothes displayed. I confided in him about how rough it's been for me since graduating college, which was when he got me the assistant designer's position. I thought he was a good guy back then, but his true colors showed soon enough.

I have to be the one to tell Logan about my past. I can't let him learn it from scum like Aiden.

Back inside, I rejoin Natalie, Tina, and Betsy, but my mind isn't on the game. At least not the hockey game. It's on whatever game Aiden is playing. I try again and again to find the words to tell Logan that Aiden is here, but I can't explain one thing without explaining everything and there's just no reason to do that. Except, well, *Aiden is here.*

I barely recognize that the firefighters have beaten the cops, ending the tiebreaker between the two. I move in a haze out of the rink, where I tell Natalie I'll see her at the bar. Then pace the parking lot waiting for Logan.

When he finds out Aiden is here, he's going to go all alpha on me. God, I don't want to tell him. I just want to handle it on my own, the way I've done everything else in life. But I promised him no lies.

The rink door opens, and a gaggle of about ten firefighters and six cops spill out with good-natured ribbing and agreements to meet at the bar.

Logan breaks off from the group, but he's joined by Tucker, Cole, and Carter. Lucky runs in circles around them.

When Logan sees me, he smiles. "Hey."

"Hey. Great game, you guys."

"Want a ride to the bar?" Logan asks.

"No, thanks. I've got my car."

The other three get into the truck, and Logan says, "What's wrong?"

"Nothing. Just wanted to congratulate you on the win."

"I guess a kiss is out of the question."

I laugh and glance at the truck with Tucker riding shotgun. He knows about me and Logan, but I'm not ready to take this to a kiss-in-front-of-others status. "I'll see you at the bar."

He climbs behind the wheel and waits until I've started the Jeep to drive out of the parking lot. I sit there, heater on high, trying to shake off the chill of the night, the rink, Aiden.

"God, what a fucking mess." I head to the bar, heavy with self-disgust and disappointment. "I finally get something really good in my life, and I manage to screw that up too."

As soon as I turn into the parking lot of the Cockloft, I know I won't get a chance to talk to Logan tonight. The place is packed, and the music is as loud as the conversations.

Well, shit. Now that I'm ready to tell him, we're in the worst possible place for a discussion like this. I know he'll want to jump in and help me, and honestly, I want to fix my own fuckup, thank you very much. Like I told Logan, I don't need a hero. All I need to do is step the hell up and end this problem.

I head inside and find the bar even busier than I imagined. A slow sigh leaks from my lungs. I'm not in the mood for this, but I work my way through the crowd, saying hello to more people than I realized I knew in town until I reach Logan. He's crouched on the floor, playing tug-of-war with Lucky, beaming, eyes bright, laughing with some of his friends.

I smile at him from a few feet away, and he lets Lucky win the game and stands. Lucky takes the toy in his mouth and shakes it hard, spinning in a circle. Logan reaches out and wraps my shoulders to pull me into the group and kisses the side of my head.

I guess we're stepping into the light after all. I'd feel better if I had Aiden behind me. Especially given he's in town.

Logan introduces me to the men, but I can't seem to hold on to a thought, let alone a name. They both say their wives are interested in coming to my next sale, and we make small talk for a bit.

I look around and see everyone laughing, smiling, talking. Women who purchased from me at the show wave and gesture to themselves wearing my designs. Their excitement thrills me. Hell, everything about this place warms me from the inside out.

Standing at Logan's side, his arm around me, feels so right. Like I'm grounded. Like I've grown roots that stabilize me. Like I've got protection from the sky falling.

Damn. I love this man.

A hot, uncomfortable current traces through my body. I've never had luck with love. As in *never*, and I have so much more to lose now than when I came to town—Logan, friends, what little self-esteem I've managed to recoup.

"Hey, look who's here." Logan drops his arm from my shoulders and steps back to take another woman into his arms for a hug. "You didn't tell me you were coming."

It's Maya, and the sight of her makes my heart plunge.

What is this? Show-up-in-Hood-River day?

I glance around, expecting to see Aiden around some corner. I check my phone, but there's no message.

"I tried to make it for the game," she says, "but I always seem to get tied up with something. Going by your smile, I'm guessing you won."

"We did," Logan says.

The men we were talking to turn and start a different conversation with others.

"Congratulations." Maya's gaze turns on me. And I brace for venom. She had to see Logan's arm around me. "Isabel."

"Hey."

"We should talk," she says, crouching to give Lucky some love. "I want to know more about this blockbuster party you had. Maybe I can look at some of your pieces."

As far as olive branches go, this one feels as big as a redwood. Still, I'd be ashamed of showing my casual wear to a designer like Maya. "You don't have to do that. You should spend your time here with Logan."

"I can always find time for fashion." She stands and glances toward the bar. "I'm going to get a drink and say hello to Cole and Tucker."

She walks away, and I'm dizzy with relief, but it's short-lived when I realize this is my chance to talk to Maya before she talks to Logan.

He faces me and slides his hands down my arms. "I sure would love it if you and Maya found even footing again."

"Yeah." I smile for his benefit, but I feel sick inside. "That would be nice. Do you mind if I go chat with her now? I'm pretty tired. I'm going to head back to the motel soon."

He tracks his thumb across my cheek. "Yeah, sure."

Then he kisses me in front of everyone and pulls back with a deeply satisfied smile.

Damn, reality is going to be one long, hard fall.

I take a deep breath and step up to the bar, turning to face Maya. "Hey."

She takes a sip of something amber in her glass. "We don't

have to talk right now. Maybe tomorrow when I can see your work."

I don't want to do this dance. I don't have time. I need to talk to Logan. "I know you don't want to see my work, and that's okay. I understand."

"I wouldn't ask if I didn't want to see it."

I feel like those roots I'd grown have been ripped out of the earth. "Do we need to talk about...anything? Other than fashion, I mean."

"You mean the mismatch between your actual work history and your Instagram profile or the stories you tell Tucker?"

Oh, Jesus. This is worse than I thought, and I'm both mortified and terrified. "How did you find out about my work history?"

"You know how it is, coworkers go out for drinks, have one too many, confidential stuff leaks into the conversation. It's the way I keep my finger on the pulse of the industry bullshit."

I bite the inside of my lip to keep the tears back.

"I mean, you're seeing my brother. I thought I should know. The whole cloak-and-dagger ruse you've been running is rather brilliant, if you ask me. You never explicitly say you're the window display styler and not the fashion designer whose pieces are on display. Then you let people think what they want so you're not technically lying. Clever. Very clever. But that approach will backfire with Logan, just FYI."

"I know. I need to clear everything up with him. Can you let me tell Logan? Tonight, after all this is over and we're alone? I really care about him. It needs to come from me."

She sighs and faces me. I'm trying to figure out if that's real compassion on her face or a facade she'll wear as she fillets me. New Yorkers are good at that. Really good.

"I don't care when you tell him," she says. "Or even *if* you tell him."

All my air rushes out. "You... I mean... What?"

"Look, I live in that world. I know exactly how harsh it can be. How many really talented designers they chew up and spit out. How completely you're expected to give your life over to your career to succeed. It's a grind, girl. You know that."

I nod.

"Just because you didn't make it doesn't mean you're not talented or that you couldn't succeed in a different venue. The fact that you stuck with it, tried over and over again to break in tells me you've still got that ambition you had when we were kids. And this facade you've built isn't malicious or directed to manipulate Logan. I'm objective enough to know you were trying to put forward as professional a front as you could with the resources that you had. We all know social media isn't reality." She smiles. "I've been known to misrepresent my life a time or twenty."

A little tension slides from my shoulders.

"I'd really like to see your work," she says. "Whether or not it's worthy of a New York runway, it's a hit here. And in the end, isn't that what we all really want—validation? Just to be seen? Heard? Considered? Hell, maybe I can hook you up with someone who could finance a small line, see how it turns out."

My mouth drops open. My heart spins. "I... You..."

"This stuttering problem is new," she says with a smile. "Don't be bothered by what you don't have or what you didn't get. It's clear you've found a few really sweet deals right here."

"Why aren't you being a bitch? This is the perfect I-told-you-so moment. And you'd be in the right."

She huffs a laugh, finishes her drink, and sets the glass on the bar. "I've got too much drama in my life as it is. What would I even gain by saying I told you so? Time is the great equalizer, my friend. We're all the same, irrelevant of where we work or what we do or who we know. In all honesty, I would have liked to see you succeed. Don't waste your talent in New York when you've got great opportunities right here."

While I'm still grappling over her grounded, sensible outlook, she looks past me and frowns. "Are you or are you not with Logan?"

I brace again. "I am. We are. I'm really crazy about him."

"Then what's your ex doing here?"

"My—" Aiden fills my mind, and all my blood drains out the soles of my feet.

"He's good-looking," Maya says, "but that's about all he's got going for him. And money, I guess."

I press my fingers to closed lids. This has turned into the night from hell. "Shit."

I'm not afraid of him. Certainly not shy about telling him how I feel. But he holds the key to my Pandora's box, and, God, I don't want that opened here, in front of all the people whose opinion of me would change, people who have been really great to me while I've been here. People who have made me feel like I'm worthy of love just as I am.

On a deep breath, I turn and find Aiden picking up a beer bottle, one finger around the neck, his gaze on me. He's completely out of place. Maybe he fits in well enough on the outside in his jeans and flannel shirt, but I know him on the inside. It occurs to me that Aiden is a lot like Emily: insecure, mean, and vindictive.

I glance around to find Logan. He's standing in a group of firefighters and volunteers, but his gaze is directly on me with a clear *What's going on?* look in his eyes. Damn, he reads me way too well.

My gut stings. I don't want to lose him. And the first step to making that happen is taking care of my shit with Aiden. The second step is telling Logan everything.

This is already the night from hell. May as well get it all over with now.

I lift a finger toward Logan in a give-me-a-minute gesture, then move toward Aiden.

I stop beside him, and he turns his head to look at me. "I never thought you'd come running back to your brother, tail between your legs."

I don't jump at the bait. "Why did you come all the way here? Why didn't you just make arrangements with me to send the gun back?"

He shrugs. "I needed a break from work. Got yourself a firefighter, huh?"

No. Not going there. "Leave, Aiden. I'll call you later with a time and place to give you the gun back."

"That doesn't work for me," he says. "I want it now."

Panic spirals through my stomach. "This isn't the time or place to push me. You're surrounded by cops."

"Bitching at me will only bring attention to yourself. And you don't want that, do you? For your brother and your firefighter and your friends to find out what your life was really like in New York."

I don't specifically remember telling him how I'd portrayed myself to my brother, but it probably came out in a roundabout way during our conversations. I sure wish I'd been more careful, but then I never imagined being in the situation I'm in right now.

"If you want to see that gun again," I tell him, "you'll get out. Now."

"And if you don't want me spilling dirty laundry, you'll take me to the gun. Now."

I clench my teeth. He's got the upper hand in the moment, and, in true Aiden style, he's working it. "Want to introduce me to your beau? He's headed this way."

My mind skips and darts before it stops on the safest location to meet him. "If you want the damn gun, meet me in the parking lot of the grocery store in half an hour."

24

Logan

I leave Royal to watch Lucky, step up beside Isabel, and slide an arm around her shoulders. From the look on her face and her tight posture, I'm damn sure this is Aiden. He's good-looking in that pretty-boy way and smug as hell.

He didn't come all the way across the country for one stupid two-thousand-dollar rifle. He came for Isabel, either for revenge or reconciliation, but neither works for me.

"What's going on?" I ask.

"Nothing," Isabel says, wringing her hands. "I was just telling him—"

"She was just telling me you're the flavor of the month," Aiden says.

Another spike of anger strikes. "This is a private event. You need to leave."

"Don't get attached," Aiden says, straightening from the bar. "You're temporary, like everything else in her life."

I lunge for him even before I realize that idea is in my head. Aiden steps back, but I still get a fistful of flannel shirt, one he bought when he got into town judging by the crispness of the fabric, and he smiles as if he's not seconds away from getting my fist in his face.

"No, no, no." Isabel grabs my arm and pulls, finally prying my hand free. Then she steps between Aiden and me, keeping me from going after him again.

Dalton steps into the situation from the left. "Looks like we've got a problem here."

"Get out," Isabel tells Aiden, "or I'll let these guys handle you."

"Couldn't have said it better myself," Dalton says. "I'll escort you to your car, just to make sure you get there."

I shoulder Isabel out of my way and follow Dalton's path. As soon as I'm outside, Isabel grabs the back of my shirt. Angry, I spin to release her grip and grab her arms. Then I freeze.

Everything slows to a crawl and vivid, split-second images hit my brain—the way my fingers indent her flesh, the shock in her eyes, the confusion in her expression.

A white-hot streak of fear jolts through me. Time returns to normal, and I let her go and step back. Way back. I just got a glimpse inside my father's head, and it's making me physically sick.

Aiden is already backing his car out of the parking lot. Dalton strolls back into the restaurant, still holding a beer. Others, standing in the doorway, ready to defend, wander back into the bar, and Isabel and I are alone outside.

"What the fuck?" I say. "Why are you protecting him?"

"I'm not. I'm protecting you. He'll litigate a broken fingernail, and he'll enjoy watching you spend your life savings trying to defend yourself against nothing."

"Why did he come all this way?" I'm not yelling, but I'm not exactly calm either. "Is there more between you two than you told me? More to the gun you have or why you have it?"

"I don't know why, but I don't care." Her words are sharp

with anger. "I just want to give him what he wants so he'll leave. I want to move forward, not stay trapped in the past."

I pace a circle, hands at my hips, head down. There's a lot of ugliness inside me right now. Anger and pain that comes from the darkness of my past. I can't seem to separate the now and then. This and that.

"Look," she says, tossing her hands in frustration. "You be however you have to be, and I'll do what I have to do."

"What are you doing? Where are you going?" My questions come out as unintentional demands. Before she answers I add, "You're not going by yourself."

"I'm sure as shit not going with you." She opens the door to her Jeep. "I stopped seeing him, because he treated me like this. I'm not going backward. Fuck that."

25

Isabel

I feel like a failure as I turn into Safeway's parking lot. Like a shitty human being. Like a loser who can't manage her own damn life no matter how hard she tries.

"I'm so fucking done with this." I've spent the last five years pretending to be something I'm not. Wishing and working and waiting, only to be disappointed and passed over time and time again. I'm ashamed of how far I've fallen since graduating. How long I let it go on without asking for help out of shame.

My heart is shredded over Logan's doubt and accusations, but I can't exactly say he's wrong. I have been telling him only part of the story. Still, it's *my* story to tell, dammit. I don't have to tell him just because he wants to hear it. And I *was* planning on telling him, just not quite like this or quite this soon.

I park toward the front of the stores, directly across from a marijuana dispensary that uses retired cops for security—it's amazing what a girl can learn in casual conversation at a bar. One of the cops is always out front. It's the next best thing to meeting in the police station parking lot.

I shut down the Jeep and drop my head back against the seat. The sight of Logan's expression when I left haunts me. I can only hope he'll listen after he's cooled off. *If* he cools off.

The sound of a car nearby pulls my eyes open to find Aiden coming up beside me. I roll my eyes to the roof. "Here we go."

Determined to remain civil, I get out of the Jeep and round the back.

"Where's your fireman?" he asks as he gets out of the car. I immediately know he's drunk. I didn't notice it at the bar, but I was distracted by a lot at the time, more concerned with Logan than Aiden.

"None of your damn business." I pull the rifle from the back of the Jeep and put the rosewood box on the trunk of his rental. "Good luck getting that back to New York on a plane."

Surprise darts through his eyes.

I laugh. "I see you didn't think ahead. Don't know why I'm surprised. Your ego eclipses all rational thought."

"I'm not the one who stole someone else's things."

"My bank account says different. And technically, this is mine. But I want to get rid of you so badly, I'm willing to let all that go." I gesture toward the box. "So there you go, asshole. Knock yourself out."

I turn toward the Jeep and emotionally release all the anger I've had pent up around that damned rifle. In hindsight, the whole situation has to be the stupidest thing I've ever done.

The second I feel his hand on my arm, I jerk away. "*Don't. Touch. Me.*"

"The gun isn't the only bad blood between us. Your exit interview reflected poorly on me."

"Damn right it did." I put a hand against his chest and push. "*Back off* or I'll knee you in the nuts."

He laughs. "Not in front of that cop, you won't."

"Try me."

I didn't mean it literally, but he steps into me and slides his arm around my waist.

"Damn you," I say as I slam my knee into his groin.

His body bends in a sharp forty-five-degree angle, his eyes bug out, and his mouth rounds into an O. Then his knees buckle. I'm not sure if he's trying to pull me down or trying to keep himself up, but we both end up on the ground.

The knee of my jeans rips, and pain shoots through my leg. "*You fucking asshole.*"

I'm trying to shove him off me and untangle myself when I find the dispensary's cop, one I haven't met, looking down at us with a here-we-go expression. "Well, good evening, folks. What seems to be the problem here?"

"He's an asshole," I say, "and he had his hands where they don't belong."

"She's a bitch," Aiden says, "and she stole my stuff."

"Ain't love grand," the cop says. "Get up, hands against the vehicle."

I'm relieved and righteous until it's clear he wants *both* of us to put our hands on the vehicle.

"It's not me," I tell the cop. "It's him. I just came to drop something off for him."

"The gun she stole."

"I can't steal something I paid for."

"Whose name is listed as the owner?" he spits back.

"Ma'am, put your hands behind your back." He doesn't wait for me to obey, just grabs one hand and clicks cold metal cuffs on both wrists.

My first thought is why me? Then Aiden's *"the gun she stole"* drifts through my mind, and I realize the cop thinks I'm the biggest threat, which is laughable.

"You can't be serious." Does this sense of shame ever end? Am I slated to continue these shitty patterns the rest of my life? I have a sickening split-second image of me barefoot and pregnant, the baby daddy drinking beer from a can on the porch in a wifebeater while listening to a ball game.

Aiden starts laughing. "God, I've got to get a picture of this. Wait till this makes the rounds through the office."

He's laughing and laughing and laughing. Definitely drunk.

A second police unit pulls into the parking lot and stops in front of my Jeep. Two cops get out, and my mortification only quadruples when I see two men I *do* know from the bar. Dennis Delgado, a man in his fifties, takes my arm and steers me toward his cruiser.

"Wait, what..." Panic sizzles in my stomach. "What's going on?"

He stops where I can lean my butt against the cruiser's fender, releases my arm, and reaches into his breast pocket for a notebook. Then cues the mic on his shoulder. "Sixteen-sixty requesting the assistance of a female officer at the Bloombridge shopping center."

I drop my head and bite my lip against tears. Angry tears. Futile tears. This doesn't happen to me. This happens to other people, stupid people who do stupid things.

Well, shit. I guess that describes me. I'm caught in a vortex of stupidity. If I ever wished a hole would open up and swallow me alive, this would be that moment.

"You're not a girl I saw getting in trouble like this," Dennis says, his voice calm, but with a fatherly shame-on-you edge. "Tell me what's happening here tonight."

I reiterate what's going on—in far too much detail, because I'm rambling, then hear Aiden's voice grow louder and louder as he is cuffed, and his life gets just as real as mine.

There is a God.

I swear an hour has passed by the time I've been searched by a female cop I don't know, and we've straightened out absolutely nothing except that Aiden was driving drunk and his hands weren't where they belonged, as was my knee. Owner-ship of the rifle is still in question.

I'm going to jail. *Jail.* How did this happen? How is this my life? What in the hell am I doing wrong to end up in shitty situations again and again?

They put me in the back of the female cop's cruiser, Aiden in the back of Dennis's. This is all very fortunate, because if my hands were free and Aiden was within reach, I might very well throttle him. For real.

26

Logan

I pace to the window and look through the open blinds for what feels like the hundredth time since I got home from the bar. I'm caught between worry and anger. I was pissed for the first few hours, but it's midnight now.

Isabel isn't answering my texts or phone calls, and I'm terrified something has happened to her. She's not at Tucker's or the fire station, not with Natalie or Maya. I've checked with all the hospitals, but no one's seen her.

Her last words to me could have been considered a breakup, and I can't get images of her and fucktard out of my head.

I shouldn't care. She does exactly what I've disallowed in relationships since my mother died—she lies. But I guess logic doesn't always line up with emotions, because I'm so crazy about her, I can't think straight.

Lucky can barely keep his eyes open, but he's watching me pace and occasionally whines, like he knows I'm stressed.

When my cell rings, I grab it off the table so fast, I fumble and almost drop it. "Jesus Christ." A split second before I hit Answer, I read the screen, and it's a number I don't know. "Hello?"

"Hey, Logan, it's Corbett."

Panic seizes my chest. Hearing from a cop tonight is my worst nightmare.

"You there?" he asks.

"Yeah." I force myself to breathe. "Is it Isabel?"

"She's fine," are his first words, and the relief is so all-encompassing, I press a hand to the back of a chair to steady myself.

"Okay."

"She's in jail."

"*What?*"

"She got into a conflict with that guy you wanted me to look into, McBride. Parker and Delgado brought them in. McBride is charged with a DUI and assault. Isabel is charged with assault."

I drop my head and close my eyes. "Jesus Christ."

"To be fair," Corbett says, "she kneed him in the balls when he put his hands on her, but she refused her phone call, and McBride insisted on pressing charges, so they had to bring Isabel in. When I came on duty, she threatened me with bodily harm if I called you or Tucker. I told her threatening a law enforcement official is a crime, but she didn't think I was funny."

I would laugh, but I'm not finding this situation funny either. It's an ugly pattern from my life—a man treating a woman like shit only to have her go right back to him. The fact that Isabel followed that pattern to a T makes something deep inside me go cold.

In my mother's case, that behavior got her killed. In victims' cases I've seen through my job over the years, that only resulted in more beatings, more severe injuries, and, on a couple of occasions I can think of, like the recent woman with a knife in her chest, a fate similar to my mother's. Now, it's Isabel, and as far as I'm concerned, there's no fixing that fucked-up mindset. I've heard of women kicking the sick habit, but I've never seen it for myself.

"I talked to McBride," Corbett says. "He says if she drops her assault charges, he'll drop his. I'm pretty sure Isabel will tell me to go fuck myself if I ask her to drop the charges. She's still fuming over the whole thing. Getting arrested for the first time can be...humbling, in an infuriating, humiliating kind of way."

I slide into a chair, prop my elbows on the table, and rub my face. "I assume this is over the rifle."

"Sounds that way. It's in evidence. We're still trying to work out who the actual owner is. I'll talk to the chief when he gets in tomorrow morning."

"Okay, I'll be there in fifteen minutes."

I disconnect, set my phone on the table, and clasp my hands in front of my mouth. I'm relieved that she's okay, but like the parent of a missing kid, the relief over finding them safe gives way to anger over having been put in the position to worry in the first place.

Trying to calm myself before I reach the jail only makes me wonder about all I still don't know, and I'm angrier than ever when I pull into the parking lot.

Inside, Corbett leads me toward the metal door of a cell. As he's unlocking it, I look through the small window and see Isabel lying on one of the benches, ankles crossed, one arm over her eyes, and I experience a whirlwind of emotions.

"Tell McBride she'll drop the charges," I tell Corbett. "I want to take her home."

Corbett nods. "I'll get the paperwork started."

He lets me into the room, then closes and locks it behind me. She lifts the arm covering her eyes and glances toward me. Then she swivels into a sitting position and yells, "*Corbett, you sonofabitch.*"

She rests her elbows on her thighs and shoves her hands through her hair, then sits back.

I lean against the opposite wall and cross my arms. "Want to tell me what happened?"

"I tried to clean up my own fucking mess. That's what happened."

"You need to drop the assault charges so I can take you home."

"That fucking bastard."

"How long have you known he was in town?"

"I saw him at the hockey game, but then lost him again, and he wouldn't respond to calls or texts."

I feel pressure building deep inside me. "He was at the *game* and you didn't tell me?"

"There was nothing to tell. I didn't know where he went."

"You could have told me he was in town."

"Why? So you could worry about nothing? You just won your game. You were so happy. I didn't want to pull you down." She rubs her face with both hands. "Go home. I don't have the energy for this."

Corbett opens the door and leans in. "She's free to go. She just has to sign some papers on the way out."

He closes the door, and I stare at the cement floor, a whole different scenario eating at me.

"He stole from you, took advantage of you, and stalked you across the country. Not only didn't you tell me he was here, but you also deliberately made contact with him." My voice rises until I'm just short of yelling. "You made plans to meet him without telling me."

"You're not my keeper. I don't require your permission to do anything."

Maybe not, but this is all too reminiscent of the sick way my parents operated. "What is this really about? Are you seriously over him, or am I just a way to teach him a lesson or make him jealous?"

She looks at me with daggers. "I don't appreciate the insinuation that I'm as fucked-up as your mother or that I used you."

I stare at her a long moment, chewing the inside of my cheek, trying to sort things out in my head. But the longer I look at the situation, the more insanity I see.

Corbett returns. "You ready to go?"

"No," she barks, deliberate but hurt. "He's leaving. I'm not. At least not with him."

"Oooookay," Corbett says. "I'll just let you two work that out."

When the door closes, I say, "Tell me the truth about him. There's more between you than a breakup. You're both way too angry for that to be the biggest rift."

She looks at the wall behind me, her jaw flexing. "He put my name in for a promotion at work," she says deliberately, like the words are being pried from her mouth. "I thought he was a good guy, and we started dating. It didn't take me long to discover he isn't a good guy, and I broke it off."

I wait, but she doesn't go on. "And?"

Her hot eyes meet mine. "And he got me fired the same way he got me hired, with a comment to the right person. I guess my exit interview caused problems for him."

"Why did you let it get that far? Why didn't you just get another job?"

"Because I'm not Maya."

"What's that supposed to mean?"

"It means Maya is successful. I'm not."

I pace the room, trying to get my head around everything. Get my heart on board. I'm crazy about her, which is exactly why I'm being so rigid about getting down to the truth. "What does that mean?"

"It means I'm a loser, Logan." She looks at me, anger and hurt in her eyes. "I never made it. After I graduated, I dried up."

I'm still trying to figure out what that means when she keeps talking.

"I graduated in the top ten percent of my class, but only the top one percent get the hot jobs in New York. I tried and tried and tried, but was always rejected. The job Aiden got me was as an assistant designer where I was previously the window display designer. I thought I'd finally broken through and that with time, I'd climb the ladder. The minute I stopped dating Aiden, he sabotaged every rung in that ladder. You want to know why I know how to do a little bit of everything? It's because I've always had two or three jobs at a time for the last ten years. Dealing cards, serving for a caterer, bartending, you name it. I didn't make it like Maya did."

I'm trying to get my mind around this. "I saw your social media. Tucker always talks about what you're doing in New York. He went to your graduation and stayed in your Manhattan apartment. He didn't stop talking about it for weeks."

Her eyes shine with tears, and she looks away. "The guy who owned that apartment was a customer at the poker club where I was moonlighting. He let me borrow it while Tucker was in town."

Poker club? My gut coils and coils. "It was all lies? Your work, your life? Nothing was real? What about your social media? It's all bullshit?"

"The window displays were mine," she says, referencing her Instagram account while avoiding my gaze, "not the clothes displayed."

"The fashion shows?"

"I worked them."

"They weren't your designs?"

She sighs.

I don't give a flying fuck what fame she did or didn't find in New York, but I sure as hell care about the way she manipulated Tucker and social media and me to shape how she's perceived. "Let's try it this way—what *was* truth?"

Tears track down her cheeks, and she swipes them away. "I'm exhausted. I can't do this right now."

Her tears should sway me, but my mother cried a lot. Cried a lot, yet never changed. Emily cried, but only in an attempt to manipulate me.

I'm struck by how twisted my perceptions have become. I'm broken. So fucking broken. One broken person plus another broken person doesn't make one whole person, let alone two. Emily was broken too. I wonder if this is a pattern in my life— choosing broken women because I was raised by a broken woman.

"Does Tucker know all this?" I ask.

"No one knows. Except Maya. She did some digging after I fixed her tire."

All my air whooshes out. So Maya knew but never told me either. I feel stupid. Stupid and pathetic. "I must have sucker written on my forehead. When were you going to tell me?"

She doesn't answer.

"You *weren't* going to tell me," I answer for her. "You weren't *ever* going to tell me."

"If you'd failed at your dream for five years, would you broadcast it to the world?"

"I'm not the world, and I care about you."

"I stole Maya's fucking scholarship," she yells at me, "then wasted it. How can you forgive that?"

"You're the only person who's ever condemned yourself for taking that scholarship." I pace a circle, my mind tearing apart everything she's ever told me. "Where you lived, where you worked, what you did, how you ended up here, it was all nothing but lies. How can I trust what you're telling me about

Aiden? How can I trust *anything* you tell me? I have no idea who you are, do I?"

"This is exactly why I didn't tell you," she says, dropping back to the bench. "Get out. I don't need this."

I open my mouth—to say *I don't need this either*, but Corbett pokes his head in again, and I decide to leave with those nasty words unspoken.

I exit the jail and sit in my truck. For how long, I don't know. My mind works to separate my mother and all the things she said and did from Isabel. I know the situations are different, but one thing is the same—the lies. Especially on the heels of Emily's whopper of a lie, one that first terrified me, then hollowed me out.

I sit there, a knife in my gut, desperate to find a way to extract it without bleeding out, but experience has taught me that once the knife is in, you leave it in until you're with professionals who are capable of handling the trauma when it comes out.

Which means it's here to stay.

27

Isabel

It's freaking freezing outside, and I wait in front of the jail for my Uber ride, which is taking forever. To be honest, I'm shocked Uber even operates here.

Hands hidden in my sleeves, arms crossed, I shift from foot to foot and concentrate on the cold to keep the anger and pain and self-disgust from sinking any deeper.

Logan has every right to be angry, but I also have every right to keep my messy past to myself. Only, the hurt and angry look on his face flashes in my mind and cuts me deep.

The only car on the road approaches and pulls to the curb. I check the license to the app, and when it matches, I pull open the back door and slide into the warm car. The heat feels so good, I close my eyes and exhale sharply.

"Hey there, Isabel."

My eyes pop open to find Larry Moore grinning at me from the driver's seat. My heart sinks, joined by dread. Larry is a retired teacher who now spends his days volunteering—at the library, the church, the school, the fire department. When he's not doing any of that, he's on a barstool at the Cockloft.

It's painfully clear this screwup will no longer stay between Corbett, Aiden, Logan, and me. Now the entire town will know what a fuckup I've become. What a liar I've been.

"Hi, Larry. Can you take me to the Cockloft, please?" He already knows where we're going. I'm just trying to get him to stop grinning at me like he's got a secret and take me to Tucker's.

He faces forward and pulls back onto the street. "So," he says with a long pause. "Jail. Sure is the last place I expected to find you."

"I don't suppose we could keep this between us."

He laughs.

I sigh and stare out the side window, thinking about nothing but the physical pain in my body. My brain is fried. My heart burns. My stomach is stuffed with a concrete pillar.

I came here to fix my life and ended up incinerating it instead.

Thankfully, it's a short drive, so I don't have to ignore Larry's questions for long.

I use the key the guys gave me and make my way up the back staircase toward Tucker's loft, dreading the conversation I know he'll want to have.

He answers the door faster than I expect.

"What—" Then it hits me. He's sleeping on the sofa, closer to the front door. Maya is using his bed. "Shit. I forgot Maya was here."

"Come on in," he grumbles, stepping aside. "I'm pretty sure you'll still fit in the bathtub."

That brings a rush from the past and how, as a kid, I used to climb into the bathtub to hide when Mom was fighting with whatever guy was in her life at the time. I'm not sure why, but when Tucker wasn't home, hiding in the bathtub behind a closed shower curtain seemed the safest place to be.

I force my mind toward other sleeping options, but it's late, and I don't feel like driving forty-five minutes to the closest Motel 6. It's also too cold to sleep in my car.

I step inside, struck by the fact that my life is still in a fucking downward spiral I can't seem to stop.

Maya comes out of the bedroom wearing sweats, her hair down and messy, no makeup. The sight shoots me right back to high school, and I'm hit by a staggering loss on top of all my other misery.

"Is everything okay?" she asks.

I'm not sure how to answer that. "Logan's fine."

The concern fades from her expression, replaced by something resembling sympathy. "Come on, sleep with me."

"No, that's okay. I just forgot you were here. I'll find another place." I turn toward the door.

"Don't be stupid," Maya says. "We've only shared a bed a couple hundred times. Get in here."

Tucker falls back on the sofa and throws his arm across his eyes. "Don't stay up all night giggling, don't eat me out of house and home, and no fucking pillow fights."

I laugh, because that's exactly how Maya and I used to spend our sleepovers when we were kids.

"We've given him sleepover PTSD," I tell Maya as I pass into the bedroom. I take one look at the rumpled sheets and add, "I see you still do gymnastics in your sleep."

"Shut up," she says without heat as she drops back into bed.

I slide out of my jacket and get a better look at what she's wearing. "I didn't even know Givenchy made sweats. How much did those cost?"

"They were a gift," she says. "Don't judge."

I don't want to know who gave them to her or how that came about, only I do. I wish we could stay up all night talking about our lives in New York. Then the chasm between our experiences hits me, and I consider Motel 6 again.

"If you try to leave, I'll tackle you," she says, reading my mind and making me smile.

I toss my jacket over a chair, then sit on the edge of the mattress to take off my boots.

"What happened with Logan?" she asks.

His angry, hurt expression at the jail instantly fills my mind, and I exhale a moan.

The first words I think are *I fucked it up like I do everything in life*, but remember he was the one who made Aiden and my life in New York a problem, not me. I didn't lie to him. I went out of my way not to lie to him. Yet we still ended up here.

"You were right. My half-truths didn't go over well with him. It's just my past coming back to haunt me." I reach under my sweater and unfasten my bra, then take it off without removing my clothes, a trick I learned at summer camp in sixth grade. A trick Maya taught me.

"Or his coming back to haunt him," Maya suggests.

"Probably both," I agree.

I slide into bed. Maya turns off the light on her nightstand, and darkness fills the room, alleviated only by the moonlight streaming in the window. It reminds me of my night with Logan, the way our bodies were lit up in moonlight and shadow. A yearning I don't completely understand hits me in the gut.

"I hear you got an interview at Threadbare in San Francisco." Maya's voice is soft, but it still seems to fill the room.

Shit. I forgot to cancel that. "How did you know?"

"Natalie told me."

I search my mind and find the memory of telling Natalie the call from Threadbare was the was the reason I left the rink, not to run after my shitty ex.

"One of the girls I interned with the summer of my junior

year works there," Maya says. "If you really want it, I can call and put in a good word for you."

I'm dumbfounded into silence, and the room seems to ring with her words long after they dissipate.

"Or not..." she adds.

"Why?"

"Why what?"

"Why would you do that?"

"Sounds like New York has embedded itself in your bones. People occasionally do good things for other people. It's called humanity. It's sometimes hard to spot in New York, but not everything in life has to be a competition or a hustle."

"Says the woman with the dream job," I say softly. I don't begrudge Maya her success. I know how hard she had to work to get it.

My mind rolls backward in time, to my three jobs, scraping by, working like a dog, never getting a break. Yeah, I guess I have viewed life as competition, and I definitely hustle. It's all I know. It's all I've ever known.

"You never answered my question." Maya rolls toward me, props herself up on her elbow, and rests her head in one hand. "What did you see in McBride? If I were a betting woman, I'd put money on his status as a narcissist."

"Wish I had that clarity. Could have saved me a *lot* of trouble."

"You probably didn't work with him very often."

"Like never."

"I've met him several times at events. Know people who know him. He's sexy until he opens his mouth."

That makes laughter bubble up. "Ain't that the truth. Doesn't matter. It's over."

"What happened after you left the bar?"

I take a deep breath and relay my story to her. She knows the worst at this point. No sense trying to save face.

"Seriously?" Maya says, as if I've just told her about unicorns and rainbows.

"Unfortunately, yes. When Logan came to get me, he was an ass, and I refused to go home with him."

"He can get a little heavy-handed now and then. It's for the right reason. He just sucks at delivery sometimes." She laughs again with a shake of her head. "You always were good at finding trouble."

"Only because I knew you'd get me out of it. Ever regret not going into law?"

She shrugs. "I deal with enough idiots as it is. Fashion isn't known for employing the most easygoing crayons in the box."

"But then there's you."

"Aww." Her face breaks into a smile. A big, authentic smile that glows in the dark. "I get into my share of debates and arguments. It's just related to fashion, not crime. Although, a lot of the designs that come out of New York are truly criminal."

That makes me laugh. Hard.

A little more tension leaves my body, but I'm struck by a hot, quick jolt of loss. I don't know if you ever get over losing a childhood best friend the way I did, but it seems safe to bet the pain hollowing me out right now tells me you don't *ever* get over it. And Maya isn't the only friend I've lost. I can add Logan to the list too.

"I wish you had told me about your mom's boyfriend instead of bailing," she says, voice softer. "I would have tied his balls in a knot."

"I wish I'd known about your mom's death before the funeral. I would have come."

My mind veers toward that time in our lives. To the decisions I made on the fly—telling Tucker about Derik, taking Maya's scholarship, leaving without telling her, and losing touch because I couldn't face what a shitty friend I'd been to the best and most loyal friend I'd ever had.

"You really have to cut yourself some slack," Maya says. "We were all just kids trying to not only parent ourselves, but stay out of the messes our parents created for us."

My phone dings with an email notification.

"If Aiden harasses you electronically, it's a crime," Maya says.

"Really?"

"Really. Save all your correspondence."

"Guess if anyone would know it's you." I'm smiling as I look at my email. I already know it's not Aiden. He would have texted or called.

"Just ju—" The last part of "junk" cuts out as I see an email from another company where I applied for a job as an associate designer.

"What?" Maya asks.

"It's from Charlie Moss. I mean, not *the* Charlie Moss, but the company."

Charlie Moss is the Donna Karen of athletic wear and has all of Hollywood in his back pocket.

"Nuh-uh." She bolts up and scoots close until we're shoulder to shoulder staring at my phone, the way we used to read each other's texts.

Now, we're reading an email that says a girl I went to school with got ahold of the résumé I sent in and recommended me for the opening. They want me to come in for an interview.

"I applied for an opening there," I say, "but I never thought..."

I never thought my résumé would make it past the lowest-level clerk in the company.

"You know Crystal Morrison?" Maya asks, her eyes wide.

"The queen bitch of bitches? I did an internship with her at Kate Spade one summer. She spits poison."

I forget just how small the fashion industry is. The only

reason Maya and I never crossed paths is because I existed on a parallel plane of reality well below hers.

"She does," I say, remembering Crystal's cold, calculating, competitive personality. "She's also an absolute genius when it comes to design. Truly out of the box. I learned a lot from her."

"I never thought she was capable of relationships."

"Oh, she's not. We weren't friends."

"How'd you get a recommendation from her?"

"Probably for saving her ass on a final project junior year. She was making some crazy-ass wraparound dress and ran out of feathers. God, she was an absolute wreck. Had a full-fledged meltdown in the studio at four a.m. We were the only two there. I ran home and grabbed a stupid boa I'd picked up—I don't even know where, Halloween or Mardi Gras or something —and let her use it to finish. She got an A, of course. She was using yellow feathers and my boa was pink, but she mixed the colors and, Jesus, how she made that thing come out worthy of a runway still baffles me."

As does this job offer. The second one in twenty-four hours. The kind I would have killed for in New York. Is this the universe nudging me toward leaving? Nudging me away from Logan?

"Associate designer," Maya says, scanning the email. "Well, I guess if you're not going to stay here and start your own thing, Morris or Threadbare wouldn't be a bad second choice. You'd rise through the ranks and be a full-fledged designer in no time. Someone just needs to give you a chance."

I've thought that more times than I can count. I thought every job I went for would be that chance. The opportunities were clearly implied in the ads, but it was all just an illusion. Over the years, I've learned that assistant designers make coffee and run errands. That merchandizing managers bow to the assistant buyers and the buyers.

So many jobs. So much bullshit. But I kept banging my

head against that wall. Always hoping. Never realizing. It's an exhausting cycle. My interest in both the jobs curdles.

My past disappointments turn my mind to Logan. To our argument. To the way he walked out of the jail.

"Though," Maya says, pulling me back from my thoughts, "I still think designing for someone else so they can profit off your work is beneath you."

"You have no idea what I'm capable of. As far as you know, I could design like a kindergartener."

"I did my research," Maya says. "I know what I'm talking about."

"I don't know who you talked to. Anyone who knows me knows I've been trapped in dead-end jobs since college."

"I talked to people you went to school with."

I roll my eyes. "That was forever ago."

"Those kinds of skills don't just evaporate."

"Doesn't matter. I learned the hard way that wizards create these job ads, and the magic fades the day you start work."

"Jaded are we?"

"After you've been lied to often enough, I guess you just start expecting everything—"

To be a lie, sticks in my throat.

All the times I've been lied to about jobs has made me cynical about believing their promises. The same way all the lies told to Logan has made him distrustful of women. And I realize I doubt all jobs the same way Logan doubts all women.

My shoulders sag under the weight of this epiphany. "Well, shit."

28

Logan

I pull into Station 21, my gut still aching.

I didn't see or hear Isabel come back to the motel last night, and there was no sign of her when I woke up. So she either came late and left early, or she stayed somewhere else— maybe even just stayed in jail.

One part of me feels like shit. Like making a big deal out of this is stupid and petty. Then there's the other part. The one that reminds me how one small lie turns into many bigger lies. That if she can lie about this, she could lie about anything.

I head into the station, praying it's a busy shift so I won't have time to stew over Isabel. Lucky runs into the engine bay, spots Master on a bench, and runs that direction. Master jumps into the closest turnout boot and hides until Lucky pokes his nose in, then swats at him. Lucky jumps back, just escaping Master's claws. This is a familiar game. One they can play for hours, only today, it doesn't feel the least bit entertaining.

Instead of going through the front door and the kitchen where I know everyone will be bullshitting and exchanging information about the prior shift, I go through the engine bay and dump my gear at my locker, then start my regular routine —safety checking my SCBA, then restocking the rig.

I'm thinking about a long run to flush out some of this edginess when Tucker and Cole come into the bay.

I stop what I'm doing and sit on the back steps of the rescue. "Did Isabel stay with you last night?"

"She and Maya shared my bed," Tucker says, leaning against the side of engine three. "I still don't know what she's more upset about, lying about her life or fucking things up with you."

Sure, guilt, jump on board. Settle your ass right between anger and hurt. Plenty of room.

"What difference does it make?" Tucker asks. "So she embellished her life a little. It's nothing we haven't done."

I lift a brow.

"Using the firefighter angle to get chicks. We've all done it," he says, spitting out examples. "The flames were a hundred feet high. We barely made it out alive. I got out of there seconds before the roof caved in. The Jaws nearly took my arm off. I grabbed one kid under each arm and ran like hell."

"That's all you, dickhead," I tell him.

Tucker glances at Cole, who's smirking.

"Okay, fine," Tucker says, "maybe that is me. My point is that she's still the same person who showed up here a little over a week ago, and you were into her then."

"Has she lied to you since she's been here?" Cole asks.

I want to say hell yes, but my memory isn't coming up with any proof. "Lies by omission."

"You sure about that?" Cole asks. "You're not taking any responsibility for maybe creating your own interpretation with the information you had?"

I push to my feet. "I need a run."

Tucker pushes me back to the step by the shoulder. "You

told me you wouldn't fuck her over."

"She's the one who created a life built on lies. How can I trust a woman who can't shoot straight? Aren't you the least bit bothered by the way she portrayed herself in New York? You came back bragging about something that didn't even exist."

"No, I'm not. It wasn't my life, it wasn't about me."

"Well, this *is* my life. And it *is* about me."

"Maybe you ought to consider other character traits before you throw in the towel," Cole says. "Like her offering to make Natalie's fucking wedding dress without taking a dime, and pitching in at the bakery when she has to drag her ass in there at an hour she finds ungodly."

"She started renovating that shithole of a motel without being asked and without expecting anything in return," Tucker says. "In fact, what has she ever asked for from you?"

I'm thinking about that and coming up empty—again—when Tucker goes on. "She sold out of all the designs she brought with her. She may not be in Bergdorf's windows, but that doesn't make her any less a designer. And she told you about fuck face."

Great, Aiden again. "Only after I found out something was going on and hounded her about it."

"But she didn't lie, did she? If you're going to make a case for lies by omission, you're going to be looking just as bad as you're making her out to be."

"What does that mean?"

"You didn't tell her about Emily," Coles says. "She heard about it from Natalie. That could be considered a lie of omission."

I roll my eyes. "That's not the same."

"Maybe not, but it could have given her a heads-up about how touchy you'd be over lies," Cole says.

"Why are you both trying to make this my fault?"

"Because it is," Tucker yells. "You're so fucking dense. And now we're going to lose her. She's got two job interviews tomorrow and the next day in LA and San Francisco. Thanks to you, she'll probably take one, you dumb shit."

A wash of cold spreads through my body. A splash of panic mixed with a whole lot of anger over something else I didn't know. "What job interviews?"

The alarm sounds before I get an answer.

Tucker points at me. "We're not done."

I outweigh Tucker by twenty pounds, all muscle, but he's got at least three inches on me and the fucker is goddamned intimidating when he wants to be. That might be because I've also seen him fight. And I've seen what the losers look like when he does.

On the way to the engines, Cole lags behind and stops as I open the rescue's passenger door. "Hey, man, Isabel isn't Emily. She's not your mom either." His tone is understanding and sober. "Emily manipulated you. Your mother was a head case. That's not Isabel, and you know it. Think about it. Her lies were designed to keep her shit from spilling over onto others. She could have told us she was struggling, asked for money, or played us, but she stood proud and dealt with her own problems. It's not her fault you're so fucked up."

"Asshole," I bite out.

I climb in the rescue, and Bobby slides behind the wheel. I'm trying to sort out the knots inside me when Bobby says, "What'd you do to fire up Medina?"

The sirens sound excruciatingly loud today, and I rub my forehead. "Long, complicated story."

I prop my elbow on the window ledge and rest my head in my hand. My mind fills with the feel of Isabel's naked thigh sliding between mine, and heat scores my skin. Then the whisper of her lips touching my neck floats in, and my heart aches. But it still wears the shadow that descended after I left the police station last night.

My mind tells me it was the right thing to do. That her lack of honesty is a problem. Would continue to be a problem. But then there are the things Cole and Tucker pointed out. Things I'd thought of on my own, but which didn't sway me back toward Isabel. It's like I've already created a concrete block between us.

Sure, I'm pissed. Sure, I'm hurt. And yeah, I guess I consider us broken up. But the idea of her moving away is a whole different kind of finality. A finality that I guess I wasn't quite ready for.

The entire eight minutes it takes to get to the mountain where climbers are stranded, I try to picture my life without her. Even though she's only been back a short time, I realize my life took on a different light, a higher-pitched buzz. And dammit, I find myself caught between the fear of living with someone I can't trust and living without someone I care about as much as I care about her.

Life just fuckin' sucks sometimes.

Three hours and several broken bones later—for the patient, not me—I return to the firehouse to find Maya in the rec room, lounging in a chair, watching television, Master and Bates in her lap.

"Hey." I wander into the living room, Lucky at my heels, and drop into the sofa. "What's up?"

Lucky wags his whole body at the sight of Maya, but when he pops his paws on the arm of the chair, Bates gives a demon-like hiss that causes Lucky to seek refuge behind my legs.

"I'm leaving early," she says.

"Why?"

She shrugs. "Bullshit at work."

"When?"

"Later today. I'll get an Uber to the airport."

"Okay." I'm disappointed I haven't had a lot of time with her. "Sounds like you and Isabel mended fences."

"Yeah." She's smiling in a way that makes me think of her as a teenager. "Basically, I decided not to hold her past mistakes against her and I forgave myself for the part I played in our breakup. It feels good."

I nod, gritting my teeth with jealousy. I wish I could do that —just forgive her and believe it won't happen again. Just forgive myself and move on.

"It's that easy, you know," she says.

"What?"

"Forgiving. We're all human. We all make mistakes. All you have to do is let it go."

A couple of volunteers are hanging in the kitchen, and I glance over my shoulder. "Can you give us a minute, guys?"

Once they head into the engine bay, I turn back to Maya. "Some of us make mistakes, and some of us make a habit of making mistakes."

"I know Mom and Dad fucked us up, but they're gone. Everything you do now is a choice."

"If Isabel had lied about something that didn't matter, sure, I might be able to let it go, but she lied about all the fundamental things that make a person who they are—where she works, what she does, what's happening in other areas of her life, her relationships. I don't have any idea who she really is."

And I don't know how to put my trust in someone like that.

"Look," Maya says, "you can either forgive or you can't. There's no middle of the road. And Isabel deserves someone who can give his all, who can love completely, not only when she's perfect, because we both know there is no perfect."

Every nerve inside me is on fire. First Tucker and Cole, now Maya. "Jesus Christ, this is turning out to be a shitastic day."

"You need to understand our career," Maya says. "It's creative, which also means it's soul driven, and every step of the way, our peers are watching, just waiting for us to fail so they can rise into the lead. One of the reasons Isabel didn't rise in the industry is because she's sweet and she's always giving—of her time, her talent, her knowledge. To do well means you have to be cutthroat. Isabel doesn't have a cutthroat bone in her body."

That rings true. She is sweet. She is giving. In fact, she's often selfless. I love that warm side of her.

"She has everything she needs to make it in this industry," Maya says. "Everything except the mean-girl streak."

"You don't have it either, but you made it."

"Oh, brother, you haven't seen me at work."

"What does that have to do with the lies?"

Maya shakes her head. "You really are dense."

I push to my feet, angry that she's right. I can't connect the dots. "I'm going to take a shower. Let me know you got home safely."

Maya stands and steps into my path, both cats cradled in one arm, the other hand against my chest. And her eyes are glittering mad. "Don't dismiss me."

"I don't want to talk about this anymore."

"Because you *know* you're wrong. You know you're wrong, and you can't stand to admit it."

"None of this matters, anyway. She'll take one of those jobs down south and disappear."

"When did you get so pessimistic and rigid?"

"Maybe when Mom lied once too often and ended up in the morgue."

"Are you going to use that as an excuse your whole life? There's always an upside to every situation, but you have to be willing to see it. The upside of my childhood was watching you stand up for me and Mom. You didn't care if you were going to get the beating he was planning for one of us. You always met the challenge head-on. You taught me to stand up for myself. And, honestly, I think that's the reason I've done so well in this industry. Isabel may have had a shitty living situation, but it was shitty in a different way. And she's a different person. What makes someone strong can make another person weak."

"Isabel isn't weak."

"But she's not me, is she?"

I don't answer, because my mind is echoing Isabel's "Because I'm not Maya" at the jail.

"And don't pretend you don't have secrets," Maya says. "Things you don't want other people to know."

I look up and lift my hands.

"Emily," is all she has to say.

"Fuck."

"You didn't tell me about it because it was embarrassing. Getting caught in the fake-baby situation makes you feel stupid and puts you in a vulnerable position. You have to choose whether to be weak and give in to Emily, maintaining the relationship out of guilt, or get your independence from Emily at the risk of being viewed as a heartless prick. How is that different from Isabel being ashamed of what she never accomplished? The one person you want to look good in front of is a guy you're interested in. Isabel is a what-you-see-is-what-you-get girl. Whether she's a millionaire or a fast-food clerk, she has the same heart she did as a kid. I, for one, am glad to see it."

"I don't know what you want me to say."

"I don't want you to say anything. I want you to listen from here." She smacks my chest. Then taps my head. "Not here. Your issues aren't Isabel's fault. Don't punish her for what Mom did. Or what Emily did. Or what any other woman in your past did or didn't do."

She stands and hands over Master and Bates. "Think about it. I'd hate for you to miss out on an amazing woman. I'll call you when I'm home."

Even though I'm mad at her, I set the cats on the sofa and give her a hug, and long after she's gone, my head is still pounding from all she said.

29

Isabel

My anger and hurt have softened into a blah type of depression. Even the designer clothes Maya is letting me borrow for the interviews don't cheer me up.

I've got a flight at 6:00 a.m. tomorrow, and Tucker got coverage to leave work early and take me to the airport. This is something I've wanted for so long, yet my heart isn't in it. I spent the night trying to get ramped up for it, imagining how fun it would be to explore a new city. Make new friends. Actually get a job doing something I love.

But with the rift between Logan and me so fresh, all I feel is loss. I need to apologize for not giving him the whole story. I don't expect him to accept it, but I have to give it anyway—as soon as I get back from these interviews. He should have cooled off by then.

I snug boots in the corner of the suitcase and look at the finished product, with my heart heavy and my interest in this whole event depleted. This just feels like a chore. A lonely, disappointing chore.

"You've got a pretty sweet deal right here."

Maya's words have been haunting me. And the more I think about it, the more I realize how much I've built here in such a short time. Friends, family, community, business. Comfort, happiness, a sense of belonging. But what's really messing with my mind are my feelings for Logan. I even miss Lucky under my feet.

But there's something I still need in my life: validation. Having a company like Charlie Moss or Threadbare value my work... It's what I've always dreamed of.

The look on Logan's face when he left the jail won't leave my head. He'd already put me behind him. He couldn't possibly care about me that much if it was that easy to shut down and walk away from what was between us. Maybe I read him just as wrong as he read me.

Maybe we're both too fucked up to find happiness.

"You ready?"

Maya's voice startles me. I stuff my feelings and smile at her standing in the doorway to Tucker's bedroom. "As ready as I'll ever be."

She strolls into the room and stares at the suitcase. "I'm leaving."

"What?" I turn toward her. "Why?"

"They need me back at work. Some fire I need to put out."

My heart sinks. "I was hoping you'd be here when I got back so we could talk about the jobs."

"There's this thing, it's called a phone..."

I return my attention to the suitcase, already feeling another wave of loss, and I ask a question that's been nagging at me. "Why do you stay in New York when you know what a jungle the fashion industry is?"

"Because I'm a lion in that jungle. My only threat is a poacher, and I've got an eye for poachers. Besides, I'm getting as much out of New York as New York is getting out of me. I won't be there forever. It's just a step in my grander life plan."

"That's mysterious."

"I'm still in the keep-it-to-myself phase."

"Well, whatever it is, I have no doubt you'll be successful."

"As will you." She opens her arms, and we hug.

"I'm sorry I let so much time get between us," I tell her.

"Me too." She pulls away and smiles at me. "Not anymore, right?"

"Right."

"If these jobs aren't perfect," she says, "don't take them. You're a gem and if they don't appreciate you, fuck 'em."

I laugh. "Says the girl with the kickass career."

"Sometimes you get a kickass career by saying no."

She gives me one more hug, then she's gone. And now I'm suffering the loss of both Robertses.

I drop to the bed and stare out the window to all the trees and the stormy autumn sky, trying to figure out what I really want and what I'm willing to do to get it.

30

Isabel

My cell pulls me from a dream. A horrible dream where Logan and Maya hate me, Tucker pities me, Cole is disappointed in me, Natalie fired me, and Aiden still holds a job I desperately want over my head.

My mind grinds through sludge as I get that bizarre where-the-hell-am-I sensation, like I've been transported during sleep. I look around the room and I'm eventually grounded in Hood River, where I fucked things up with the best man I've been with in years. Pain and loss crowd my chest and drag my mood even lower.

I grope the nightstand for my phone. I hurt, physically, mentally, and emotionally, and after everything that's happened, I feel like I need a month's vacation in Bali to clear my misery, heart, body, and soul.

Instead of looking at my cell, I look at the bedside clock, which is showing 4:10 a.m., and wonder if my flights have been changed. Which brings to mind the interviews. And that bottoms out my stomach.

"Fuck," I groan, pulling the phone to my ear and offering a groggy "Hello?"

"I am so, *so* sorry to call this early." It's Mike, the Cockloft's head cook. My mind floods with the hard times his daughter is going through, and I instantly know he needs me to work.

The interviews flash in my mind and a tug-of-war launches inside me—what I should do versus what I want to do. And that confuses me, because what I want is to get the job I've been chasing for years. At least that's what I've wanted for the last decade.

"Hello?" Mike says in my silence.

"Yeah, sorry." I force my mind back. "Are you okay? Is Tori okay?"

"She's got a raging fever and has been throwing up all night. I'm pretty sure she has another abscessed tooth."

I sit up and dangle my legs off the edge of the bed. "Oh, jeez. Poor thing."

"I'm so grateful the bar provides insurance for us, or we'd be on the street by now. I hate to ask, but I'm in a real bind, and all the guys are working."

I rub my eyes, but my brain hasn't kicked into gear yet. "What do you need?"

"I left work early last night, because Tori was sick, thinking I'd go in early and get the food prep done this morning, but I've got to take her in and there's no telling how long it will take."

"Food prep, got it."

Mike starts rattling on about what's on the menu and what food is where in the kitchen. All that needs to be done is staggering. But not near as staggering as watching your daughter suffer.

"I'll handle it," I tell him, cutting him off. I won't remember a fraction of what he's saying anyway. "You just take care of Tori."

"Oh my God." His voice fills with emotion. "I don't know

what I'd do without you. You've been a lifesaver. I haven't had anyone I could count on like this since Cynthia died. I can't even tell you how much I appreciate everything you do for us."

My heart softens and saddens, thinking about leaving and setting him adrift again. "Thank you. Now go take care of your girl."

I hang up and rub my face. Since I'm up, I may as well get started.

I dress and sleepwalk my way downstairs. First things first, I put on a pot of coffee, then lean against the counter thinking about how to juggle everything. I'll have to change my flights. I'll have to hand the baton here over to one of the guys when they can get out of work, then rush to the airport which is an hour away. Longer if I leave here after 6:00 a.m. and hit traffic. One of the other guys will have to take me to the airport, since Natalie and Tina will be at the bakery. Or I can try to get an Uber, but at this hour, there's no telling if that will be possible.

The coffee sputters into the glass pot, and I watch the slow, meditative sight of the filling carafe. My mind slides back into standby. I'm in a fog. Thoughts ping and clang around my brain.

I'm struck by how many options I have. How many people I could ask for a favor, knowing they would make it happen. Tucker, Cole, Natalie, Tina, Betsy, Mike, half a dozen other firefighters at the house, half a dozen locals I've befriended here at the bar, another half dozen women I've sold clothing to. And even after everything going to shit with Logan, I know without question, he would be there for me if I really needed him.

"Jesus," I murmur. "This is my village."

This. Is. My. Village.

The realization brings the burn of tears to my eyes and a balm to my soul.

I *belong* here. I can't leave. No—I don't *want* to leave.

I think of Mike's gratitude for all he has even in the worst of times. The way he juggles everything without complaining puts me to shame. True shame. His gratitude in light of those hardships turns my brain another direction—to all I have to be thankful for. Not only the people here, but the natural beauty and calm, my health, all the skills I've developed throughout my life. Flexibility, tenacity, persistence.

I'm a cat. I always end up on my feet. Only now do I realize I'm grateful for that resilience. That I've looked at my life as a struggle, when what I've really been doing is adapting. Surviving.

But here, I've thrived.

Thrived.

That hits me, makes my mind crank, and wakes me up. I think back through the years, searching for any other time in my life that's given me so much contentment, peace, or belonging, but come up empty.

I feel expansive here. Nurtured. Needed. Loved.

That last one brings Logan to mind. "Man," I say, rubbing my eyes. "I fucked that up."

31

Isabel

I've gotten a lot done in the last two hours. I've chopped and diced all the meats and veggies for the day ahead, made half a dozen different sauces, breaded this, whipped that, mixed the other.

I turn a bag of Portobello mushrooms upside down and dump them into the sink under a stream of water, then proceed to take a brush to each before tossing them into a strainer.

I search inside myself, trying to figure out what's going on in there. I feel relief and loss and fear. So much fear. How will I make money? Where will I live? What does my future look like?

I guess I should have known changing the direction of a career I've wanted for over a decade wouldn't be easy. Nothing about this situation is easy.

"Hey, man, I'm glad you're here. I slept like shit and—"

The deep voice makes me jump. I turn and face Logan with a hand on my heart. "You scared me."

He's wearing jeans and a long-sleeved Henley, the soft fabric following the contours of his wide chest and tight abs.

I'm not ready to face him. I don't have what I want to say figured out, but it looks like I'm going to have to ad-lib. Lucky is dragging behind Logan, but comes to me for pats and plops on the floor at my feet.

"What are you doing here?" He glances at his watch, then at me again, his brow furrowed. "Tucker said you had a six o'clock flight. Where is he?"

My stomach flutters over the missed flight, the change in plans, the uncertain future. "I don't know. I—"

"He left the station right before me. Why are you doing this? What's going on?"

"Mike called—"

"I know about Mike and Tori. He called Tucker this morning. That's why I'm here, because Cole is helping Natalie in the bakery this morning and Tucker is supposed to be taking you to the airport."

I frown. "What time did Mike call Tucker?"

"About five."

"He called me at four. I told him I'd handle it. I texted Tucker to tell him I wasn't going to the airport."

"Then where did he—" I can read the shift on Logan's face like a headline.

"The flight attendant," we say at the same time.

"That fucker," Logan says. "What a shitty thing to do. He should have covered the kitchen so you could get to California." He rubs his eyes. "Can you call and reschedule? Maybe until later today? I can take you to the airport right now. The flights are about an hour and a half. It's only six. You still have time—"

I slam the handle on the faucet to shut off the water and face him again. "Can you stop talking over me for a second?"

He pulls keys from his pocket. "Let's go. Just leave this. I'll finish it when I get back."

He turns and walks out the kitchen door, leaving it swinging. Lucky stays put. I stare at the door, my hip against the sink, arms crossed. *Five, four, three, two—*

The door opens, and he sticks his head into the room. "Come on. Do you want to make those interviews or not?"

"Not."

He steps into the kitchen. "Did you already reschedule them?"

"No, I canceled them."

"Canceled? As in you're not going *at all*?"

"That's generally what canceled means."

He presses a hand to the counter. "What's going on?"

"I've done a lot of thinking since jail."

His eyes close. "About that—"

"Let me finish," I say, trying not to sound annoyed, but I'm tired and frustrated and I've missed him, even if it's only been barely a day since we were together.

When he crosses his arms and sets his feet, I know I have the floor.

"When it came down to leaving for the interviews, I looked deeper into the job descriptions. They sound good, but over the last few years, none of my jobs turned out to be as advertised. They get dressed up and put on display, but they're often just cardboard facades, and the job doesn't turn out to be even close to what was promised."

I cross my arms and build up for what has to come next. "I realized last night that if you're lied to often enough, you start to distrust everything."

The frustration in his expression dims, and he lowers his gaze to the floor.

"Which made me realize how you must feel about people lying to you. After a lifetime of your mom's lies, and then Emily's lies, I could see how what I did made you doubt me."

He looks up, his expression pained. "I overreacted. I'm sorry."

I didn't realize how badly I'd hoped he'd say that until right this moment. "Me too. For what it's worth, I was going to come clean about Aiden and the mess of my life in New York after the party, when we were alone. Then he showed up at the bar, and all my plans went to shit."

Logan nods.

"I'm not leaving." The words, said aloud, ground me in a way I've never felt before. "That's what I told Tucker, and he evidently took the opportunity to do something so Tucker-like instead of staying at work. I won't be applying to other jobs out of the area. I won't be entertaining offers anywhere else. I'm staying. I'm staying and I'm going to show you that you can trust me."

The tension leaves his body. "Are you sure? I don't want you feeling stuck here."

My smile is instant and big and makes my heart happy. I stroll toward him, slide my hand down his chest, and wrap my arms around him. He returns the gesture, and my fears fade.

"I don't feel stuck here," I tell him. "I *want* to stay. Maya was right about one thing: everything I want is right here. Including you."

He cups my face with one hand. "I should have trusted you. I know you don't have one mean bone in your body. You've shown that to me over and over. I was blindsided by Aiden, and yeah, jealous. I'll do better."

He drops his mouth to mine, and I open to him, craving his taste. When his tongue meets mine, I know we have some catching up to do.

"I have a peace offering," I tell him, "you know, in case the apology wasn't enough."

"I hope that's you. Naked. In my bed."

I smile. "That works too."

I turn, open the fridge, and pull out one of Natalie's chocolate silk pies.

Logan groans and smiles. "I know exactly what plate I want to eat that from."

I raise on my toes and kiss him again. "Then let's go. We can come back and take care of this later."

He hugs me back, kisses me deep, and finally presses his forehead to mine. "Great minds think alike."

Logan

Two weeks later

I'm in the engine bay when my cell rings, but I'm in an intense tug-of-war with Lucky over a toy Sorenson, of all people, brought in—a sloth in a bunny suit with a squeaker somewhere inside.

As soon as Ken gave it to him, Lucky took ownership and won't leave it anywhere. He even grabs it when the alarm sounds and runs to the rescue, jumping in with the damn thing in his mouth. Needless to say, he's won Sorenson over. I may even have seen the boss napping in a lounge chair with Lucky tucked beside him a time or two.

Lucky's really grown in the month since I found him— physically and emotionally. He's silly and sneaky and sweet, and he brings joy to everyone he comes into contact with. Sure, he's constantly getting into trouble, but that really just makes him one of us.

"Don't answer that," Tucker says. He's got twenty bucks bet on Lucky giving up on the tug-of-war before I do. Bobby, Cole,

Carter, and Royal are in the pool, each cheering on their hopeful winner.

To answer my phone, I'd have to let go with at least one hand, and Lucky's stronger than he looks. I'm pretty sure he'd rip it away.

I glance at the phone and see Corbett's number on my screen. "Sorry, guys, I gotta take this."

I let go of the toy to everyone's disappointment, and Lucky was pulling so hard, he does a backward somersault before righting himself and running away with the bunny-sloth, which gets the guys laughing again.

With all the commotion in the engine bay and voices echoing off hard surfaces, I head outside to answer the phone right as Isabel pulls to the curb.

"Hey," I answer the phone, "can you hold on a sec?" Then I ask Isabel, "Which design did Tina pick?"

"The one with Trevor's newborn footprint."

All the tattoos she sketched for Tina were beautiful. "That was my favorite."

She gets out of the car. "We're going into Portland tomorrow to find a tattoo artist. Who's that?"

"Corbett." I put the phone on speaker and say, "What's up?"

"After reviewing all the evidence, the chief has declared the rifle belongs to Isabel. The sales receipt has been authenticated, and while it may show McBride as the owner, it clearly states Isabel was the person who paid for it. And that makes her the legal owner, despite what the auction house wrote on the receipt."

Isabel sucks in a breath, eyes still on the phone, like she's expecting the other shoe to drop.

"I relayed that message to McBride," Corbett says. "He took it about as well as you can imagine. Hung up on me."

She drops her head back, closes her eyes, and says, "*Yes.*"

McBride went back to New York the day they released him

from jail, but did exactly what Isabel said he would do in a conflict and contacted a lawyer about getting the gun back.

"I've got even better news," Corbett says, bringing Isabel's gaze back to the phone. "My uncle is a bit of an antiques buff. He's not into weapons, but he knows someone who is, a guy named Malcolm Wells. Wells runs an auction house in Pennsylvania, an area rich in history and lots of antiques. So my uncle asked him about the rifle. After explaining all the details and surveying the rifle over Zoom, Wells did some research and told my uncle the rifle is definitely a valuable antique. From the decorative silver and ivory, he identified the gun as one customized for and owned by General John Sullivan, who fought in the American Revolution, under George Washington. That dates the rifle back to the late seventeen hundreds."

Isabel's eyes are wide, but she doesn't seem to understand the significance any more than I do.

"I don't know anything about antiques," I say. "Can you put it in layman's terms for us?"

"In layman's terms, that rifle is worth a shitload of money. As in high five digits."

She grabs my arm, but speaks to Corbett on the phone. "Are you serious?"

"I'm serious."

"That's why Aiden was being such a prick," Isabel says. "That's why he wouldn't let this go. It didn't have anything to do with me."

"I don't know about that," I tell her. "He may have found out what it was worth and decided not to have you ship something that valuable, but he obviously thought he could kill two birds with one stone and get you back too. Otherwise, he wouldn't have put his hands on you."

"Wells said he'd sell it at his auction house if you want," Corbett says. "He gets a fee, of course, but my uncle says that fee would be paid back ten times over because of the higher price you'd get for the rifle back east. He says it was in Sullivan's possession when he crossed the Delaware. As concrete a piece of the past as there ever was."

Isabel presses both hands to her cheeks. "Holy shit."

"Thanks," I tell Corbett, "and thank your uncle for us, will you? I'll get back to you about selling—"

"No," Isabel cuts in. "Sell it. For God's sake, sell it. Just let me know what we have to do or get me Wells's contact information."

"Will do."

"Corbett?" Isabel says before he disconnects.

"Yeah?"

"I'm sorry I called you a sonofabitch."

Corbett laughs. "Apology accepted."

When I disconnect, Isabel throws herself into my arms. "Oh my *God*."

I hug her tight. "This is *amazing*. You'll have the money to kickstart your business."

"Think of all the amazing upgrades we can make to the motel," she says, pulling back with stars in her eyes. "It'll be up and running for the summer season kickoff."

I tilt my head. "I meant your design business."

A big smile brightens her face. I'm not sure I've ever seen her happier. "Sounds like there will be enough money to do both. And I've been thinking about asking you about us going in on the motel together. It could be *our* business, you know? Our baby, so to speak."

Lucky streaks out of the firehouse, toy still clamped between his teeth and jumps on Isabel. Since she's decided to stay, she and Lucky have become nearly inseparable. We moved Isabel into the apartment and built a workspace for her in room 7. Lucky follows her around like a tail at home and always tries to get in between us in bed, snuggling up to Isabel. Needless to say, he hasn't stayed between us long, and if I have anything to say about it, he never will. One of my greatest joys is having Isabel in my bed every night.

She leans down and picks up the squirming, tail-wagging, face-licking devil. "Don't worry, buddy. You'll always be our first baby. In fact, I got you a present."

"He's getting spoiled," I say. "All these presents are going to ruin him."

Isabel reaches into the pocket of her Hood River Fire & Rescue hoodie and pulls out a red strap, then holds it up. "His first collar."

I grin and slide my arm around her waist, pulling her up against my side. "That's great."

She takes the silver tag in the shape of a Maltese cross between her fingers and shows me the engraving. Lucky's name on one side and on the other, both our phone numbers, labeled as Mom and Dad.

She's assured me she's staying because the corporate design life doesn't call to her anymore, and because she wants to be with me, but up until right this minute, I didn't realize I doubted that commitment.

"We're in this together," she tells me, her voice soft, like she knows exactly what I'm thinking. "We're living together, we've got a—potential—business together, and a puppy together." She kisses me and her dark eyes shine with joy. "I love you, Logan. I'm staying. We're solid."

And just like that, my outlook turns around.

"I love you too." I pull her close and kiss her again. "Which means there's nothing left to see but good."

She nods. "*All* good."

ALSO BY SKYE JORDAN

FORGED IN FIRE

Flashpoint

Smoke and Mirrors

WILDFIRE LAKE SERIES

In Too Deep

Going Under

Swept Away

THE WRIGHTS SERIES

So Wright

Damn Wright

Must be Wright

MANHUNTERS SERIES

Grave Secrets

No Remorse

RENEGADES SERIES:

Reckless

Rebel

Ricochet

Rumor

Relentless

Rendezvous

Riptide

Rapture

QUICK & DIRTY COLLECTION:

Dirtiest Little Secret

WILDWOOD SERIES:

Forbidden Fling

Wild Kisses

ROUGH RIDERS HOCKEY SERIES:

Quick Trick

Hot Puck

Dirty Score

Wild Zone

COVERT AFFAIRS SERIES:

Intimate Enemies

First Temptation

Sinful Deception

Keep up to date on all my new releases by signing up for my
newsletter here:

http://bit.ly/2bGqJhG

Get an inside view of upcoming books and exclusive giveaways by
joining my reader group here:

https://www.facebook.com/groups/877103352359204/

ABOUT THE AUTHOR

Skye Jordan is the *New York Times* and *USA Today* bestselling author of more than thirty novels. She was born and raised in California and has recently been transplanted to Northern Virginia.

She left her challenging career in sonography at UCSF Medical Center to devote herself to writing full time, but still travels overseas on medical missions to teach sonography to physicians. Most recently, she traveled to Ethiopia and Haiti.

Skye and her husband are coming up on their thirty year wedding anniversary and have two beautiful daughters. A lover of learning, Skye enjoys classes of all kinds, from knitting to forensic sculpting. She is an avid rower and spends many wonderful hours on the Potomac with her amazing rowing club.

Make sure you sign up for her newsletter to get the first news of her upcoming releases, giveaways, freebies and more! http://bit.ly/2bGqJhG

You can find Skye online here:
Skye's Starlets | Website | Email

Made in the USA
Monee, IL
07 May 2021

66905068R00146